Hard

MOTIVELESS MURDER

Hardcastle & Young

MOTIVELESS MURDER

Liz Vincent

Troubador Publishing Ltd
Unit E2 Airfield Business Park,
Harrison Road, Market Harborough,
Leicestershire LE16 7UL
Tel: 0116 279 2299
Email: books@troubador.co.uk
Web: www.troubador.co.uk

ISBN 978 1 83628 109 2

British Library Cataloguing in Publication Data.
A catalogue record for this book is available from the British Library.

Printed and bound by CPI Group (UK) Ltd, Croydon, CR0 4YY
Typeset in 11pt Aldine by Troubador Publishing Ltd, Leicester, UK

Matador is an imprint of Troubador Publishing Ltd

To the village of Alrewas, for giving me inspiration

CHAPTER ONE

Murder.

Yes, the idea appealed to him; Very much.

But could he get away with it?

This thought flashed across Clive's mind as he slowly awoke from a television induced doze. Then all his senses went on high alert. There was a smell that he didn't like. A smell that shouldn't be there.

'What the bloody hell?' he muttered grumpily as he hauled himself off the settee and headed for the kitchen. 'What's she done now?'

Murder. The thought was there again, shouting at him this time.

He pushed open the kitchen door to be greeted by a dense cloud of oily smoke. Fighting down his panic, he put his hand over his mouth as he felt his way across the room. His girlfriend, Debs, was nowhere in sight.

Oh my God, I can't breathe! His heart was pounding, his eyes were streaming, and he could feel the pulse in his neck going into overdrive. He thought he was going to be sick as he coughed and spluttered his way to the back door. He flung it open and went outside, the cloud following on swiftly behind. When he had got his breath back, he could see the cause of it. The chip pan, with the gas still burning underneath it.

'That bloody woman. I'll swing for her, I swear.'

He switched the gas off and wondered what to do next.

He had a brainwave.

'Tea towel.' He grabbed it, ran it under the tap, and threw it over the pan. Fortunately, it hadn't caught fire.

Then he saw Debs. Lounging on a sunbed, with a glass of vodka and tonic in her hand. She was talking to herself again, and laughing at her own answers.

'Hi, Clive.' She waved her free hand in his general direction and giggled. 'Come to join me?'

He marched over to her, his anger reaching boiling point. 'You stupid cow.'

'You stink.' She wrinkled up her nose as he got to her. 'God, what's that smell?'

'Chip fat.' His eyes were bulging. 'You left the pan on.'

'Did I?' She looked genuinely confused. 'Don't remember.'

'No.' Clive sprayed her with furious saliva. 'You never do. You're always pissed, that's why.' She waved her half empty glass at him and laughed. 'You'd better get to bed, you've been on that stuff all day.'

'Ooh, you coming with me?' She grinned.

'No,' he said firmly, 'I'm going out.'

'You're always out.' She pouted now. 'You got another woman? You fed up with me?'

Clive winced. How could she be so drunk and yet so perceptive? He was tempted to tell her the truth, but wasn't sure how she would react. He didn't want her to burn his house down for real. He took a deep breath before he spoke again.

'Tell you what.' He tried to sound kind. 'I'll fetch you another drink. Then you can enjoy the evening sunshine.'

'Aw, Clive, you're so nice sometimes.'

'Tell me about it,' he muttered as he went back indoors and up to her bedroom. He knew she had bottles of vodka stashed in the wardrobe. Their one and only attempt at counselling had given him vital information like that. He grabbed one and took it out to her, gave her a peck on the cheek, and left her to it. She had completely forgotten that today was his birthday, and he wasn't about to remind her. As far as he was concerned, if she wanted to drink herself to death then she could get on with it.

It would save him the job of strangling her.

He smiled as he left the ex-farmhouse, walked to his big black Mercedes, and drove the short distance into the village of Hawksmere. Soon he was on the A38, heading towards Burton on Trent.

Debs has sussed I'm seeing someone else, wonder how she managed that? If I tell her, will she clear off? Could I ever get that lucky?

Clive drove through the town towards the hospital, and pulled up outside a row of terraced houses. He wasted no time in knocking at the door of one of them.

'Hello, Connie.' He smiled at the woman, whom he likened to Marilyn Munroe. This one was also shapely and sexy.

He stepped inside as she reached for him. She pushed the door shut as he kissed her. Again, and again.

'Och, I've missed you,' she murmured.

'It's only been three days.'

'Feels like a lot longer.' She looked up at him and smiled. 'Anyway, happy birthday.'

'It will be now I'm with you.' He smiled. 'And soon I hope to be with you all the time.'

'Aye.' She looked unsure. 'Maybe.'

'Definitely. When I've sorted things out at home. Trouble is, she's always so out of it, I can't get through to her.'

Connie gave him a pleading look, and he knew he should change the subject. Quickly.

'Come on. I've got a table booked at La Dolce Vita, and we've got time for a couple of drinks first. I'll get a taxi to take us into town.'

'I love Italian food.' She looked happier now.

The pub they went to reminded Clive of The Red Lion in Hawksmere, with its beams in the ceiling, Victorian fireplace and stained-glass panels. Compared to the village, Burton was the bustling metropolis. Fifty or so years ago, it had been the brewing capital of England. The older locals still swore blind they could smell hops in the air; either that, or it was the Marmite factory.

'You alright, Clive?' Connie was asking.

'Yeah. I was just thinking about how we met. I never expected going to the gym to be so good.'

'Get out of it.' Her laugh sounded like tinkling music. 'You hate the gym. I have to whip you into shape every time you go there.'

'Mm.' He winked at her. 'But you do it so well. It's been three months of very enjoyable torture. And I've lost some weight.'

'Some good's come out of it, then.'

Cheeky bugger.' He looked around them. 'This pub's nice. Old World. Can't stand those modern plastic things.'

'I don't mind them,' murmured Connie. 'You live in Hawksmere, don't you?' He nodded. 'I've never been there. What's it like?'

'Great. It's got old black and white thatched cottages, a pub and a canal. What more could you want?'

'What, no sheep, cows, fields of green?'

'Oh yeah, we got them too,' Clive answered. Then he realised she was taking the micky. 'Church bells as well, on a good day.'

Connie laughed. 'Sounds lovely, but I'm a city girl. Not sure about the countryside.'

'I'll have to see if I can convert you.'

'Or I you.' She lowered her eyes as she spoke, and Clive knew she was saying a lot more than those three words. Maybe he wouldn't be going home later, as he usually did. That would make this birthday the best ever.

This thought stayed with Clive all through the meal and the rest of the evening. Nothing was said as such, but he knew he was going to be staying the night. He was on cloud nine as he drove back to Hawksmere the next morning. It was nearly lunchtime when he got home. His house was up a driveway, and as his Mercedes glided along it, he frowned when he saw a police car. Nearer to the house was another vehicle. A white van, with Forensics Investigation Unit written on it.

'Oh God, what's she done now?' Clive groaned as his imagination went into overdrive.

A police officer approached the car as he attempted to park it outside the garage. He couldn't actually get anywhere near it. His drive was cordoned off with blue and white police tape.

'Sorry sir, and you are?' the young male police constable asked him, after he had wound the window down.

'Clive Morrison. I live here.'

'I see. Stay there.'

'What's going on? Is Debs alright?'

'That would be Miss Deborah Hunt?' Clive nodded. 'Your partner?'

'I suppose so.' Clive had never regarded her as his partner. Pain in the backside was more like it. 'What's she done? Is she okay?'

The constable didn't answer, but looked over to another man, who was walking towards them. They had a brief discussion, then the plain clothed officer approached Clive's car.

'Mr Morrison, is it? I'm Detective Sergeant Young.'

Clive never remembered what happened next, but he was told about a sequence of events. His cleaner had arrived at her usual time, let herself in, and begun her work. When she reached the kitchen, she had seen Debs outside asleep on the sunbed. She hadn't taken too much notice, as it wasn't the first time she had found her like this. Later, she made herself a cup of tea, and had gone into the garden to ask Debs if she wanted one. She had shaken her to get her attention. Then she had screamed. Debs' body was as stiff as a board.

'You mean… ' Clive was struggling to understand. 'She's dead?'

'I'm afraid so, sir.'

'But,' Clive almost stuttered. 'What happened?'

'That's what we're here to find out, sir.'

Clive put his head in his hands in despair. He could see it all coming. The police were going to want to know where he had been last night, and who with. He groaned as he thought of Connie.

He needed to think.

And fast…

CHAPTER TWO

At Brodewell police station, Detective Inspector Vic Hardcastle breezed into the CID office, his eyes gleaming. Something needed his attention; he could feel it in his bones.

'Wot's 'appening, then?'

DC Nikki Singh answered him. 'Stuart's just brought someone in. There's been a suspicious death in Hawksmere.'

'Murder?' Vic asked, his heart beginning to race.

'Could be.' She glanced up at him. 'Looks like it.'

'Oh, ar?' Vic smirked. 'Anyone told the Super? After all, she is the one in charge of the Major Crime Team for this area.' A dreamy look came over his face. 'An' with a bit of luck, I'll get made up to acting DCI again, like last time.'

Nikki didn't answer.

'That's the second murder I've dealt with since I bin 'ere.' He scowled now. 'Bloody villages, I hate 'em. Always something dodgy going on. Dunno why I didn't stay in Tipton.'

'Nor me.'

He heard the muttered comment, but decided to ignore it. This wasn't the first time it had happened. Still, he wasn't here to win any popularity contests but sometimes he did wonder why he had come to such a backwater place.

'Where is he?'

'Interview Room Three.'

Vic hurried along there, to find his Sergeant sitting opposite a well-built man in his early fifties, who looked like he could take care of himself. DS Young was setting up the interview recorder.

'Morning.' Vic directed the comment towards Stuart but the other man looked up as well, so he thought he had better introduce himself. 'I'm DI Hardcastle, and who's this, then?'

'Clive Morrison,' the man said, 'and I don't know why I'm here.'

'His partner was found dead in the garden this morning,' Stuart explained, for Vic's benefit, 'by his cleaner.'

'Where's she?'

'Next door. Nikki'll be talking to her.'

'Good.' Vic sat down. 'Well then, sir. It looks like you've got some explaining to do.'

'It's nothing to do with me.' He crossed his arms over his chest. 'I wasn't even there.'

9

'First things first,' Vic said firmly. 'Name and address, for the tape.'

'Clive Morrison, Byre End Cottage, Hawksmere.'

'And your partner is – was – Miss Deborah Hunt, aged thirty-four?' Clive nodded. 'You like 'em young?'

Vic saw the look Stuart gave him. Maybe he was getting too personal. His people skills were a bit lacking.

'Never thought about it.' Clive did look surprised.

'How long were you together?' Stuart asked.

'About a year. She was alright to start with, then I realised she had a drink problem. I tried to help her, counselling and stuff, but she didn't want to know. I gave up in the end.'

'She was found in the garden, you say?' Vic looked at Stuart. 'She'd been there all night?'

'Suppose so.' Clive nodded. 'She often did that. I usually threw a duvet over her if she'd crashed out on the sunbed. She got all arsy if I woke her up. Better to leave her to sleep it off.'

'But not last night?'

'No.'

'Why's that, then?' Vic leaned forward. 'You were out?'

'It was my birthday yesterday.'

'You went out on your own?'

'I couldn't take her anywhere any more. She'd show me up.'

'Where did you go?'

'Oh, I dunno, here and there.'

'You'll have to do better than that, sir.'

Clive squirmed a bit and looked uncomfortable. Vic and Stuart exchanged glanced and nodded to each other. Clive saw them.

'Alright, alright, I went for a meal. La Dolce Vita in Burton.'

Stuart made a note of that and Vic smiled.

'On your own?' he asked.

Clive didn't answer. Vic was watching him closely, wondering what he was hiding.

'Would you say that things were good between you and Miss Hunt?' Stuart was asking.

'Yeah, fine.' Clive looked at his fingernails, then looked up at them both. 'Well, I suppose we just worked round each other really.'

'But you weren't trying to help her any more, with the drinking.'

'She was past help. Told you, she didn't want to know.'

'That must have been difficult for you, sir.'

Clive shrugged his shoulders, then slumped them. 'I didn't really know she had a problem until she moved in with me. Suppose I shouldn't have let her do that.'

'Does she have any family?'

'Dunno. She never mentioned any.'

'We'll make enquiries.'

'Why am I here?'

Vic and Stuart looked at each other in amazement. Did he really have no idea? Vic rolled his eyes to the ceiling, so Stuart answered.

'It's standard practice to interview everyone who knew the victim.'

'She ain't a victim, she drank herself to death.' Clive looked annoyed. 'Nothing to do with me.'

'The facts haven't been established yet, sir, so until then, this is a suspicious death.'

'And you think I killed her?'

'We don't think anything yet.' Vic leaned forward and stared into his face. 'But you ain't doing yerself any favours by acting all outraged. We'll check your story, and if we find you've bin lying to us, you'll be in a lot of trouble.'

Clive sat back in his chair, not looking so sure of himself now.

'I – I just don't understand,' he said quietly.

Vic looked at Stuart, and rolled his eyes again.

'Let's go and see what the other one has to say,' he murmured to Stuart. Clive looked surprised as they both stood up.

'Interview terminated at two fifty,' Stuart said as he switched off the recorder.

'We'll be back.' Vic pointed a finger at Clive. 'We'll leave you to do some thinking.'

Clive stared after then as they left the room. Then he buried his face in his hands.

'Gawd, I've got better things to do on a Friday afternoon.' Vic complained as they went to the monitoring room. There they could watch any interviews via downlinks to dedicated computers. 'Let's see how Jigsaw's getting on.'

'Nikki, Guv,' Stuart said quietly, 'her name is Nikki.'

'Everyone's got a nickname, son, and I'm still

working on yours, don't know you well enough yet. And yes, I do know what people call me.'

Stuart gave a nervous laugh, but made no comment.

The interview had only just started. Clive's cleaner had a cup of tea in front her, and looked nervous.

'I've worked for Mr Morrison for three years,' she said. 'It used to be an easy job, he don't make much mess. But that woman –'

'Miss Deborah Hunt?'

'Yeah. She was a messy cow, lazy too. Spent half the day in bed and the other half boozing. I had a right game getting to clean her room.'

'So, they had separate bedrooms?'

'Not to start with, but the last few months, yes.' The woman leaned forward. 'I think he was fed up with her. They used to row a lot. He was always going on at her over the drinking.'

'Was he ever violent towards her?'

'Not that I saw. He's a nice bloke, but he can get his hair off if something upsets him. He had his car serviced a while back, and there was something they didn't do. Gawd, you should have heard him, ranting and raving down the phone, he was. I cleared off out of the way.'

'Don't blame you.' Nikki laughed.

The cleaner smiled. She looked more relaxed now.

'Lately I've been clearing off a lot. I dread going there sometimes.'

'Mm.' Vic looked at Stuart. 'Not quite the way he described it.'

'No,' Stuart agreed. 'Looks like he's got a temper. He could have lost it with her.'

'Probably did. He's hiding something, that's for sure. Tell ya summat, she's good at interviews, ain't she?' He looked back towards Nikki.

'Yeah, she's a people person. Certainly better at it than I am.'

'And me,' Vic admitted. 'I feel like ripping their heads off half the time. Get the truth out of the bastards.'

'Yes, Guv, I had noticed.'

'You wouldn't be much of a detective if you hadn't.' Vic chuckled.

'He's been going out a lot these last few months,' the cleaner was saying. This brought Vic's attention back to her. 'Debs thought he might have another woman on the go, although he's got a mate he goes to the pub with.'

'Do you know his name?'

'Phil, don't know his other name. They go to the Red Lion. Case of having to, I s'pose. There's only one pub in Hawksmere.'

'That could give us some good info,' Vic muttered. 'Pubs are good for gossip. Wonder if -?'

He looked back at Nikki. Stuart was about to say something when a young PC came rushing into the room and handed Vic a sheet of paper.

'Post mortem report.' Stuart had thought as much. 'Oh well, this is interesting.' Vic smiled. 'Bruises on the arms and lower chest, consistent with a struggle. Severe bruising in the osofo – throat, suggesting a hard object was forced down there. Cause of death, asphyxiation. Shortness of breath, in other words. This proves it, son. Deborah Hunt was murdered!'

CHAPTER THREE

After what seemed like forever, Clive was allowed to leave the police station. His head was swimming from the experience, all the things he had seen and heard. Like a lot of people, he had never had any direct contact with the police. The worst thing about it had been the dreadful cardboard cup of coffee they had brought him. He doubted whether anyone would be able to think straight after drinking the stuff.

He got a taxi back to Hawksmere, wondering what he was going to find when he got there. His car was still parked halfway up the drive. Had he locked it? It hardly mattered now. The house looked empty and alone, no signs of activity. He supposed he wouldn't have been allowed back into it until everyone had finished whatever it was they had to do in there.

He let himself in through the front door, not sure

what sort of state his home would be in. Apart from some patches of grey fingerprint powder, it was pretty much the same as he had left it. He heaved a sigh of relief and went to put the kettle on. The bitter taste of cheap coffee was still in his mouth.

He stood by the sink and looked out into the garden. All he could see was the pale green sunbed. Last time he had seen Debs she had been lying on it, talking to herself and laughing. Now there was nothing, and never would be again. So many times he had wished her gone. Now he could hardly believe he had been contemplating murdering her. What had he been thinking?

I just wanted her to go, I didn't really want her dead. Oh, who am I kidding? She did my head in. I could have killed her ten times over.

'But I didn't,' he said aloud, still staring out of the window.

Someone had. He had been told that the post mortem report had arrived, and an object had been the cause of her death. A bottle was the obvious culprit, but who had rammed it down there?

'It wasn't me.' Clive began to cry. 'I wasn't even here.'

But to prove it, he had to involve Connie. He was going to have to tell her about this. He couldn't face that at the moment. In the back of his mind, he was wondering how long it would take the police to find out about her. He knew they would, they always did. He had watched enough television crime dramas to know that. They were going to pry into every aspect of his uneventful life. Nothing was ever going to be private again.

The kettle boiled and switched itself off. He ignored it. A large gin and tonic seemed more appropriate now. Or he could go to the pub. No, he couldn't face anyone yet. Not even his best friend, Phil.

He pulled open the ice shelf at the top of his freezer. Empty.

'Bollocks,' he shouted as he slammed the door shut. The fridge magnet, a picture of an angel that Debs had bought, clattered to the tiled floor.

He repeated the word several times as he staggered towards the lounge, his tears blinding him. He collapsed onto the settee and let them come. They kept coming for a long time, and he knew why. He wasn't crying out of grief; it was sheer guilt.

'I've got to speak to Connie, before the police get to her.'

This realisation came to him when the tears had stopped and he had calmed down. He knew he had to salvage what he could from their developing relationship. Connie had been his escape from all the hassle Debs had sent his way, but now what? He had to find out. He would have to go to see her.

After a shower and a change of clothes, he drove over to Burton with a heavy heart. He wanted to see Connie, but at the same time he was dreading it. She was being dragged into a situation that was none of her making, and he knew the police, especially DI Hardcastle, were going to have a field day with it. He would lose her after this, he was sure.

Connie's house was a small two up and two down, but it was very homely. He felt more comfortable there than in his own property, which didn't have many personal touches. He had never had a woman in there long enough to make any. He had imagined Connie living with him, bringing light and laughter into his life, but now…

He knocked on the door with shaking hands, his nerve starting to fail him. Perhaps he should have rung her first.

'Clive.' The surprise on her face was obvious when she opened the door. 'I wasn't expecting – och, Lord, what's happened?'

'I need to speak to you,' he said quietly.

Come in.'

The front entrance led straight into the living room. Connie waved him towards the settee and sat in an armchair at right angles to it. She sat still, looking at him and he knew he should just get on with it.

'Problem?' she prompted.

'A big one.' He nodded, then took a deep breath. 'Debs is dead.'

'What?' Her mouth fell open. Her eyes were wide as she continued. 'You haven't -?'

'No.' He nearly choked on the word. 'Someone beat me to it. She's been murdered. Last night, while I was out with you. I've been at the police station all afternoon.'

Connie gripped the arm of the chair. 'They'll be wanting to speak to me, then.'

'I haven't told them about you, but they're bound to find out. Oh, Connie, I don't know what to do.'

'Neither do I,' she muttered.

Clive wasn't taking much in, but even he could see she was worried. More concerned than she need to be, surely?

It was as if she was hiding something, and, at the moment, he didn't want to know what it was. It was time to chatter.

'The police station was horrible.' He had no wish to relive the experience, but it was taking his mind off her anxious face. 'They asked me all sorts of questions I couldn't answer, and they've given me a – what was it? Oh yeah, a family liaison officer. Can't see the point of it, I told 'em I haven't got any family.'

'None at all?'

'Nah. I'm an only child and my parents died years ago. Car crash. They were touring round Italy.' He stopped to think. 'Might have some uncles and aunties somewhere, but if I have, I never hear from them.'

'What about Debs? She must have someone.'

'Dunno.' Clive frowned. 'She never said. I never told her about mine either, I hardly ever think about them now. It's been over twenty years. I took over Dad's business and kept it going for a while before I got into property.'

'Someone'll need to find Debs' family,' Connie said quietly. 'For the funeral.'

'I suppose so.' The reality of the situation was only just starting to sink in. Things would need doing. Things Clive knew little about.

'Maybe there's something in her room.'

'I should think the police will have searched it, but I'll have a look.' Clive sighed. 'Oh, God, it's all such a mess. I was with her for over a year and I know next to nothing about her. Parents, brothers, sisters, nothing.'

'You don't know much about me, either. There are some things you ought to know.'

19

Clive stared at her. 'Connie, I've got enough to deal with without –'

'The police will find out once they've got my name, and I'd rather you heard it from me.' Clive buried his face in his hands. His brain felt like it was about to explode. 'I don't want to lose you, Clive, but I'm probably going to.'

He shook his head. After the day he'd had, he couldn't take any more.

'The thing is,' she continued. He wanted to scream at her to shut up. Whatever it was, he didn't want to hear it. I haven't been entirely honest with you.'

Clive whimpered. He put his hands over his ears but he could still hear. Her voice was like a soft dentist's drill burrowing into his soul.

'I left Scotland for a reason. I came down here to get away from someone. I wanted to start again, meet someone I could spend my life with. I thought I'd found that with you, but now it's all gone wrong.'

'I know,' Clive groaned.

'No, you don't. Oh, Clive, I'm so sorry. I'm married. I've got a husband back up in Glasgow.'

CHAPTER FOUR

Everyone in the CID office knew what to do even before their tasks were assigned. It was a small team, and as they already had other cases to work on, Vic decided to lighten the load and involve two uniformed officers from the front office.

'It'll be good practice for ya,' he told them. 'Off yu go.'

PCs George Nicholls and Richard Comer needed no urging. George had lived in Hawksmere when he was growing up and knew the village well. As they drove up the A38, he explained to his colleague what life was like in a small community.

'It's not like Midsomer Murders. People don't leave their places unlocked, and they ain't in each other's houses all the time neither. Then again.' He grinned. 'They do have their moments. Might tell you about that sometime.'

Richard looked across at him but he was concentrating firmly on his driving. George was only a year older than him, but he treated him like a baby sometimes. He knew he wouldn't get any more out of him until he was ready.

'Suppose it's hard to keep things quiet. Secrets and stuff.'

'Bloody impossible, mate,' George laughed. 'We'll go to the Co-op, the hairdressers and the butcher to start with. Bound to get something from one of those.'

'You reckon?'

'Sure. Women know all sorts of stuff.'

They parked near the shops in Hawksmere, and headed straight for the Coop. There were two people on the tills, and they looked at each other with raised eyebrows as the PCs walked in. Richard had a photo of Deborah Hunt ready in his hand.

'Do you know this woman?' he asked the cashier nearest the door. Her staff badge told him her name was Lesley. She took a glance at the picture and smiled.

'Oh yes, we know her, don't we Sarah?'

Sarah took a look, and laughed. 'She's in here all the time. Our vodka sales have never been better.'

'She did buy the odd sandwich sometimes as well.'

'Do you know if she had any friends?' George asked. They both shook their heads.

'How's Clive?' Sarah sounded serious now. 'It must have been a shock for him, finding her dead like that.'

'I'm not surprised,' Lesley said. 'She bought vodka nearly every day. She must have been packing it away at a right rate.'

'So, you never saw her with anyone apart from Mr Morrison?'

Sarah shook her head. 'She seemed to be a bit of a loner.'

George and Richard left the shop, having held up the queue to get served. They could hear the gossip starting as they went through the sliding door. Why were they there? What was going on?

'Routine enquiries.' Richard said to similar queries after they had walked across the road to the hairdresser. That wasn't enough to satisfy anyone's curiosity, but it would have to do for now. They got no joy there either.

'She must have been a real loner.'

'A lot of people who drink are.' George looked thoughtful. 'But someone must have known her, apart from her partner. This is a village, for Christ's sake.'

'A friendly one?'

'Not particularly. Aldermarsh is better.'

'Worth going there?'

'Might be.' George looked at the time. 'Let's try the pub. It should be open now.'

'They only got the one here?' George nodded. 'Gawd, how boring.'

The landlady of the Red Lion looked at the photo and frowned.

'She used to come in here with Clive, but not for a while. He just comes in with Phil now, and sometimes his partner. I haven't seen this one for ages.'

'Was she friends with Phil's partner?'

Don't think so. She never really spoke to anyone. Just sat staring at her drink, that's all she was interested in. Not surprised she drank herself to death.'

'Do Clive and Phil drink anywhere else?'

'Yeah. They go over to Aldermarsh sometimes after they've been in here. Bit more going on there. Bigger village.'

'Okay. Thanks for your help.'

Richard and George walked back to the car and set off for Aldermarsh, two miles up the road.

'This place has changed since I lived here,' George said quietly as they drove out of Hawksmere. 'Lot's of new people from outside. Brummies in particular.'

'They gotta live somewhere.'

'Yeah. Suppose so.'

There were three pubs in Aldermarsh, and the village had a different feel. Everyone seemed more cheerful. As they drove down the Main Street. They could see small groups of people chatting and laughing. It felt like a happy place.

'Shall we try the shop here?' Richard asked.

'Nah. Don't see why she should use this one, especially as she didn't have a car.'

'Makes sense.'

The pub in the centre of the village had the biggest car park, so they pulled up on there and went inside.

'I've never seen her.' The landlord took a good look at the photo. 'Clive and Phil come here sometimes.'

'With anyone else?'

The landlord shook his head. 'Phil's got a girlfriend, but she's not keen on this place. They come here for boy's only, I think.'

'Where's next?' Richard asked when they got back to the car.

'The White Hart, it's round the corner. The other one doesn't open till later.'

'Looks posh.' Richard noticed as they walked inside.

'Yeah. It's been refurbed. Turned it into a sort of gastropub.' George didn't look impressed. 'It was better as it was.'

One end of the old building was a smart restaurant, but they had kept the small comfortable snug which overlooked the car park. The barman seemed to like this area. He was lurking there, with nothing to do.

'Good morning, officers,' he greeted them cheerily. 'Coffee and cake, is it?'

'Not just now, sir,' George gave Richard a warning look and muttered, 'we haven't got time for that.'

Richard's face fell, but he said nothing.

'We're making enquiries about this woman.' George put the photo on the bar. 'Do you know her?'

'Oh, yes,' he said with no hesitation. 'Now, what was her name?'

'Deborah Hunt, sir.'

'Oh, crikey, is that the woman who died in Hawksmere?' George nodded. 'Oh, I see.'

George doubted whether he did, but made no comment.

'Yeah. She started coming in here a few months ago, with another woman. Haven't seen either of them for a week or two.'

'This other woman – do you know her name?'

George and Richard glanced at each other. They might be getting somewhere at last.

'Mm, let me think. She was tall, slim, blonde. Good looker. Oh yes, I think her name was… oh, what was it… Shelley. That was it. Shelley.'

CHAPTER FIVE

Nikki left the police station feeling cheerful. She had got herself a bit of overtime and was pleased to be doing something to help. All she had to do now was talk her other half into driving out to Hawksmere for a drink, as Vic had suggested. Her thoughts were on this as she drove from Brodewell to Walsall. She had lived in the town all her life, but was now longing to leave it. It didn't seem to suit her any more.

When she got to the large detached house, she was surprised to see Zak's car was already on the drive. These days she beginning to wonder whether he had a job at all. He had told her he worked in IT, and did a lot of foreign travel connected with it, which was one of the things that had attracted her to him in the first place. Now she didn't know what he did all day. He always seemed to have plenty of money though.

She let herself in through the front door, and immediately heard raised voices coming from the living room. Zak's parents were rowing again. As she headed towards the back of the house she heard a muffled thud, and her eyes widened.

'Hi, Nik,' Zak greeted her as he came out of the study. He looked subdued, not his normal self at all. He looked past her. 'They're at it again. Shall we clear off? Leave them to it?'

'Good idea.' Nikki nodded. 'Yeah, let's get out of here.'

Nikki really wanted to get into some different clothes, but she didn't want to give him time to change his mind. She followed in his brisk footsteps down the hall. His parents were still talking in Punjabi, but at least the shouting had stopped.

'We'll take your car,' Zak was saying. 'I'm low on petrol.'

In other words, I can drive and you can drink. Typical.

Nikki's car was a small blue Italian job that she couldn't pronounce properly, so she called it her Chinky Dinky. It was parked next to Zak's black BMW four by four, which towered over it.

'God, I'm glad to be out of there.' Zak heaved a sigh of relief. 'They wanted us to go to some do at the temple, so at least we're out of that.'

'Good,' Nikki said as she backed off the drive. 'Once a week is enough for anybody.'

Zak didn't answer, so Nikki drove out of Walsall onto the Lichfield road, and concentrated on her driving. She wasn't used to having Zak as a passenger.

'When we have a baby we can get our own place,' he eventually said. 'You'd like that, wouldn't you?'

'We've only been married for three months. We hardly know each other yet.'

'What's that got to do with anything?' From the look on his face, she could tell that he genuinely didn't understand.

'I don't see why we couldn't have had our own place to start with. It's not much fun living with your parents.'

'Yeah, I know, but it's difficult.'

'You're telling me.'

'Anyway, it's good in a way. You don't have to do anything. Mom does all the cooking and cleaning.'

'Yeah. Things a wife should be doing. I don't even feel as if I'm married. We should be on our own, doing our own thing. In private, not with other people breathing down our necks and interfering.'

Zak fell silent now. All the way to Hawksmere. When they arrived, she parked at the back of the Red Lion, and led her sulking other half inside.

The Red Lion was an old building, that had benefitted from several refurbs which hadn't ruined it. There was still a wooden bar, stained glass panels and a real fireplace. They stood at the bar, as they usually did when they went to a pub. One or two of the locals gave them a second look, and Nikki could understand why. They were the only Asians in the place.

As Zak ordered a pint of lager and a white wine spritzer, she took a look around. There were two men standing by the fireplace and a young couple who were sitting holding hands and looking into each other's eyes.

Nikki and Zak had never done that. If they sat in a pub, he was always glued to his mobile phone.

Nikki wondered about the couple. How did they meet? She supposed the internet had a lot to do with it these days. Her own relationship had been arranged by their mothers, who both went to the same temple.

She looked at the fireplace again, and noticed that one of the men had gone. The one remaining fitted Stuart's description of the murder suspect, Clive Morrison. There was no one she could see that looked like his best friend, Phil.

The front door rattled open, and in walked a tall, well-built man with very little hair and a twisted nose. He glanced at Clive, smiled, then came to the bar to order two pints.

'Hi, Phil,' the landlord greeted him. 'Usual?'

Nikki had the right people. Now all she had to do was watch and listen.

'Not a bad pub, this,' Zak said as he checked his change.

'That's what I'd heard,' Nikki replied, keeping one eye on her targets to make sure they didn't disappear.

'Who told you about it?' Zak was looking suspicious.

'No one,' she lied. She was getting far too good at lying. 'Read it in a magazine.'

Phil was standing next to Zak as his pints were being pulled. Nikki took the opportunity to get a good look at Clive. Considering his partner had just died he didn't look very upset. She remembered the cleaning woman's statement, which said they fought all the time. She supposed that, in that situation, things could come to a head, and one of the partners could snap. Her thoughts flew to her in-laws, and for a moment she speculated on what might happen there.

'Mate.' Phil handed one of the glasses to Clive. 'What can I say?'

'Nothing, Phil, no need. What's done is done.' Clive took a long slurp of lager. 'God, that tastes even better than the first one. I needed to come out. Try to feel normal for a while.'

'Yeah, I –' Phil hesitated. 'I was going to say I know how you feel, but I don't. I can't even begin to imagine it.'

Clive looked at the floor.

'Do you know what happened?'

'Not really.' Clive shook his head. 'The cleaner found her. Must have been one hell of a shock for her. Should ring her really and tell her not to bother coming in for a while. She probably won't anyway. She's a funny bugger at the best of times.'

'I should've brought Michelle; she'd know what to say. Women are better at this sort of thing.'

Clive grimaced. 'I'm glad you didn't, Phil. I just want to enjoy a couple of pints tonight.'

As Nikki watched, a man in his thirties wearing a high-vis orange jacket walked up to Clive with his hand outstretched. He looked like a construction worker.

'Clive,' he said, 'sorry to hear the news, mate.'

'Thanks, Mick.'

'Is there anything – you know -?'

Clive shook both his head and his friend's hand, and said something that Nikki didn't catch. Zak was busy boring the bar staff senseless. Now Nikki could get back to the job in hand.

31

'You'll be getting a lot of that,' Phil said, as Mick wandered off.

'Looks like it's reached the Co-op.' Clive sighed.

'Never takes long.' Phil drained his glass. 'Done anything about the funeral yet?'

'Give us a chance, haven't even thought about it. Suppose I'll have to try to find her parents or whatever. If she's got any.' Clive put his hand to his head.

'Want another pint?'

'Yes. Definitely.'

Phil came to the bar again, and this time stood next to Nikki. He smiled at her and she turned away, not wanting to get into conversation with him. He got served quickly, and went back to his friend.

'Seen her at the bar?' he said quietly. 'Very easy on the eye.'

'Yeah.' Clive looked over at her as she pretended to be reading the specials menu. 'But I think I'm going to be off women for a while.'

'Really?' Phil grinned. 'So you won't be going to the gym any more, then?'

'Meaning?' Clive raised an eyebrow.

'I reckon Connie's got the hots for you. I've seen the way she looks at you.'

'She's very nice.' Clive looked embarrassed.

'Bit more than nice, Clive.' Phil laughed.

'I know.'

'Oh, yeah?'

'Shut up, Phil.'

Nikki turned back to face the bar as the two men drank their beers. She gave her own drink her undivided attention for a while. After a few minutes, she heard Clive say he was leaving. Going home, things to do.

'Okay,' she heard Phil reply. 'If you need anything.'

'Thanks, Phil. See you.'

Nikki's glass was suddenly empty. She had drunk most of it without noticing. She looked at Zak and gave him the brightest smile she could manage.

'Shall we have another one?'

'Yeah, it's alright here. Might even have something to eat. They're bound to have a curry on the menu.'

'Something else would be favourite,' Nikki muttered. All his mother ever cooked was curry, and not very good ones at that.

'You going all English on me?'

'I am English, you daft sod.'

He looked at her as if he didn't understand what she was talking about, and she sighed. Her upbringing must have been a lot different to his, and she was glad. She was free thinking and independent. At least she had been until she married him.

Nikki picked up a menu and took it to an empty table. She imagined herself here with someone else. Someone who valued her for who and what she was. Someone like…

For some reason, Stuart Young had just popped into her mind. She knew why. She had a report to write out and give to him tomorrow. She was pretty sure he would be pleased with what she had found out. Already she had a warm feeling spreading through her body as she thought about it.

Or was it there for some other reason?

CHAPTER SIX

As Stuart left the police station and walked to his silver Ford Fiesta, his brain was trying to rearrange all the facts of this case and get them in the right order. Most coppers hated paperwork, but Stuart found it reassuring. He liked details, he felt at home with them. They were the glue that held everything together. In his opinion, without them people only had half the story.

Wish the Guv felt like that.

This thought was going through his mind as he reached his car, noticing the recent addition to the team climbing out of the back of the Forensics van. She had started work at Brodewell just after him.

'Hello, Frankie,' he called over.

'Oh, hiya. Off out?'

'Yeah, on enquiries. How you doing?'

'Okay, getting used to it. It's a lot different to Manchester.' She laughed. It was the dirtiest laugh Stuart had ever heard.

'It's not much like Bristol either,' he chuckled.

'That where you're from?'

'Yeah. I passed my sergeant's exam but there wasn't an opening for me, so I transferred up here. If I'd known who I'd be working for, I might not have bothered.'

'Shorty?' She laughed again. 'Glad I don't have to see much of him. Is he as bad as they say?'

'Worse sometimes. Still, I suppose I'll have to get used to it. At least I've found a good place to live. Got a flat in Lichfield. What about you? Found anything yet?'

'Still at my mum's in Rugeley. It's okay, it's working out alright. This lot are keeping me busy.'

'Were you on the Hawksmere case?' She nodded. 'Me too. Off to check the boyfriend's alibi.'

'I'd better let you go, then. Catch you later.'

Stuart got into his car, feeling more cheerful than he had before. Frankie seemed to have that effect on everyone, and it was a pleasure having her around.

It's not all bad, he decided as he drove out of Brodewell and onto the A38. *What's this place called again?*

La Dolce Vita was the name of the restaurant he was going to visit. How original, he thought as he overtook a lorry with a Romanian number plate, and vaguely wondered what cargo it was carrying.

Stuart didn't know Burton very well, he hardly ever went there. He didn't do much in Lichfield either. His activities were pretty much confined to the nearest supermarket and the nearest pub, and these were only about once a week.

He had been told that close to the railway line was a big hardware store with a large car park. It was well signposted, so he found it easily. It was only a short walk into the town centre, where parking was more difficult. He didn't know how long he was going to be either. He might break the habit of a lifetime and have lunch somewhere, if he liked the look of the place.

To get to La Dolce Vita, he had to walk through the two main shopping centres. Both undercover, he noticed, and full of people. Stuart was impressed with what he saw, and nearly let himself get led into a very attractive coffee shop in the middle of Cooper's Square. This too was busy, and the smell of coffee and croissants was alluring. Maybe afterwards, on his way back.

Five minutes later he was entering the restaurant, which could seat about thirty people. The floor was red tiled, the tables plain scrubbed wood, and there were photographs of Naples, Sorrento and Capri on the magnolia walls. Now all he had to do was find the manager, one Silvio Verde, whom he had telephoned earlier to warn him he was coming.

There were no customers in the restaurant yet, but two waiters were floating about laying tables. One of them spotted Stuart as he was reaching for his ID, and came over with a frown on his face.

'Si, Signor?'

'I'm here to see Mr Verde. He's expecting me.' He waved his warrant card.

'Ah si. In the office, Signor.'

'Thank you.' Stuart walked towards the door that was being pointed at.

'Ah, de polizia,' the man inside greeted him warmly. 'Please, take a seat.'

'Detective Sergeant Young, sir,' said Stuart as he shook his hand, thankful that he didn't try to kiss him on the cheeks. As he sat down, he weighed him up. He wore an expensive suit, and looked like an archetypical Italian. Dark brown eyes, slicked back black hair, and a tidy moustache. He obviously liked his food, from the look of his waistline.

'How can I help you?' He came straight to the point. Stuart liked that. He wasn't much good at small talk.

'This man.' Stuart slid a photograph of Clive Morrison across the tidy desk. He was fumbling for another one of the dead woman.

'Si, si, I know him.' Signor Verde was nodding. 'A regular customer, every four to six weeks. Always leaves a good tip and drinks mucho vino.' He laughed.

'I see.' Stuart had found the picture of Debs now, and placed it on the desk next to the one of Clive. Even in photographs they looked an unlikely couple.

'Ah si, I know her too, but he hasn't brought her here for a while. The last few times he come alone.'

Stuart was disappointed to hear this. He hoped this visit wasn't going to turn into a dead end.

'Was he in here on Friday night?'

'Si.' Signor Verde nodded again, 'but not with this lady.'

'Oh?'

'Another blonde lady. He likes de blondes, he tell me. He likes de Marilyn Munroe, his favourite lady.' He looked as though he agreed with Clive. He now had a slightly lecherous look about him. 'I not seen this new lady before.'

'Do you think you would recognise her again?'

'Oh, si, si. Very attractive lady, very, how you say, er, full of life.'

Stuart made a note in his pocketbook. 'Is there anything else you remember about her?'

'Mr Morrison, he can no take his eyes off her.' He smiled. 'Very new lady, I would say.' He hesitated. 'She no from round here, different voice.'

'A foreigner?'

'No.' He didn't sound too sure. 'One moment, I fetcha de waiter.'

He went to the door, opened it, and rattled something off in high speed Italian. The conversation lasted for a few sentences, then he came back.

'Scotland, he say. Scottish accent. She very nice lady.'

'Very interesting,' Stuart murmured. That narrowed things down by quite a lot. 'Thank you very much.'

'Mr Morrison, is he in trouble?' Signor Verde didn't look concerned, so Stuart guessed he was just being nosy.

'I wouldn't say that, sir, just making enquiries. It's this one we're really interested in.' He picked up the picture of Deborah Hunt.

'He no look at her the same way as the new one,' Signor Verde said quietly. 'He no like her no more.'

'Yes, that does seem to be the case.'

'She okay?' Now he did look anxious.

'As I said, sir, just making enquiries.' Stuart put the photos back together and reached for his pocket. 'Can you remember what time Mr Morrison arrived?'

'Si, he always comes at seven thirty and stays till we close at eleven. Like I say, mucho vino.' He smiled mischievously. 'They both had a very good time.'

Stuart made a note of the times along with the other information he had been given. The alibi had been confirmed, but the presence of another woman was cause for further investigation. Why hadn't he mentioned her? There was something funny going on here.

Stuart stood up. 'Well, thank you for your help. We'll be in touch if we need anything else.'

'Always glad to help de police.' Signor Verde shook his hand again, this time with a beaming smile.

As Stuart left his office and walked through the restaurant, he could almost smell the burning curiosity coming from the waiters. By the time he was going through the front door he could hear them jabbering away in even higher speed Italian than before.

Outside in the street, Stuart looked around himself. The town was still busy, and he wondered if he should go for that coffee. He checked the time on his phone, nearly twelve-thirty. It wouldn't matter if he ate in town instead of the station. It would make a change, and he had noticed a cafe a few doors down.

As he walked toward it, he wondered about this mysterious blonde woman with the Scottish accent. Had she and Clive Morrison been in this together?

Could she be an accessory to murder?

CHAPTER SEVEN

Clive was half awake and aching all over. He felt as though he had been run over by a truck. What had happened? Where was he? Not in his own very comfortable king-sized bed in Hawksmere that was for sure.

Then he smelled something and his eyes flew open. A horrible sense of déjà vu was coming over him. He sat bolt upright and shouted.

'Debs!'

He looked around the room with wide eyes. This wasn't his house. The smell of sausages and bacon was getting stronger as he looked down and realised he was sitting on a strange settee. He must have been there all night. That would account for his aching neck and back.

Connie came into the room, drying her hands on a tea towel. She looked nervous.

'Breakfast is ready,' she said quietly.

'Full English? I'm supposed to be watching my weight,' he spoke quietly too, remembering that they had important things to discuss.

'You had nothing last night. You need to keep your strength up, especially now.'

'Yes, we need to talk.'

'I know.'

He hauled himself off the settee and into the back room where the dining table was. A galley kitchen sat behind there. After they had eaten they stayed at the table, staring at each other.

'I had to tell you, Clive, else I never would. I know it was a lot on top of everything else. You were in such a state, you crashed out soon after.' He didn't answer, so she went on. 'When I met Andrew, I thought he was alright. Very charming and persuasive. He'd been to good schools and got a good job. It was only after we got married I found out he was a control freak, and violent with it.'

She slid her top off one shoulder and Clive saw a long white scar. He hadn't noticed it before. As he stared at it, his eyes wide, she quickly hid it again.

'He did that, amongst other things. I went for him with the carving knife, but he got it off me and laughed. Och, Clive, his eyes. I knew then I had to get out. I sold everything I had and moved as far away as I could. I ended up here and working at the gym.'

'Oh, God, Connie.' He reached for her hand.

She started to cry. 'Once the police get my name, they'll find out about him. I can't go back. I can't stand another trip to the hospital. I've changed my name by deed poll, but I'm still scared he'll come after me. He said many times that he'll never let me go.'

'We'll work something out, I promise. It's me the police are after, not you. They'll only want you to check my alibi, and if your surname's different to his they'll probably leave it at that.'

'Oh, Clive, do you really think so?' She looked hopeful now.

'Well, that's what I'd do.'

'Aye, you're probably right. It's just that I've been so worried about telling you. I didn't want to lose you.'

'You haven't, Connie. You're the best thing that's ever happened to me. I can't imagine life without you.'

'Nor me without you.' The words came out in a rush of relief. 'Och, thank heavens.'

He reached over to her and wrapped his arms around her.

'We shouldn't see each other again for a while, to be on the safe side,' Clive said after a while. 'The cops have said they'll want to speak to me again. After they've done some checking up.'

'Aye, that's sensible. But I'll miss you.' She smiled.

Later Clive drove slowly through Burton, his mind still processing everything she had said. He couldn't for the life of him understand why anyone would want to hurt such a lovely person as her. His blood boiled at the mere thought of it.

He joined the A38 at Branston. For once, the dual carriageway was quiet. Darkness was falling fast, so he switched on his headlights. As usual, he kept just below the speed limit, to keep himself out of trouble. His car's engine was over five litre capacity, so it was easy to ramp the speed up.

He had only gone a few hundred metres when he noticed a large vehicle coming up behind him. Very quickly. When it flashed its headlights at him, he wondered why. He wasn't doing anything wrong.

'Bloody prat,' he muttered as the glaring lights bounced off the interior mirror and nearly blinded him. He reached up with his left hand and knocked it downwards.

The headlights flashed again, and Clive wondered if it was someone he knew. He was trying to work out what make of car it was, but he couldn't see it properly. All he knew was that it looked more like a lorry than a car.

Don't know anybody with a thing like that.

The driver of the mystery vehicle blew his horn. Over and over again. He was as close to Clive's back bumper as he could possibly get, with his headlights on full beam. Clive was starting to get worried. What the hell was he playing at?

Clive shook his head and squinted against the bright lights. He could hardly see where he was going. Whoever was driving this thing was obviously trying to make him go faster, but Clive wasn't that stupid. Instead he pulled into the fast lane, and flicked his left indicator to tell the other driver to go past. For a second his eyes felt normal again, and he heaved a sigh of relief. Halfway through it, he realised the car was behind him once more. Doing exactly the same as before.

'What the fucking hell is going on?' Clive hissed between gritted teeth. 'What's this idiot trying to prove?'

He pulled back into the inside lane as he went past the turnoff for Riversholme. The one for Hawksmere was several miles ahead, but he had already decided to come off at Aldermarsh and go home through the lanes.

The next thing he knew, his car was rammed from behind. Clive's body was thrown forward and his chest slammed into the steering wheel, knocking most of the air out of his lungs. He began to panic as he realised he could hardly breathe. Black flecks appeared in front of his eyes and he felt faint. He gasped for air, his mouth wide open in a grimace of fear and pain. The thought flitted across his mind that the other driver might be Connie's husband, but surely that wasn't possible? Unless he had been stalking her and watching the house. From what he had heard, he was quite capable of doing both.

'Should've come off at Riversholme,' he realised as the pain began to subside and he put his foot down. There was only one thing to do. Get away from this mad bastard. His speed crept up and up, but he barely noticed.

Clive's breathing was coming back, but now his whole body was shaking. He gripped the steering wheel even harder as the thought of being run off the road by a jealous husband refused to go away. He was perspiring, cold sweat running down his back. He had heard the expression blind terror but had never known what it meant until now. His eyes were wide as he tried to focus on the road.

Shit, he can't find out where I live. Shit, shit.

He saw the sign for Aldermarsh and automatically reached for the indicator stick. His shaking hand hovered over it, then he put it back onto the wheel. Let the other car go speeding off in the direction of Lichfield. By the time the driver realised what had happened, Clive could be miles away.

The turnoff was approaching and he knew he was going too fast. He needed to slow down, but daren't. Not yet. Whoever was behind him wasn't messing about.

Clive's breathing sounded like a tired old steam train as he saw the ramp to come off the A38. He would need to go round a small island at the top, to go over the flyover. He would be doing it on two wheels if he wasn't careful. His mind went blank as he stared at it. It was getting closer by the millisecond.

He nearly closed his eyes as his Mercedes flew onto the ramp. He braked as hard as he could, gritting his teeth as he stamped down hard on the pedal. The tyres squealed in protest, and he thought he could smell smoke. The car responded a lot quicker than he would have thought possible and by the time he got to the top, he was doing a normal speed. It was just as well. A motorcyclist was coming onto the island from his right.

Clive drove round the island carefully, now aware that his hands were aching as well as his chest. There was a closed off lane to the left up ahead, so he pulled into it and stopped. He leaned back in his seat and groaned with pain. His body seemed to be shaking on the inside as well now. He felt so tired, like he could sleep for a week, if he ever got into his bed. His body twitched and he got the driver's door open just in time. He threw up beside the car, fighting for breath. His eyes prickled with tears. He wanted to go home and lock himself away from the world. Never face it again.

After a while his breathing came back under control and he stopped shaking. He went over the incident in his mind and told himself not to be so stupid. It couldn't have been Connie's husband, it was just some nutter on an ego trip.

This thought reassured him that he had overreacted. Then he panicked again and looked all around himself for signs of a vehicle. There was nothing.

He was alone. Scared – but alone.

But what if it was him? What will he do to Connie?

CHAPTER EIGHT

Stuart eventually drove back to Brodewell, feeling better for having spent an hour in the cafe in Burton. He had drunk two cups of tea, and eaten a jacket potato with cheese and beans. The best thing about it was that no one had known who he was. It had been so pleasant to relax and do ordinary everyday things without being disturbed by anyone. He didn't feel the slightest bit guilty either.

On the way back he decided he ought to do this more often, but maybe not in Burton. There must be somewhere in Lichfield he could use, preferably a place he could walk to. He needed to get out more. He was turning into a boring young old man.

He got back to the police station halfway through the afternoon, and found a note on his desk from Nikki. She wasn't around, and he frowned. He read the message, and smiled himself. She had been to the pub and gleaned some useful information.

He supposed he had better speak to Shorty before he did anything else. Stuart knocked on his office door, and responded to the grunt he got in reply. Stuart often wondered what it was that Vic had got to be so bad tempered about.

'Wot's 'appening, then?' It was the usual greeting.

'I went to the Italian restaurant.'

'You've been gone long enough to have a three-course meal.' Vic scowled at him. 'Did you?'

'Of course not, Guv, but I did have something to eat while I was out.'

'Right. Fair enough, I suppose.'

'Anyway, Clive Morrison was in there on Friday night. With a new woman.'

'Was he now?' He was looking interested now.

'Yeah. Blonde, very attractive, Scottish accent.'

'Another bird on the go.' Vic actually smiled. 'So, he'd want to get the old one out of the way.'

'I suppose so.' Stuart wished he would shut up so that he could finish his report. 'And it looks as though Nikki found out some good stuff. A woman called Connie was mentioned. Also a gym. Sounds like she works there.'

'Told you to send her to the pub.' Vic looked very pleased with himself. 'Women are nosy. Good at getting that sort of information.'

Stuart stared at him in astonishment. Whether he realised it or not, Vic had just given the whole of womanhood the most amazing back-handed compliment. Wow. Things were looking up.

'Get 'er to find this woman.' Vic opened the top drawer of his desk, frowned, and closed it again. 'Then we'll have to speak to them both before they have a chance to get together and cook up a story.'

'Probably already have,' Stuart murmured.

'Yeah, you're probably right.' Vic sighed. 'In the meantime, find this Connie woman. And speak to that mate of Morrison's. He might give something away.'

'Yes, Guv.'

'Off you go, then.' Vic waved a dismissive hand.

Stuart went back into the main office and saw that Nikki was back at her desk. He immediately felt better. He wished he had someone in his life that could cheer him up like that. It would be so much nicer than going back to an empty flat every night.

'Hi, Stuart. Did you get my note?'

He nodded. 'Excellent work, Nikki, just what we needed.' He smiled at her.

'Not looking good for the boyfriend if there's another woman in the picture.'

'Yeah. Can you get onto that, see if you can find her?'

'Already on it. I've got the names of all the gyms in the area.'

'Good. Sorry you've got all the boring stuff. We need more staff.'

'I don't mind.' She gave him a beaming smile. 'Someone's got to do it, and I enjoyed the pub. Wouldn't mind going there again.'

'They got some smashing pubs out in some of these villages. Much friendlier than the town ones.'

'That's coz everyone knows everyone.' Nikki

laughed. 'I fancy living in a village. Thought I was going to be, but it never happened.'

'Everything alright at home?' he asked quietly.

'Sure.' She glanced at Vic's office door and shook her head slightly. Stuart got the message, and cleared his throat in embarrassment as he tried to think of something to say. Something connected with work.

'The Guv's asked me to speak to Phil Bateman, the boyfriend's best mate. See if that throws anything up. Might do. When I talked to Clive Morrison I got the feeling he was hiding something.'

'Connie?'

'Maybe. Probably.'

'I wonder how long that's been going on?' She looked thoughtful.

'The restaurant owner seemed to think it was a new relationship, and I think he's right. He must see loads of couples like that in his job.' Stuart laughed. ' I bet there's a few he could blackmail.'

'Yeah, I'll bet.'

'Oi,' a detached male voice shouted from the next office. 'Stop chatting up the birds and get yer arse in 'ere.'

'All charm as usual.' Stuart sighed.

'Yeah. Know what you mean.' Nikki chuckled.

'Oi, sunshine, I haven't got all day,' Vic's voice rang out again.

'You'd better go.'

'Yeah. Catch you later.'

Stuart opened the door just as Vic was draining his Stoke City Football Club coffee mug. 'Guv?'

'Just heard about a spate of car thefts in the area. Gawd, just coz I've bin made up to DCI, she thinks she can dump it on me.' Vic waved him to the chair on the opposite side of his desk. 'You heard anything on your travels?'

'No, Guv.'

'Keep yer eyes open, Fatso's on the warpath over it.' Stuart raised his eyebrows. 'Yeah, I know. Uniform should be dealing with it. She's only got her knickers in a twist because it's high-end motors being nicked, and she's got the latest Audi.'

'Lucky her,' Stuart muttered, but Vic heard him.

'Yeah. All I've got is a clapped out Volvo.' Vic laughed. 'Think I'm safe.'

'And me, with a Ford Fiesta.'

'Dunno about that. Your model of car is about the most popular one to get stolen these days.'

'Thanks, Guv. That's really cheered me up.'

'Dunna worry, son. These geezers are after Jags and stuff. Posh cars the likes of us can't afford. Do you know, there are two Maserati's in Hawksmere, and I've heard that some flash git in Aldermarsh has got a five litre Ford Mustang.'

'My dream car,' Stuart murmured, a faraway look in his eyes. 'A silver one.'

'You dream on, son, coz that's all you'll ever do.' Vic laughed, but there wasn't much humour in it. 'As if we ain't got enough to do. What's yer mate up to?'

'Tracing this Scottish woman. Shouldn't take her long. She's good at stuff like that.'

'Yeah, she's a good cop,' Vic said, then stared at Stuart. 'But don't you go telling her I said that.'

'Yee-haa!.' Came from next door.

'What the 'ell?' Vic grumbled, nodding his head towards the next office. Stuart went to investigate.

'I've found her.' Nikki looked at him with shining eyes. 'Works at that big gym on the edge of Burton. Connie Mackenzie. Gotcha!'

CHAPTER NINE

Phil was excited. Today his latest project would be finished, and he couldn't wait to try it out. He had seen one on a rugby trip to America, and had wanted one ever since. He could hardly wait to show it off to Michelle, and anyone else he could talk into coming round. He was sure that no one else in the area had one, and he had beers and white wine cooling in the fridge ready for the grand opening. Of his brand new hot tub.

Halfway through the afternoon, he was in his swimming trunks and climbing into the warm bubbling water with a can of lager in his hand. There was a bench seat all around the tub, which would easily seat six people. His imagination went into overdrive as he pictured Michelle opposite him dressed in a bikini, or even less. Oh yes, he couldn't wait for tonight.

Then he remembered Clive. The poor bloke was very

unhappy but Phil could hardly understand why. All he had done for months was moan about Debs, so what was the problem? At least Phil didn't have any issues like that, although Michelle didn't always share his enthusiasms. Her favourite activity seemed to be shopping trips to Birmingham, not his sort of thing at all.

He was halfway down his beer when he heard his phone ringing.

'Oh shit,' he complained, and decided to let the answerphone pick it up. When he heard a male voice begin to speak, he changed his mind. It was a Detective Sergeant Young, and no one messed the police about if they knew what was good for them. He hurried out of the tub to answer the call.

'I understand you're a friend of Clive Morrison?' the voice said.

'Yeah, that's right,.' Phil replied, feeling rather puzzled.

'I'd like to speak to you about him.'

'What do you want to know?'

'I'd like to come round later this afternoon, if that's convenient.'

No, it ain't, I got plans. 'Er, yeah, okay.'

'Four o'clock?'

'Yes, that's alright.'

Stuart repeated the address to Phil to make sure he had got it right, then rang off. Phil looked at the tub half buried in the garden as if it had done something really wicked, and cursed. He was still cursing when he put on a fluffy towelling bathrobe and walked inside the house to get dressed.

'Bloody police,' he muttered. 'What the hell do they want to see me for? I don't know anything.'

He was dancing his way into his underpants when the phone rang again. This was turning into one of those days when nothing went right, and he was beginning to wish he hadn't even bothered to get up. Once a day started like that, it rarely got better.

'Hello,' he snarled into the phone.

'God, somebody's got out of bed the wrong side.' Michelle's voice soothed him somewhat. 'What's up with you?'

'Got the sodding police coming round in a bit.'

'What for?'

'I don't know. Something about Clive and Debs, I suppose. Dunno what they think I can tell them.'

'Perhaps they think he killed her?'

'Trust you to think of that. Of course he didn't kill her. You've got a nasty suspicious mind.'

'Of course I have, I'm a Brummie.' she laughed. Phil sometimes wondered about her past. She never talked about it. It was as if she hadn't existed before he met her. 'He might have, you know.'

'Michelle, get real.'

'It happened on his birthday, didn't it?' she persisted, 'and he wasn't out with you, was he?'

'Give over, he didn't kill her. He wouldn't. He couldn't.'

'I wouldn't be so sure.'

'You'd better stop saying things like that. It's bad enough I've got to speak to the police, without you starting.'

'Okay, okay. Shall I see you later?'

'Dunno. I'll see.'

She started to say something, but Phil had had enough, so he hung up on her. Today was turning into a nightmare, and about all he wanted to do now was get pissed and have an early night. There didn't seem much point in doing anything else. Michelle had really annoyed him, suggesting his best friend was capable of murder. How dare she?

He finished getting dressed and cleaned his teeth to get the smell of beer off his breath before the police arrived. He didn't know why they were bothering. He didn't know anything. He had hardly known Debs.

Two cops arrived at two minutes past four, both male. Detective Sergeant Young introduced himself and the young PC in plain clothes, who made notes as they talked.

'So,' Stuart began. 'How long have you lived in Hawksmere?'

'About five years. Since I retired.'

Stuart looked surprised, then asked him what he did before.

'I was a professional rugby player, mainly county stuff, but I made the England team for a while,' Phil said proudly. Stuart looked suitably impressed. 'Then I did TV commentaries, and coached a youth team. In Warwickshire.'

'What made you come here?'

'Always liked the place. Had enough of cities. I think most people who live here feel like that.'

Stuart nodded as though he understood. 'And how long have you known Clive Morrison?'

'Since I moved here really. Met him in the pub.'

'You're good friends?'

'He's my best mate.'

'Deborah Hunt. Did you know her?'

'Hardly at all, he didn't bring her out much. He did to start with, but she always got drunk and loud. Made a prat of herself and embarrassed him.'

'Were they together when you moved here?'

'No, they'd been together for just under a year. I don't know how they actually met, but I think Clive soon wished they hadn't. He wanted to get shot of her, but he didn't know how to do it. Said she needed someone to look after her. She couldn't cope on her own.'

'So it wasn't a close relationship?' Stuart glanced at his colleague, who nodded slightly. What that was all about, Phil had no idea. He just wished they would hurry up and go. They were making him feel uncomfortable.

'Only for a few weeks. Until he realised she was an alkie.'

'Did she get treatment?'

Phil shook his head. 'Didn't want to know, just after someone to latch onto. Clive got himself well and truly lumbered.'

'Do you know if she had any family?'

Phil shook his head. 'Not a clue. Like I said, I hardly knew her.'

'What about your friend. Was he seeing anyone else?'

Phil didn't know what to say. How honest should he be?

'I dunno really, he has been – well – a bit distant lately, but that could be anything. He owns a lot of properties

57

and I know he gets problems with them sometimes, so I can't really tell you.'

Stuart nodded. 'Last Friday, did you see him?'

'Yeah, it was his birthday. We went to the Red Lion for a couple of pints, then he went off for a meal.'

'What time was this?'

'Ooh, I dunno. Got there about half five, I suppose. He left at seven. He'd got a table booked for half past.'

'Birthday meal on his own?'

Phil thought Stuart looked sceptical, but tried not to react to it.

'He often went on his own. Always goes to the same place, he likes his food.' Stuart was still looking at him. 'Some Italian place in Burton.'

'Well.' Stuart stood up. 'You've been very helpful, sir.'

Phil showed them out, trying not to smile as he did it. Inwardly he was heaving a sigh of relief. He knew he had confirmed his friend's alibi, but only for part of the evening. What if Clive had murdered her? He knew he had a temper, and he also knew that Debs had been very good at winding him up.

Phil's blood ran cold.

Oh God, what if he really did kill her?

CHAPTER TEN

Clive was getting ready to go out for a walk, a thing he rarely did, and was wondering what to wear. A pub was going to be involved too, so he shouldn't be too scruffy. A drink at the end had been the big incentive. He knew he should get more exercise, but most of the time he couldn't be bothered.

The idea had come from Phil, with encouragement from Michelle. Clive still wasn't sure about her. He was convinced that she was more interested in what Phil had got in the bank than the man himself. Maybe his own situation had influenced his thinking. He had decided that now this had changed, he ought to give Michelle the benefit of the doubt. Perhaps she was genuine after all.

'Right,' he said to the empty bedroom. 'Jeans, sweatshirt and trainers. That'll do.'

He met Phil and Michelle by the canal bridge and they set off to walk to The Swan. It was an old pub at the junction of two canals and was a popular watering hole, especially in the summer. It would take forty-five minutes to walk along the tow path, and Clive was actually looking forward to it. He smiled at Michelle and she looked surprised. He could understand why. He usually ignored her.

There wasn't room for them to walk three abreast, so Michelle fell behind. She had her phone in her hand, and Phil tutted.

'She lives on that thing,' he complained quietly. 'Dunno why, she don't seem to have any friends. Not round here, anyway.'

Clive didn't answer, so Phil changed the subject. 'Heard anything yet?'

'Yeah, the cops have got hold of Debs' dad. He says he'll arrange the funeral but I've offered to pay for it. Seems the least I can do.'

'I had the police round yesterday. Wasn't sure what to tell them.'

Clive looked over his shoulder. Michelle had stopped several metres behind them, and was typing.

'You're the only one who knows about Connie. Keep it to yourself, will you? At least for now.'

'"Course I will. Mind you.' Phil glanced back too. 'Who's she going to tell?'

'I suppose the police will find out about her, but I'll cross that bridge when I get to it.'

'Might be that one up there.' Phil grinned at the one he could see in the distance.

When they got to The Swan, they sat at a table outside the front of it. Phil went inside, leaving Clive alone with Michelle.

'Are you alright, Clive?'

'Getting there.' He looked at her. She seemed genuinely concerned.

'Yeah,' she said quietly, 'and you've still got us.'

She leaned across the table and kissed him gently on the cheek. Clive was embarrassed, especially when he caught her eye when she sat back. She didn't fancy him, did she?

Clive looked away towards the narrow boats at the canal junction. One was mooring up close to the shop next to the pub. Out of the corner of his eye he was relieved to see Phil coming back carrying a tray of drinks. As he put it down, someone he knew came running along the towpath. He was a boater friend who drank in the villages. He looked worried, but his face broke into a smile as he spotted the three some.

'Graham.' Phil greeted him, 'how's it going?'

'Could do with a bit of help, from both of you.'

'Sure.' He said as he stood up. 'Keep our seats, Michelle, it's getting busy.'

'Huh.' She was reaching for her phone.

Clive and Phil walked towards the lock, which was close to The Swan. The other man seemed to be in a tearing hurry.

'What's the rush, Graham?' Clive asked.

'Need to keep the boats where they are. Got swans in the lock.'

'Eh?'

'Mum, Dad, and five cygnets.' Graham was getting breathless. 'If some prat lets the water in at full pelt, they'll drown.'

'Oh.'

Phil rushed after him, wondering how the birds had got into the lock in the first place. Or was Graham having them on? He was known as a bit of a joker.

'You stay here.' Clive was told. 'And you get down the other end, and don't let anyone do anything,' he said to Phil. 'I'll fill the lock and let them out.'

Nobody argued. It seemed their mate was telling the truth. Sure enough, there were seven swans way down in the lock. Graham wound the paddles up only a few centimetres to let the water in slowly. Even so, the cygnets started to panic. They began to swim around in circles, cheeping furiously. Clive didn't know what to do, so stayed where he was. There was a boat approaching from his end, so he called to it to stop. When he explained why, he could tell the people on it didn't believe him, but they moored up anyway and waited.

The lock filled up a lot slower than usual, and complaints were coming from both ends. Graham took no notice. Everyone knew he was a stubborn blighter. He lived on a boat a few locks down towards Aldermarsh, and was very aware of, and concerned about, nature and the environment. He was a real water gypsy, and proud to be so.

Clive had one eye on the swans. When the water was nearly at the top of the side wall, the adults began to attempt to climb out. One of the cygnets had a go too but had no success at all. Eventually the bigger swans got out. One of them stayed on the grass, and the other one waddled off in the direction of the lock gate. This was opened carefully a few minutes later by Graham, who had been talking quietly to the swans all through the operation. Normally he had a gruff voice, but not at the moment.

'Come on, you little buggers,' he said with a smile as the five cygnets glided effortlessly through the open gate, cheeping with happiness now. When they were well out of the way, he called to the boat which was waiting to come through at Phil's end. 'Okay mate. Panic over.'

Everyone went back to what they were doing before. Michelle had finished her glass of white wine and was looking at her phone again. Phil rolled his eyes at Clive, who fought back a smile. They both picked up their pints and took a long slurp.

'Well, that was a bit of excitement.' Phil chuckled.

'All that fuss for a few poxy birds.' Michelle tutted, and reached into her handbag.

'You're in the countryside now. It's different to the middle of Birmingham.'

'Tell me about it,' she muttered sullenly.

'You chose to come here.'

Clive could tell Phil was annoyed, and thought he had better change the subject, having no desire to be stuck in the middle of a domestic.

'I was thinking of buying a narrow boat a while back.'

'Why didn't you?' Phil seemed to be playing along.

'Don't think I'd ever use it to be honest, and you lose money on them in the long run. Bought some gold instead. Can't lose on that.'

'Never thought of doing that.' Phil looked thoughtful. 'Not a bad idea. Bit dodgy having it in the house, though.'

'It's in the bank. Should be safe enough there.' Clive laughed. 'It'd better be.'

'Perhaps I should buy a boat. Just for the hell of it.'

'Where you gonna go on that?' Michelle snorted. 'Up and down the canal?'

'That seems to be the general idea of them. Fancy it?'

'Not a lot.' She went back to her phone.

'Got the hot tub working, Clive.' Phil smiled. 'That was fun.'

'Never been in one of those.' Clive wasn't sure he fancied it. The thought of being barely dressed in front of strangers made him feel uncomfortable.

'You'll have to come round and have a go. Got plenty of beers in the fridge.'

'Yeah, we'll have to do that sometime.'

'We'll keep you to that.' Michelle was smiling at him again. Now Clive was sure he didn't want to do it. 'Anyway, who's going to get me another drink?'

Clive was about to offer when his phone started to ring.

'Oh God, now what?' he grumbled.

'Mr Clive Morrison?' There was a female Walsall accent, and Clive wondered who she could be. Probably in one of his rental properties. 'My name is Detective Constable Nikki Singh. We'd like you to come into the station at Brodewell again, to give another statement.'

'Is that really necessary?' Clive didn't like the sound of that.

'Yes, sir, it is,' Nikki said firmly. 'We have some new information.'

Clive could guess what it was, and was worried. It looked as though they had found out about Connie.

How was he going to talk his way out of this one?

CHAPTER ELEVEN

'He's on his way.'

Stuart looked at Nikki and had to admit he was nervous. Vic had insisted that he should take the lead in the interview with Clive Morrison, and that Nikki should be there too.

'She needs the practice,' he had said. 'And anyway, you'll be gentler with him than me. I'll be in the monitoring room.'

Great, Stuart thought. *My every move being watched. Can't wait.*

Feeling like he was the one about to be interrogated, Stuart headed for Interview Room One, with Nikki walking behind him. The Family Liaison Officer had been informed that Clive was to be interviewed again, but as he had no family, she wasn't going to be involved any further. Stuart wasn't looking forward to seeing

Clive again. He hoped he had calmed down and lost his aggressive attitude. Maybe that was why Vic was keeping out of the way. He never had ripped anyone's head off, but Stuart got the feeling that he might make an exception in the case of Mr Clive Morrison.

Stuart took a deep breath as he pushed open the door. Clive was sitting at the table on his own with his hands clasped in front of him. Stuart and Nikki sat opposite him.

'Mr Morrison, thank you for coming in,' Stuart began. 'For the benefit of the tape, I am Detective Sergeant Stuart Young. Also present is Detective Constable Nikki Singh.'

Clive nodded towards Nikki, and almost smiled.

'Don't really know why I'm here,' Clive said quietly. 'I haven't done anything.'

'Maybe not, sir.' Stuart looked back at him. 'But you haven't told us the whole truth. We've checked your story and found something rather interesting.'

Stuart stopped, hoping Clive would respond. Silence.

'The lady in question is on her way here. We'll be speaking to her soon.'

Clive squirmed.

'Connie Mackenzie.' Nikki added.

'Yeah, okay. I know her. I go to the gym she works at, that's where we met.'

'And she was with you on your birthday. At La Dolce Vita.'

'That's not a crime, is it?'

'No, sir. But withholding information from the police is not the best thing to be doing,' Stuart said firmly. 'Would you care to explain?'

'No. It's private.'

'Surely you can see how it looks? You go out with another woman, then the one you've got at home gets murdered.'

'That just proves it wasn't me, if I was out with another woman.' Clive glared at Stuart. 'Doesn't it?'

'You have an alibi for the time up until eleven pm. After that, you can't prove where you were. We know you weren't at home, as I was the one who greeted you when you returned to your house the next day, at eleven forty-five.'

Clive growled and ran his hand through his hair. Then he spoke quietly.

'I was with Connie. All night. Okay?'

'She'll confirm that, will she?'

'Of course she will. God, you people.' Clive rolled his eyes.

Stuart glanced at Nikki. Neither of them knew what to say. Stuart wished Vic was here. He could feel his beady eyes on him and could almost hear him saying, 'yer making a hash of this.'

Except he wouldn't have used the word hash.

'Would you like a cup of tea, Mr Morrison?' Nikki asked.

'Yeah, I'm parched.' He held her eyes for a second. 'Let's hope it's better than your coffee.'

'Yes, it is a bit grim.' Nikki smiled as she reached for her phone. 'Doesn't do much for your temper.'

Stuart smiled at Nikki. It seemed she had rescued the situation. He nodded at her and she understood. He was letting her take over now.

'This is all very awkward for you, sir,' she spoke softly. 'And quite embarrassing.'

'You're not wrong there.' Clive sighed. 'The business with Debs was over, had been for quite a while. I wanted her to move out, but she just wouldn't go. I couldn't get through to her.'

'She could have gone back to her family, surely?'

'She never talked about any. They couldn't have been close. I don't know what the situation was there. Or what set her off drinking. I wasn't much help to her.'

'Dealing with a problem like this is very difficult.'

'I didn't know what to do. We went to counselling once, but she wouldn't go again. I was out of my depth with her, I couldn't cope.'

'That must have been very frustrating.'

'It was. I tried to talk to her about it but all we did was argue. She wouldn't accept that she had a problem. I mean, what can you do with someone like that?'

'Did you ask her to leave?'

'Loads of times, that's when she turned the tears on. Meeting Connie saved my life. Well, my sanity anyway. My birthday was the first time I'd stayed the night with her. I never gave Debs a thought.'

Too busy having a good time, Stuart thought. *Can't say I blame him.*

'Debs must have had some friends,' Nikki was saying. 'Perhaps someone came round to keep her company while you were out.'

'Can't imagine who that would be.' Clive looked thoughtful. 'The only time she went out was to the shops. To get booze, of course. That was all she was interested in. I can't see anyone else wanting to get involved with her.'

'Did she ever ring anyone?'

'Not that I know of.' Clive frowned. 'I used to hear her talking in her room sometimes, but she talked to herself a lot when she was pi – drunk.'

Nikki glanced at Stuart. He could tell she was running out of things to say, but she had done better than he ever could have. He wondered what Vic was thinking.

The tea arrived, and they let Clive drink it in silence.

'Just popping out for a sec.'

'Detective Sergeant Young is leaving the room,' Nikki said as he went through the door.

Stuart found Vic with his head in his hands.

'Are you alright, Guv?'

'Headache. Had the missus on the phone last night. She does me 'ed in.'

'Oh.' Stuart looked towards Clive. 'What d'you think?'

'You've covered everything I can think of, and a few other things besides.' Vic sighed. 'Reckon we can leave Nikki to talk to the woman. Don't think we'll get much different out of her. They'll alibi each other and there ain't a thing we can do about it.'

'No. You can't blame him for getting involved with another woman. I feel sorry for him in a way.'

'Yeah,' Vic muttered. 'That's probably what I should have done.'

'Right, then.' Stuart didn't know how to answer that.

'Stay single, son.' Vic sighed. 'Much easier in the long run.'

'Mm.'

'Any road up, get back in there and wrap things up. We ain't gonna get anything else out of 'im. If that woman's here yet, don't let him speak to her. Smuggle him out the back way.'

Stuart had visions of slinging a blanket over Clive's head and leading him past a gang of screaming and shouting reporters while cameras flashed. He must have been watching too much television.

'Yes, Guv,' he said with a smile.

After Clive had gone, Stuart and Nikki went to the kitchen.

'You were right about the coffee,' he said as they walked down the corridor. 'Perhaps that's why Shorty's in such a bad mood all the time.'

'Haven't seen him today, what's he up to?'

'Not sure really, he doesn't seem his normal self.'

'Got one on him?'

'No, very quiet.'

'Heck.' Nikki grimaced. I don't like the sound of that.'

CHAPTER TWELVE

On the quiet, Vic was feeling fragile. He had done his best to hide the fact from everyone, mainly by keeping out of the way. He had the hangover from hell but it wasn't his fault. The stupid woman he had once been married to had been on to him last night, and given him a load of grief about their daughter, Faye.

Vic hadn't seen Faye for years, not since his wife had walked out. He went back to his office as memories of the past began to overwhelm him. He closed the door behind him and buried his face in his hands again. He felt awful.

He had been seventeen when he met Roz. In no time flat she had become pregnant and that was when the trouble had started. How was he to know she was only fifteen? His family had thought it was hilarious, and his father had even congratulated him for being able to get it up. That had been the first time Vic had thought he was worth anything. He was usually being beaten into submission by one of his three much bigger older brothers. He felt like he had got his fifteen minutes of fame.

The girl's family were a different lot altogether, even if they did live in the same rough area as Vic. They had given him three choices. Death, marriage or prosecution. Vic had gone for the easiest option.

The call from his ex-wife had led to several pints in a bar somewhere, followed by a load of Scotch at home. Now his head was woozy, his stomach felt raw, and his eyes were behaving as though they belonged to someone else. He had spent half the morning trying to think up a believable excuse to go home, so far without success.

The phone rang, and he jumped out of his skin. It wasn't usually that loud surely? Praying it wasn't the Super, he answered it. He was in luck. It was a Detective Sergeant from Lichfield.

'Thought you'd like to be kept appraised of the ongoing situation,' the posh male voice said.

Vic nearly swore at him. Why could nobody say what they meant these days?

'Yeah.' He didn't even try to sound enthusiastic.

'There's been another car theft,' the voice said.

'Oh, ar?'

'Yes, sir.' The voice rattled off some details, then politely rang off, ending with a phrase that Vic detested. Have a nice day.

'I'll give you nice day, you bleedin' twat,' he muttered as the phone went silent. 'Shove it right up your posh squeaky arse.'

Ooh, me head.

Coffee. That might help. He had already had two, which hadn't, but he lived in hope.

'Nikki,' he yelled. Then he winced. Shouting wasn't a good idea at the moment. The word was banging around in his brain like a ball bearing in a pinball machine. Weee, ping, clunk. 'Oh Gawd,' he muttered. 'Looks like I got to fetch me own bleedin' coffee.'

He wandered down to the kitchen, hoping he wasn't going to get a cheery 'good morning,' from anybody. So far there had been nothing good about it whatsoever.

He dismissed the thought as he entered the kitchen and headed for the counter. Stuart was walking away from it with a cup in his hand, but Vic barely noticed. Nikki was in front of him, making tea. She must have felt his presence, as she turned to face him.

'Oh, hello, Guv.'

'Yeah, whatever.' He gave the mug a dirty look. 'Don't take all day over it. You got another interview to do.'

'Yes, Guv, I know. She hasn't arrived yet.'

Vic reached for the kettle, his head beginning to throb now. 'I need black coffee,' he growled. 'Now.'

Nikki turned away, and Vic suspected she was trying not to laugh. He must look worse than he felt. He got his drink and hurried back to the office. Today wasn't getting any better. Perhaps he should go home, and not bother about any excuses.

Back in the safety of his own personal space, Vic tried to relax. He knew from experience that as the day wore on he would feel better. He had never been a morning person at the best of times. And sometimes forgot he had to get up early. That had certainly happened last night. He had been in a foul mood and was now in the process of regretting the antidote to it.

'Stupid cow,' he muttered as he glanced up at the enormous clock over his office door. 'More money off me. Hope she's spending it on the kid.'

Their daughter probably wasn't a kid any more, and Vic wondered exactly how old she was now. He hadn't seen her for what – at least twelve years. He thought back over the conversation with his wife, which had degenerated into the usual slanging match. He felt a flash of pity for Faye. Maybe he should get in touch with her. She must be in her twenties by now.

He slurped the lukewarm black coffee without even noticing. Why did it taste so bloody awful? He let out a low slow groan.

The phone rang again. It didn't seem as loud this time, which was good news. The coffee must be working at last. He picked up the receiver and growled into it. Then he sat bolt upright and straightened his tie as he realised who was on the other end. Fatso. Superintendent Joanne Lowe.

'DI Hardcastle,' she began. While Vic was mentally yelling that there wasn't an R in castle, she continued. 'How are things?'

'Fine, ma'am, everything's under control.' If she had been standing in front of him, he might have been tempted to salute her. 'Anything I can help you with?'

'No, just touching base.' There was a slight pause. 'What exactly are you dealing with at the moment?'

Vic sighed. How did she get to be Super? He reeled off his current active cases. 'Suspicious death in Hawksmere, and some geezer in Riversholme has had his Aston Martin stolen.' *Serves him right, the flash git.* 'I've passed that one on to uniform.'

'I asked you to deal with the stolen cars.' She sounded annoyed.

There isn't an R in asked either. 'Oh yes, ma'am, of course. What I meant was, I've passed on the details.' He smirked. 'They need to be kept appraised of the ongoing situation.'

'Of course, of course.' She sounded a bit happier now. 'Nice to see you're being so cooperative.'

'I do my best, ma'am.' Vic winced. He sounded like a right creep. Still, it never hurt to suck up to the boss.

'How many cars is that now?' she was asking.

'Too many. Four, ma'am.'

'This has to stop. You'd better make this your top priority.' Vic almost groaned again. 'Any developments on the suspicious death?'

'Interviews are in progress, ma'am, as we speak.'

'Good, good.' She actually sounded pleased. Vic allowed himself a small smile. 'Well, you seem to have everything under control, excellent.' There was a pause. 'Er, you know, of course, that the Chief Superintendent is retiring?'

'No ma'am, actually, I didn't.' He smiled. So that was the real reason for her call. He wondered what might be coming next.

'No matter. We're arranging a party for him. I want you to make sure there's a good turnout. We want him to know how much he's appreciated.'

'Yes, ma'am.' Vic rolled his eyes to the ceiling. That was two retirements in one month. The other had been the Chief Constable, whom he had never met.

Superintendent Lowe gave him the necessary details, which he dutifully noted down. Then she rang off. Now he really did growl. Another boring retirement do, where everyone had to be on their best behaviour for someone they hardly knew.

Then again, someone usually manages to get drunk and do something interesting. Mmm. Maybe it won't be so boring after all…

CHAPTER THIRTEEN

For a short time Vic was lost in the past again, calling to mind some of the more memorable moments from past parties at various places across the county. He chuckled a few times. His eye caught the clock – it would be difficult to miss – and knew he should get back to work. He hadn't done much today as it was.

I'm feeling better, good. Knew the coffee would work if I drank enough of it.

'Right, wot we got,' he muttered, shuffling through the files on his screen. 'Oh, ar, stolen cars. Gawd.'

Still thinking that somebody else ought to be dealing with such a mundane matter, he got reading. It was only high-end cars that had gone missing. Four of them, but they all had something in common. The owners hadn't seen them for several days before realising they had disappeared. At last, something of interest in this case. Vic started going through all the statements again, looking for the missing link.

The CID office was quiet, so there was nothing to disturb his concentration. He made notes as he went along, hummed and haahed a few times, and tapped his pen on the desk every now and then while he was thinking.

Until he heard a Frankie Baxter laugh.

'Oh, fer –'

He could hear female voices and they were getting closer. One was Frankie, obviously, but it took him a while to realise that the quieter one was Nikki's.

'Just finished another interview with Stuart,' she was saying. 'When it's typed up, I'll have to show it to the Guv. What you been up to?'

'Been to see my manager, and now I'm stocking up the van. You wouldn't believe how many evidence bags I get through.'

'There's plenty of work for all of us. This station is pretty understaffed.'

'Yeah, I've noticed. Must be coz you only deal with rural stuff.'

'Yes, we're a bit of a backwater.' Nikki laughed. 'No one takes much notice of Brodewell.'

'Hey, when are we going out again? Must be overdue for a drink together.'

'Mm, it's been a while.'

Vic's ears stood to attention. So, these two were friends. An unlikely combination. Today was full of revelations. He sat still and listened to the rest of their conversation.

'What about Friday?' Nikki was saying. 'I've told Zak I'm going to Mom's for the weekend. He'll never know.'

Vic frowned. Nikki had not long got married. Secrets already? He moved quietly over to the door so he could hear better.

'You haven't seen her for a while, have you?'

'Not since the wedding. Me and Zak had a right row about it, but I told him he could sod off and I'm going to see her. Or words to that effect.'

'Good for you, gal.' Vic heard what he presumed was a high-five going on.

'She's my mom. I've got every right to see her.'

'She lives in Walsall, doesn't she?'

'Yeah, just across town from where we're living. It's not as if I'm going to the other end of the country, and it wouldn't make any difference if I was.'

'What's up with the bloke?' Frankie asked.

'I dunno. Seems to think he owns me now. He's changed a lot since we got married. I don't even like him anymore.'

'Sounds like you need some time off from him.'

'Do I ever.' Nikki laughed.

'Right. Friday night it is.'

'I can get a hotel room somewhere, then go to Mom's on Saturday.'

'You can stay with me, if you don't mind sleeping on the floor. Mum won't mind, so long as we're quiet.'

'You sure?' Vic guessed that Frankie was nodding. 'That'd be great.'

'She'll put the kids to bed. She usually does.' Frankie gave another of her laughs, and Vic winced. Nikki was welcome to a night out with her, he decided. 'She loves having the girls at hers, and I don't think she minds me too much either. She never liked Paul anyway, so I think she's quite glad we've split up.'

Vic's mind was racing as they put the finishing touches to their arrangements. So that's why Frankie Baxter had moved down here. And the way things were going, it looked as though her mate might soon be manless as well. He wondered if he should warn Nikki off, but it was none of his business.

'I'd better be going,' Frankie said. 'That van won't stock itself.'

'Yeah, see you Friday, if not before.' Nikki sounded happier now.

Vic went back to the files, only half aware what the common denominator was on the car thefts. One owner had been on holiday abroad, and one was away on business and had used the train. There seemed to be nothing on the other two. It was all very mysterious, and not a little irritating.

A knock came on his door, so he grunted his usual greeting. Stuart walked in, with two sheets of paper in his hand.

'Wot ya got there?'

'Statements from our two lovebirds. Picked them up on me way through.'

'Good. I like to see stuff on paper. Sling 'em in the in-tray.' Vic was still distracted. His mind, although clearer now, still wasn't up to full speed.

'And me.' Stuart looked at him. 'You look fed up.'

'That's one way of putting it. I bin going through

this car theft stuff, but I can't get anywhere with it. It's really annoying.'

'Don't suppose there'll be anything useful in these statements either.' Stuart sounded resigned to that fact. 'It's turning into one of those days.'

'Tell me about it, I've had the Super on the phone. Talking of annoying, we've got a retirement do coming up.'

'Oh? Anyone we know?'

It's only the bloody Chief Superintendent. He's been here since the year dot, about time he buggered off. Bloody nuisance, I know that.'

'Oh. That'll be nice.'

'No, it won't.' Vic was sure about that. 'It'll be as boring as hell.'

'Free bar?' Stuart looked hopeful.

'Get real.' Vic laughed.

'Oh, well.' Stuart sighed. 'When is it?'

'Dunno yet, she ay told me.' He jabbed a thumb towards the ceiling. 'I think I'll get meself run over by a car.'

'A posh one?' Stuart couldn't resist.

'Ar.' Vic grinned. 'Know anybody with a Ferrari?'

Stuart laughed as he shook his head. He looked at the files in front of Vic.

'Surely you can find one in amongst all that.'

'Don't think anyone round here is that posh, son.' Vic reached for his in-tray. 'Anyway, let's have a look at these statements.'

They each read one then swapped over, exchanging a knowing glance. They were virtually identical, even down to the wording.

'So.' Vic was the first one to speak. 'As we thought, they have got together to cook up a story. They must have been planning this for weeks.'

'Does look suspicious.' Stuart agreed.

'Just a bit.'

'So, what do we do now? We can't prove anything without any evidence.'

'No, we can't.' Vic frowned. 'That's the thing with murders. Most of 'em happen between people who know each other. And some of them never get solved. This looks like one of them.'

'So, we just have to forget about it, then?'

'Yeah, seems that way. We'll have to write this one up as unsolved and move on. But I've got a feeling we haven't heard the last of Mr Clive Morrison.'

CHAPTER FOURTEEN

On Friday afternoon, Frankie got into her Ford Mondeo and followed Nikki's car off the police car park. It was easy to keep her Fiat 500 in sight, and before long, they were in Lichfield. They parked at the big supermarket on the edge of the city, then walked down Greenhill into the centre. Wetherspoons was their objective.

'Fish and chips,' Frankie said as they found a seat. She was clutching a pint glass with ice, and a bottle of cider. Nikki had her usual white wine spritzer. 'Unless you want to go for a curry?'

'Nah.' Nikki shook her head. 'Zak's mom feeds me curry till it's coming out me ears. She won't cook anything else.'

'So, what shall we do? Have a couple of drinks and eat in here, then go to Rugeley? There's a pub we can walk to from Mum's house.'

'That sounds good.' Nikki smiled. 'Don't want to get stopped by the police for drunk driving, do we?'

Frankie laughed, which turned a few heads in their direction. 'Gawd,' she said, 'I wish I didn't laugh so loud. Can't help it, just comes out that way.'

'I don't mind. I need some laughter in my life.'

'What's going on, Nikki? You've been really down since you got married.'

'I walked eyes wide open into a trap. He told me he works in IT, and goes all over the world. I was promised the earth, moon and stars, but it was lies. All of it.' Nikki sighed. 'We went to look at a lovely house in Aldermarsh, and I thought he was going to put in an offer on it. I've always fancied living in a village. I had the shock of my life when he took me to his parents after the so-called honeymoon. Just for a while, he said, until we get you trained in our ways.'

'God, Nikki, I don't like the sound of that.' Frankie was deadly serious now. She put her elbows on the table and leaned forward. Nikki did the same. The conversation needed to be private.

'No, neither did I. They're trying to turn me into a submissive little wimp who'll just do as she's told. If that's what he wanted, then why didn't he marry one? Now he's saying we'll get our own place when I have a baby, but I don't believe him. He's the youngest of I don't know how many, and I don't think his mom wants to let him go. I think she's frightened of his dad.'

'You're in the shit there alright.'

'You're not kidding. Anyway, I've made a decision.

I'm going to look for somewhere to rent, either in Brodewell or in Lichfield. I like this place.'

'Can't you go back to your mum?'

'Yes, but they'll come after me, won't they? Don't want Mom caught up in all that. She's had enough trouble in her life.' Nikki downed the remainder of her drink, and stood up. 'Want another one yet?'

'No, I'm okay for the minute.'

Nikki went to the bar, and Frankie's eyes followed her. What a mess she had got herself into. No wonder she was downing her drinks so quickly. Frankie liked a drink herself, and had to admit, she had been doing more of it since Paul had walked out on her. It numbed the pain, and helped her to forget.

'Anyway,' said Nikki when she came back. 'That's enough about my shit life. What's going on in yours?'

'Not much. Paul wants to meet me to talk about the girls. Access, and all that. I'm dreading it.'

'But you'll be glad to see him?'

'Dunno. In a way yes, but he's not going to come back.'

'Maybe if he sees the girls, he'll realise what he's missing.'

Frankie shook her head. 'It's too late now, he's happy with his new woman. She doesn't work, so that'll suit him. Dunno how they'll manage for money, though.'

'What does he do?'

'Painter and decorator, self-employed, but he doesn't earn enough to keep a family going. I mean, Rosie wants to go to France with the school, but there's no way she could go unless I pay for it. Paul lives in La Land. He wanted me to be a full-time wife and mother, but we just couldn't afford it. He was always moaning about me being on call, and going out at all hours, but what else could I do? I love my job.'

'You'd be bored stiff at home all day.'

'Too right. Don't get me wrong, I love the kids and all that, but I need more than just being a housewife.'

'Yeah. So do I. I couldn't stand being at his parents' house all day with his folks for company. I'd slit my wrists.'

'At least we had our own place, bit of privacy.'

'That's the worst part,' Nikki looked embarrassed. 'I mean, our bedroom is right next to theirs. It's really awkward.'

'I'll bet.' Frankie laughed, a bit quieter this time. 'That's when I miss Paul the most, at night. We had a good sex life.'

'I've hardly got one at all, and I don't even want it any more. Not with them listening. I just want out.'

'Don't blame you. Right.' Frankie picked up the menu. 'Shall we get something to eat?'

'Yeah. At least it'll be a change from curry.'

'Ya can't beat good old-fashioned fish and chips.'

'No,' said Nikki seriously, 'you can't.'

Within half an hour, the food had arrived, and had been completely demolished. Nikki was still going on about mushy peas and tartar sauce as they left the pub to walk back up the hill to the supermarket.

'Dump the cars at Mum's, then we can go for it,' Frankie said happily. 'Couple of bottles of wine, or something?'

'You not sticking on cider?'

'Nah, sends me to the loo too much. Waste of valuable drinking time.'

Nikki laughed. 'Can't argue with that,'

By the time they wobbled back to Frankie's mum's house, it was nearly midnight. Nikki couldn't stop giggling, and Frankie wasn't much better. They shushed each other as they entered the house and crept up the stairs. They took it in turns in the bathroom, then Nikki snuggled down in a sleeping bag on the floor.

'That was a good night,' said Frankie, as she switched off the bedside light.

'Yeah,' Nikki slurred back. 'Thanks, Frankie, I needed that.'

'So did I. Night, love.'

The next day, they both got up late. Nikki had been looking forward to meeting Frankie's two daughters, but when they got downstairs, they discovered that Grandma had taken them into town. Frankie did them bacon sandwiches, then decided that the washing machine needed emptying.

'You off to your mum's for the rest of the weekend?' she asked as she opened the door, and frowned as a sock fell out.

'Yes. She'll feed me up, as usual. She's always cooking.'

'She'll be pleased to see you, I expect.'

'Yeah, I haven't seen her for ages. That lot seem to think I don't need my family any more, like I belong to them now.'

'The sooner you're out of that, the better, by the sound of it. You sound like a prisoner.'

'I feel like one, but I don't know what Mom's going to say when I tell her I want to leave. It was her that set me up with meeting him in the first place. Our mom's go to the same temple.'

'Ah, that could be awkward.'

'I know she only wanted the best for me. I don't know how I'm going to explain all this. I hope she'll understand.'

'Should do, from what you've said. At least you knew yours before you married him. Must have been terrible for her, being dragged off to a foreign country to marry someone you've never even clapped eyes on.'

'I know.' Nikki seemed lost in thought, and Frankie could only guess what was going through her mind. 'It took her ages to learn English too. My sister says Dad never liked her using it. I don't remember him, I was only six months old when he died.'

'How old's your sister, then?'

'Twelve years older than me. Me brother's nine.'

'You see them?' Frankie had all the washing in the linen basket by now, stray socks and all.

Nikki shook her head. 'He's in Dubai, and Lyn works in London. For the Inland Revenue, of all things.'

'Married?'

'No, they've both managed to avoid it so far. Looks like I'm the only one stupid enough to get dragged into it, and now I feel like I was.'

'Well, get out before you get pregnant.'

'Don't worry, I intend to.' Nikki looked determined. But scared too.

'If you need any help, you know where I am.'

'Thanks, Frankie. I may need to hold you to that.'

CHAPTER FIFTEEN

Nikki gave Frankie a big hug before she left to drive back to Walsall, and her previous home. How she wished she was still there, in the terraced house in Pleck. She shuddered as she drove past the road where she lived with Zak and his parents, and dreaded seeing his BMW coming the other way. He had objected fiercely to her having this weekend away from him, and she couldn't understand why. She had every right to see her mother.

'Lovely to see you, Norinda,' her mother greeted her as she opened the front door.

'Oh, Mom, you know I don't use my Indian name.' Nikki frowned a little. Her mother's accent seemed to have got stronger.

'Sorry, Nikki.' Mom seemed to have tears in her eyes. 'It's just that since you left, I've hardly seen anyone.

If I didn't go to the temple, I wouldn't see anyone at all. I miss you, darling.'

'Come on.' Nikki decided to take control. 'Let's put the kettle on, and you can tell me all about things.'

Mom closed the door and Nikki saw stains on the door mat and carpet just behind it. That was unusual, and she didn't remember seeing them before. Then she noticed the smell, and crinkled up her nose.

'Yes,' Mom said, 'I know. I've tried everything to get rid of it, but it keeps coming back.'

'What is it?' Nikki was dreading the answer.

'Someone put dog mess through the letter box. I got up one morning, and there it was.'

'Oh, Mom! Have you reported it? You really should, you know.'

'Don't be silly, Nikki, the police won't want to know, especially in this area. It was probably kids.'

'What a disgusting thing to do.' Nikki was appalled.

'Yes. I was nearly sick when I cleaned it up. I've taped the box shut now. I don't get much post anyway.'

'I can't believe anyone round here would do anything like that.'

'Nor me. Anyway, that's enough about it. Let's go into the kitchen.'

Mom led the way, and Nikki could smell the curry that was brewing up in a big pot. It almost turned her stomach, then she remembered that her mom was a much better cook than Zak's. Onion peelings and discarded pepper seeds were still on the chopping board, so Nikki swept them into the pedal bin before she filled the kettle with water. She could feel her mother's eyes on her as they waited for it to boil. She wanted to say something, Nikki could tell, but didn't seem to know where to start.

'I'm sorry I haven't been before, Mom.' Nikki had to break the pregnant silence between them. They were like strangers all of a sudden.

I understand, love, I know you're busy. First being married can be a bit confusing. It takes a while to adjust.'

'You're telling me,' Nikki muttered, while knowing it must have been a lot worse for her mom. Now she was going through it herself, she didn't know how her mother had coped with it. She had no choice, she supposed. At least Nikki had a fighting chance. She had a job and her own money, she had made sure of that. To begin with, Zak had wanted her to put her wages into a joint account, but she had flatly refused. That was when she had taken her bank details to work, to hide them. There was no way his family was getting their hands on her well-earned money. Or anything else of hers, come to that. 'So.' She tried to smile brightly, and failed miserably. 'What have you been up to?'

'Nothing much. Cooking, that's about all.'

'You're a good cook, Mom.'

'I've had plenty of practice.'

'That's true.' Nikki managed to laugh. The way her mom went about things, the local temple must have more food that it knew what to do with.

'There are always people that need food.' It was as though her mom had read her thoughts. 'I should know. I was one of them.'

'I know, Mom,' Nikki said gently. 'It must have been terrible for you.'

'I don't know which was worse. Being married, or being destitute.' She turned to Nikki and tried to smile. 'I know living with your in-laws is hard, but at least you're saving money. You'll get your own house one day.'

Nikki didn't know what to say. Her mom and Zak's mother were friends, mainly through the Sikh temple. That was how she had met Zak. Only now did she realise that she didn't even know what his real name was. Most of the younger Sikh's adopted English names. It seemed to make things easier somehow. The one he had chosen suited him. He fancied himself as an ultra-modern poser.

They took the tea through to the living room, and Nikki's thought were all over the place. She wondered what Armajit had been saying. Probably that everything was alright, and that the young couple were very happy. How was she going to be able to burst that bubble?

Nikki sat next to her mom on the shabby settee, with her mug of tea in her hand. It was the same mug she had used for years when she had been living at home, and the feel of it brought her back to some kind of normality. She glanced around the room, and saw that nothing had changed, whereas her life now was completely different. She stared at the glazed tiles around the Victorian fireplace, then looked above it at the photographs of her family. Her sister and brother, her mom and herself, all smiling and happy. Tears filled her eyes, then began to fall.

'Hey, hey, what's all this?' Mom took the mug from her, and stared at her in confusion. Nikki looked at her, then fell into her arms.

'Oh, Mom,' she wailed. 'I wish I was back here. I wish I'd never married Zak.'

Mom held her tight, and let her cry onto her chest. She didn't say anything. After a few minutes, Nikki recovered a little, then it all came flooding out. The pressure, the oppression, the lies.

'I don't know what to do,' she ended by saying.

'It's early days yet. Marriage takes time,' her mother said quietly.

'I don't want to be married.'

'Neither did I. I was only sixteen.'

'Oh, God, Mom, how did you cope with all that?'

'I don't know, I just did. I didn't have any choice.'

'Well, I do,' Nikki said firmly. 'I've got a good job, and my own money. I'm not giving that up to become somebody else's doormat. This is the twenty-first century, and I'm my own woman.'

'This is all my fault.' Her mother began to cry now. 'I brought you all up to be strong and independent. I've made you too English.'

'I should have married an Englishman, not an Indian. I'm not Indian at all, not like – that lot.'

'Armajit always comes across as very English. Very modern.'

'Well, she's not, I can tell you that for nothing. Neither is his dad. And I'm not giving up my life to be like them. No way.'

Now it was Nikki's turn to comfort her mom.

She did her best to reassure her that none of this was her fault. She had been duped as well. Zak had turned Nikki's head with his stories of foreign travel, and all things exotic. She had imagined herself travelling the world with him, staying in luxury hotels, and dripping with gold and jewels. She should have known it was all too good to be true.

The rest of the weekend was a bit strained, as mother and daughter fought with their emotions and memories of the past. When Nikki went to her old bed on Saturday night, she cried herself to sleep. What a difference this was to last night, when she had felt so happy and carefree. She had to hang on to that feeling, especially when she went back to the other side of Walsall.

When she finally got to sleep, she wished she hadn't. She began to dream that she was just sixteen years old, living in a remote village in India. Someone told her she was going off to a new life in England, and she was both excited and scared. A woman met her at the English airport, and she was taken on a long journey in a car. She had never been in one before. Everything was so different here, and she knew it was going to take her a long time to get used to it.

She was taken to a Sikh temple, which was something that was more familiar to her. After being washed she was dressed in fine clothes, and led towards a group of people. She wasn't sure what was going on, but a little while later realised she had been married to a man who looked a lot older than herself. She didn't even know his name.

She didn't like the way he was looking at her, as though he was undressing her with his eyes. Later he undressed her for real, and she was terrified. He was rough with her, and hurt her a great deal. Several times. She didn't understand what was happening to her, but it kept on happening, night after night. She only knew one thing. She hated this man, and was prepared to do anything to get rid of him. Then she found out she was having a baby, and he said it was to be the first of many. She knew she would never escape now. She was well and truly trapped.

Nikki awoke in the morning, and burst into tears again. Her life was awful, but not as bad as her mother's had obviously been. She stayed in her room until she had pulled herself together, then got through the day somehow.

She returned to her own prison on Sunday evening, with a heavy heart and a very full stomach, glad she had had some time to think things over. She hadn't said much more to her mother. It seemed like rubbing salt into the old wounds, although she never talked about her own marriage, aside from the odd very telling comment. All Nikki could do now was keep her head down and pretend to go along with what Zak's parents said for a while. But only until she had found herself somewhere else to live.

Alone and free.

CHAPTER SIXTEEN

'Ashes to ashes, dust to dust . . .'

As the vicar warbled on at the graveside, Michelle was reminded of an old song from the nineteen eighties. She had been twelve when it came out, and she had loved the video that went with it. She had always wanted the big lumbering piece of machinery in the background to run over the clown dressed in white and crush him. People had often told her she had a weird sense of humour. She couldn't understand why they would say that at all.

Michelle sighed. This funeral seemed to be going on for ever, and she hadn't known the person they were burying. She had only come because Phil had nagged her into it. She could see why. The turnout was extremely low. Debs' parents and the three of them. To add insult to injury, it had started to rain.

Oh, shut the fuck up, you boring old fart.

The vicar must have heard her thoughts, as shortly

afterwards he did just that. Michelle walked briskly to Phil's car. She stood by the side of it and saw a lot of handshaking going on.

What the hell? Come on, let's get out of here.

After a few minutes, Phil joined her. He didn't look very happy.

'What's your rush?' he asked.

'It's pissing down, in case you hadn't noticed.'

'Only a bit of drizzle. Thought you could've hung around to say goodbye to her folks.'

'I don't know them. Hardly knew Debs even.'

'Nor me. Came to give Clive a bit of moral support really. And show my respect.'

'Come on, let's get out of here. This place gives me the creeps.'

'Pub?' Phil looked hopeful.

'If we must.' Michelle found the Red Lion boring. The same people were in there day after day, ones she didn't know. She supposed that was her own fault. She never spoke to any of them. 'Is Clive going?'

'Yeah. When he's finished with them.'

'Seems to be finding a lot to say to someone he's never met before.'

'Michelle, their daughter has just died.'

'So what?' Michelle was bored with this conversation, which didn't seem to be going anywhere. 'People die all the time.'

'God, you're a heartless cow sometimes.'

'Just stating a fact.'

'He's paying for the funeral.' Michelle didn't know this. 'He's probably talking about that.'

'Oh well. Let's go. He can catch us up.'

'Yeah, suppose so.'

Michelle got into Phil's car, a big white Chelsea tractor of a thing, and made herself comfortable. She had been looking through a holiday brochure earlier, and New York was still on her mind. It seemed a good place for a shopping trip.

They didn't speak on the short journey to the Red Lion. Michelle was still in holiday mode and as for Phil, well, she had no idea. She had met him at a party a few months ago, and thought she had hit the jackpot. He was rich and easy going, generous too, and had been on television. He was boring though. He had a big designer built house in the village of Hawksmere and several cars, but he never wanted to do anything or go anywhere. Michelle guessed she would be going to New York on her own, which would be no problem. Just as long as he gave her his credit card.

Phil went to the bar when they reached the pub, and Michelle headed for a table opposite the fireplace. She rummaged in her bag for her mobile phone, which was the best friend she had. She had never had many friends, she didn't have time for them. She was always too busy chasing after money.

A glass of wine was placed on the table in front of her, but she didn't notice. Facebook was opening up, and she was keen to see what her friends had been doing today. Not that many of them were real friends. People sent her requests every now and then, and she accepted all of them. She didn't want to be known as Billy no mates.

As text and images scrolled up on the screen, she realised there was something she had forgotten to do. Earlier she had cooked a lasagne and a chicken and vegetable casserole. She enjoyed cooking and filling up the freezer. It gave her something to do during the long boring days in Aldermarsh. Usually she put pictures of everything she had done on Facebook, for all her friends to see. There wasn't much else for her to do. Messing around on her laptop or phone was a good way of filling the time, and she seemed to have plenty of it to waste since she had moved here. She needed to get out more. Take herself off places on her own. New York was calling to her again.

She was looking at a photograph of a pair of flip-flops that someone had washed and wanted to show off. A small 'huh' escaped from between her lips. She had a much better pair herself. Tomorrow she would upload a picture of them to prove it.

'Anything interesting?' Phil was asking.

'Nah. Load of crap, as usual.'

'Dunno why you bother with it, then.'

'Huh.' This one was a much louder one.

'Clive's taking his time.' Phil looked towards the door.

'They're probably trying to talk him into paying for something else.' Michelle wasn't really paying attention.

'Michelle.' Phil was looking at her all old-fashioned.

'What?'

The conversation went no further. Clive had arrived. He smiled at Phil but barely glanced at her as he walked up to the bar.

'Fancy a Chinese later?' Phil asked.

'No. I've been cooking this morning.' She didn't look at him. 'Might as well eat some of that.'

'Okay.' He nodded. 'You're a good cook.'

'Did you say cook?' She smiled.

'Yeah, that as well.'

Phil moved back to the bar to talk to his mate, so Michelle went back to her phone. She would go home in a minute. Leave them to it. Boys talk didn't interest her in the slightest.

Later in the evening, she glanced across at Phil and sighed. They had eaten half of her lasagne, opened a bottle of white wine, and now he had fallen asleep. She looked at the clock and sighed again. It was only ten o'clock. The night was young, but here she was, sitting in an armchair watching her latest squeeze sleeping like a baby. He couldn't get any more boring if he tried.

'Oh, bugger this,' she murmured after a few more minutes. 'Might as well go to bed.'

She went upstairs and turned on the television. The remainder of the bottle of wine was on her bedside cabinet. She got changed, then poured herself a glass as she tried to find something to watch. The content was about as exciting as Facebook had been earlier. An old crime series was halfway through, repeats again. She got into bed to watch the rest of it.

What's happening to me? Things never used to be like this. What the hell did I come here for? If I was still in Birmingham I'd be getting ready to go out about now.

She knew very well why she had left Birmingham, she had upset a lot of people there. Rich men seemed to all know each other, so now they all knew about her. Over the years she had been round them all, and had done very well out of it. However, even she had enough sense to realise when she had overstepped the mark, and worn out her welcome. It had been time to make a move. Fresh start somewhere else, where no one knew her. Aldermarsh.

Michelle sipped her wine as she thought about the past. She missed the city of her birth more than she had imagined possible, and still went back there on shopping trips. She knew she would be safe in the daytimes from running into anyone she knew. Most of the things she had got up to were a lot later in the day. About now, in fact.

Yeah, go there tomorrow, bit of retail therapy. Get meself in the mood for New York.

Next day she waited until the worst of the rush hour traffic had gone, then drove into the city. She had a few things she wanted to check on. These were things she hadn't told Phil about. The three properties she owned for a start off.

She kept the smallest of them for herself, in case she needed a bolthole. It was a one bedroomed flat that she had used a lot in the past, when she was between men, and she couldn't bring herself to give it up. She was wondering whether to stay for a few days, but that might be dodgy. She decided to leave that option open. See what the day would bring.

After visiting various people and establishing that everything was alright, Michelle thought it was time for lunch. An upmarket sandwich was called for. That, and a large mocha latte.

She found a café that looked suitable, and nabbed the last available table in the window. The place was busy, but nobody looked at her. She was used to this. The village she now lived in unnerved her a bit. People said hello to her even though she had no idea who they were, and she couldn't understand why. In a city mere eye contact could be dangerous, so she always avoided it. Anonymity suited her.

She ate her sandwich and drank her coffee. She was debating whether to have a second one when the door opened and a man walked in. Michelle ignored him as she looked down at her large designer handbag. It felt like Facebook time again.

'Hello, Michelle,' a deep voice said quietly.

Michelle looked up, and her heart nearly stopped.

'Tony,' she breathed.

She was looking into the face of her ex. He had been the best lover she had ever had. He knew all the buttons to press, and in exactly the right order. The only genuine orgasms in her life had been with him.

He was also dangerous.

An irresistible combination.

CHAPTER SEVENTEEN

Tony nodded towards her empty glass cup. 'Latte?'

She half nodded back, not knowing what to say. As he went to the counter, she eyed the front door, wondering if she should make a run for it, but there was a group of youngsters in the way. By the time they had decided there was nowhere for them to sit and charge their phones, Tony was back.

He sat next to her, and she almost fainted. She could smell his aftershave and it was bringing back memories she would rather not remember. Her hands were shaking as she reached for her coffee.

'Dunno how you can drink that stuff,' he was saying, his eyes twinkling and making her even more nervous. 'Too milky for me.'

'Milk's good for you.'

'Since when have you done what's good for you?'

Michelle laughed, and noticed it sounded more than a little hysterical. 'What have you been up to?' As soon as she said it, she wished she hadn't.

'Oh, you know me. Bit of this, bit of that.'

'Yeah, I can imagine.'

Michelle didn't know the details of Tony's criminal activities, only that he was well feared in and around Birmingham. He always played his cards very close to his chest. Safer that way, he had told her. She could see his point. Whatever he was into now, he was unlikely to tell her about it.

'Wanna go for a drive when you've finished that?'

The words purred into her ears and she felt a flash of excitement. Sexual excitement. This, and any other kind, had been in very short supply since she had moved away. Tony was irresistible indeed. Despite this, she tried to play it cool.

'Can't. Need to get back.'

'Yeah.' He smiled. 'I'd heard you'd moved away. Where did you end up?'

'Oh, nowhere much. Somewhere quiet.'

'You don't do quiet,' he murmured.

More memories were attacking her mind now, and she wished he didn't know her so well. He could get her to do anything, in bed or out, and that had been the main reason she had left. She didn't mind sailing close to the wind, but she had no desire to end up in prison. She knew he had been there a few times.

'I'm in love,' she said. After a few seconds' silence.

Tony stared at her. Then he burst out laughing, nearly choking on the dregs of his Americano. Several people turned round to gawp at him. He noticed them, and tried to bring himself back under control.

'You? Oh, come on.' He chuckled.

'Yes. Me. Honestly, I am.'

'Well, I know how to cure that.' Now his eyes were hard and glittering. The sort of eyes you didn't say no to, not if you knew what was good for you. 'Come on, drink up. We'll go for that drive.'

Michelle gulped. She knew she had said the wrong thing and had made him angry. When she had been with him, he had regarded her as his personal property. He didn't like competition. He wouldn't put up with it. Another reason she had moved away.

Tony stood up, still looking at her. Why on earth had she sat in the window, for all the world to see? She was still cursing herself as she followed him out of the café. The lunchtime lull was over. The streets were busy again.

Michelle was led to a bright yellow Ferrari, and raised her eyebrows when she saw it.

'Beauty, isn't she?' Tony said proudly.

'Suppose so. Is it yours?'

'Of course.' He opened the door for her. 'No point being in the car game and not having the best.'

So that was what he was into now. From the look of things, he was several levels up from the traditional archetypal second-hand car salesman. Michelle's nose was twitching. She could smell money from a hundred paces away. And this was big money.

She half climbed and half fell into the passenger seat, and felt as if she was sitting half a centimetre from the ground underneath the car. It was parked on double yellow lines but there was no ticket on the screen, even though a traffic enforcement officer was a mere three cars away. Tony noticed him and winked at Michelle. Despite herself, she couldn't help but smile. Money and power. She had almost forgotten what they felt like.

The engine roared into life, then screamed in agony as Tony flipped the throttle pedal. The enforcement officer looked up and gave them a cheery wave as they drew away from the pavement. The streets were crowded, so Tony had to drive slowly.

'Bloody traffic,' he muttered. 'We'll get out of the city. Show you what she can do.'

'Okay.' Michelle knew she had no choice. She could hardly leap out and do a runner. Besides, she was still excited. She wished she wasn't. She knew what was likely to happen later. Still, Phil would never know.

Somehow Tony managed to find a quiet stretch of road, and let rip with the accelerator. The speed nearly took Michelle's breath away and she had to admit, she was impressed. Only Tony could have a car like this, and she tried not to wonder what he had done to get it. It wouldn't be anything legal, that was for sure.

Eventually he brought the car back to something like a normal speed, and turned to her, smirking now.

'Now I'll show you what I can do,' he said quietly. 'And you might as well phone lover boy and tell him you won't be home tonight.'

'I – .' She was trying to think of a suitable protest, but no words would come. 'Yeah, alright.'

'Might even take you to dinner. If we've got time.'

These words excited her even more. She clamped her knees together to stop them from shaking.

'Okay,' she heard herself saying.

'There's this nice hotel I know. I'm sure we can find something to do for a few hours.'

'Yeah,' she laughed. 'I expect so.'

A short time later, they were at the hotel. Now Michelle wished she had dressed up a bit more. The place was extremely upmarket. She hung around pretending to read a poem in an ornate frame while Tony checked them in. He was soon back with their key card.

'Just need to make a quick phone call, won't be a sec.'

Michelle sat down in one of the comfortable armchairs, and reached for her own phone. He glanced at her and seemed to be satisfied that she wasn't paying any attention.

'Zak, it's Tony. Won't be needing you tonight.' There was a pause. 'Yeah, get back to you tomorrow.'

She was getting interested in Facebook when he nudged her elbow and nodded towards the lift. She shoved the phone back into her bag, alongside the few bits she had bought today. When she had left home, she had no idea that today was going to be so interesting. She shivered in anticipation. The button pressing was about to begin.

It went on for several hours. Then they had a shower together and went out for something to eat. So far conversation had been in short supply, but Tony made up for it at dinner. He told her all about what he had been doing for the past few months. When Michelle left to go home the next day, she didn't feel guilty about cheating on Phil. Tony had given her a good time, as he always did. This worried her, though. She never felt as if she was in control when she was around him, and she didn't like feeling that way. Best keep away from Birmingham for a while.

On the drive back to Aldermarsh, her thoughts went over what they had talked about. Not only had she slept with him, she had made another mistake as well.

CHAPTER EIGHTEEN

The funeral was over, and Clive's sense of relief felt like the world had been taken from his shoulders. He hadn't realised how stressed he had been and now wanted to laugh and cry in equal measure. The police had finished with him too: at last he was free.

But the guilt wouldn't go away.

'Are you alright, Clive?'

Connie was by his side, hanging onto his right arm. Clive shook himself out of his daydream and looked around. They were on Cannock Chase, walking through trees which towered above them, and bracken that wet their legs. Clive had lost the path, and Connie was looking concerned. Sunbeams filtered through the canopy of pine trees. They stopped by the gnarled trunk of an old oak tree, its leaves shining silvery green. Near to it was a Rowan tree, with shiny red berries. A squirrel appeared out of nowhere in its branches, and Connie shrieked in alarm. Clive didn't notice it.

'Sorry,' he mumbled. 'I was miles away.'

'I'd never have guessed.' She laughed as she squeezed his arm, the squirrel forgotten now. 'It's so peaceful here. I think the countryside is growing on me.'

'Need some peace after the last week or so.'

'It's over. You can get on with your life now.'

'Once the gossip dies down. I hardly dare go out for people looking the other way and muttering. Half the village thinks I killed her. I'm pissed off with the place at the moment.'

'There's nothing stopping us from clearing off for a while. Would that help?'

'I reckon it would.' He smiled at her and pulled her towards him. 'Come here, gorgeous. You're a genius.'

'Oh, Clive!'

When Clive got home he got to work on his laptop, searching for hotels in Cornwall. Soon they were heading south down the motorway towards Falmouth. Connie was bubbling over with excitement, and chattered about everything. Clive wished she would shut up, but he didn't say anything. He knew she hadn't visited many places outside Scotland. He planned to show her the entire world.

It was early evening when they reached the hotel on the seafront. Their room was on the top floor, and from the large window they could see the sea. A small boat was whizzing across the bay at high speed, bouncing through the water, foam flying everywhere.

'Wow, that looks like fun.' Connie said from just behind him.

'Looks ruddy dangerous to me, but then again, I can't swim.'

'Neither can I,' she said quietly. 'There are so many things I haven't done.'

'That's all about to change.' Clive wished he felt as confident as he sounded. Guilt was still swirling around in his mind. ''Just stick with me, kid.'

Connie laughed, and it melted his heart. Considering what she been through in the past few years, it was a wonder she could laugh at all. Now all Clive wanted to do was look after her, protect her. Sod her husband, the police and the village. Their happiness was top priority now.

'We haven't got time for exploring tonight,' he said as he looked at his watch, 'but I happen to know there are some good restaurants down by the harbour. And Italian and a seafood one for starters.'

'Couple of drinks first?' she asked. 'All that driving had made me thirsty.'

'Who was doing the driving?' He raised an eyebrow.

'You must be very thirsty, then.' She winked at him.

Clive smiled as he pulled his toiletries and razor out of his travel bag. 'Come on.' He nodded towards the door.

They wandered the short distance into the town, and he took her to an old pub that overlooked the harbour. They managed to get a table in prime position by the window. Connie sat admiring the window boxes in full bloom, an explosion of red, yellow and pink, while Clive went to order their drinks. It was starting to get dark by the time she looked out at the harbour properly.

'Do ferries run from here?'

'Round the corner, yes,' Clive answered. 'Over to the other side of the estuary. St Mawes for one. Pretty place. Fancy a trip over there?'

'Anywhere with you, Clive, you know that.'

They gazed into one another's eyes like a pair of lovestruck teenagers. Time appeared to stand still for a while, until they recovered themselves and remembered where they were. People were looking at them.

'We should be moving,' Clive realised as he glanced up at the clock above them, 'or we won't get a table.'

'Och, yes.' Connie followed his gaze.

After breakfast the next day, they left the hotel and walked down the hill towards Gyllenvase Beach. It was a lovely day, sunny and warm. A large bay was spread out around them, along with a huge sandy beach. People were everywhere, a lot of them heading for the large café. There was another place selling ice cream and everything both adults and children could want for the beach. There were children everywhere, laughing and playing. Connie watched them, and smiled.

'One of each?' Clive suggested as he saw her.

'Ten of each.' She laughed.

'I don't know about that.' He laughed too. 'Don't think I've got enough bedrooms.'

'I was only joking.' She didn't look as though she was. 'Maybe one day. Maybe.'

Clive didn't know what to say. He didn't know if he really wanted a family now, but the thought of it was appealing. Like she had said, maybe one day.

They both fell silent after glancing at each other. Clive set off along the pavement towards the café, and Connie followed him without a word. The gardens along the path were full of all sorts of exotic plants with neither of them could name. Connie stopped and leaned on the rail, looking at the sea below. Clive stood next to her, and put his arm around her shoulder.

'You seem sad,' she said, without looking at him.

'I wish my parents were still around so that you could meet them,' he said quietly. 'They died a long time ago.'

'What were they like?' She turned to face him now.

'My father was a successful businessman. Trouble was, he was so busy making money that he sort of forgot he had a wife and son. We had to make the best of things together, he wasn't around much.'

'Neither of mine bothered with me either. I was the youngest of six. We lived in Edinburgh, but not in a very nice area. I married Andrew to get away really. Stupid thing to do.'

'You'll soon be out of that.' Clive kissed the top of her head. 'They still alive?' Connie nodded. 'Mine died in a car crash. Killed instantly.'

'Were you very young?'

'Thirty-three. They left me some money, which helped to ease the pain, but I've been lonely ever since. Moving to Hawksmere was the best thing I ever did. And now I've found you.'

Connie hugged him tightly. She didn't need to speak; Clive could tell she felt exactly the same. They had both been given another chance at love.

'It'll be alright now,' he murmured into her hair. 'Nothing bad will happen to either of us from here on in.'

'No.' She sounded very sure. 'It won't. It can't.'

'Shall we go for a coffee?' He nodded towards the busy café.

'That'd be lovely.' She smiled up at him. 'And afterwards, a long walk along the beach. I love the sea. It feels like freedom.'

'Yeah,' he murmured, 'know exactly what you mean.'

Shortly afterwards, they picked their way through the crowds to the waters' edge. Connie paddled in the surf and he looked for shells a few metres away, smiling as he watched her. She looked like a naughty schoolgirl jumping in puddles.

'Enjoying yourself?' he asked.

'I can't begin to tell you how much.' Her eyes were shining.

'Good.' He grinned back at her. A wave washed over his shoes, but he didn't notice. 'We're going to have a wonderful life together,' he said quietly. 'That is, if you want to be with me?'

'What do you think?' She looked up at him, her eyes serious now.

'I love you, Connie. I want to be with you always.'

'I love you too. I always will.'

They hugged each other, not hearing the laughter and chatter around them. Even the soft crashing of the waves over their legs had disappeared.

'You know the best thing of all?' He kissed her forehead. 'We've got all the time in the world.'

'Aye,' she murmured. 'For ever.'

CHAPTER NINETEEN

At work on Monday afternoon, Nikki couldn't concentrate. Over the weekend all she and Zak had seemed to do was snipe at each other, and she was exhausted. All she could think of was ways to leave him, yet none of her ideas seemed to gel. She knew she had to do something. She couldn't go on like this.

Need to go round some estate agents, get myself a flat or something. Oh, God, what's Mom going to say?

Thinking about her mother, all alone in the Pleck, made her feel guilty. If she went through with what she was thinking about, she would be seeing even less of her, but she knew she couldn't stay with Zak. That had been over before it even began.

'Oh, God,' she groaned as she covered her face with her hands.

'No need to tell everyone.' Came from behind her.

Nikki froze. Vic had just walked into the office. There was silence for a few seconds, so she thought she had better face him. He was giving her a funny look.

'Hello, Guv,' was all she could think of to say.

'Quiet round here, ain't it?' Without waiting for an answer, he carried on. 'Tell you what, why don't you call it a day? You did overtime going to the pub. You're due a bit of time off.'

'You sure, Guv?' Nikki could hardly believe her ears. Or her luck.

'Yeah, go on. I'll stick around for a bit longer.'

'Thanks.' She was already on her feet, car keys in hand.

As she drove into Lichfield, Nikki was thinking he must be a mind reader. She parked the car and headed for Bore Street, where all the estate agents' offices were. She started at the top and worked her way down, promising herself a large glass of white wine when she had finished.

She was in luck at the last but one. They had an apartment for rent which was well within her budget, and she could view it immediately. Nikki could hardly believe it. This must be meant to be, but it all seemed to be so easy. She was wondering what was going to go wrong.

An hour later, she was back at the estate agent agreeing to take the flat. Some paperwork had to be arranged, and she was told they would be in touch in a few days. She left the office feeling happier than she had for a very long time. It was nearly done. She was almost free.

She hurried to the nearest pub, got her drink and took it to a quiet corner, the euphoria wearing off a bit now. She was dreading going back to Walsall, but was comforted by the fact that it wouldn't be for much longer. Getting her possessions out of the Singh family home was her next worry. How would they react? Would they try to stop her? She needed to keep her plans as quiet as she could. Try to disappear into the woodwork.

She parked next to Zak's four by four BMW, which loomed over her Fiat 500 like a big black alien monster waiting to pounce on her. Every time she came back to the large detached house she felt like this. Once it had been full of life, with Zak's brothers and sisters, but now it was just the four of them. Occasionally a sibling came to visit, but never to stay. Nikki could understand why. Zak's father wasn't the friendliest of souls.

She let herself in the front door, and could hear raised voices coming from the living room. He was rowing with Armajit again, although it sounded as though she was trying to calm him down.

'Benchaud!'

Nikki froze as she heard Rahul shout the word. She only had a smattering of Punjabi, but she knew that was a very rude word indeed. She heard Armajit cry out, then everything went quiet. Far too quiet. She headed for the study; it was the nearest hiding place.

Zak was in there, which was no surprise. He was on the computer, but as she walked in, he began to shut it down, looking decidedly shifty about it.

'Hi,' she forced herself to say. 'Busy?'

'Just work.'

She could tell he wanted to change the subject,

and hoped he wouldn't get onto the usual ones. She had heard enough about staying at home and having babies.

'You're a bit late.'

'Traffic was bad,' she lied. Very easily, which was worrying.

'Yeah.' He smirked. 'It's better when it's not. You can have a bit of fun then.'

'Oh, yeah?'

'The other night me and this bloke had a race, but I won. Done it a few times, but always on different roads. M42, A38 –'

'That's pathetic, no wonder you get speeding fines.'

'It's only a lark, no harm in it.'

Nikki couldn't agree and was annoyed with him. She went to make a cup of tea. As she left the room, she heard the front door slam. She could hear Armajit crying, so hurried towards the kitchen. Unfortunately the living room door was open, and she had been seen.

'Norinda.' Armajit looked shocked.

Nikki was embarrassed. Was that a bruise she could see on her cheek? She didn't want to get involved but it seemed she had no choice. Armajit was patting the cushion next to her.

'Where's Rahul gone?' Nikki asked as she joined her.

'To the temple.' Armajit dried her eyes, and winced as the tissue brushed against her cheek. 'I'm going there too in a minute.'

The gold bangles on her left wrist jangled together as she moved. One was a Kara, a religious symbol of Sikhism. The others Rahul had bought her, as if to tell the world he knew how to spoil his wife. He was certainly doing that. But not in the right way.

'Where's your Kara?' she asked. Nikki knew she was trying to take her mind off what had just happened.

'I can't wear jewellery at work.' Nikki had told her this a thousand times already. What she hadn't told her was that she had never worn one. Ever.

'Work.'

Nikki couldn't tell if she had said the word out of derision or envy. She didn't want to continue the conversation to find out.

'Has he hit you?' The words were out of Nikki's mouth before she had a chance to stop them.

Armajit tried to smile, but didn't succeed. She half shook her head, then shrugged her shoulders.

'Sometimes I'm not a good enough wife,' she said quietly.

Nikki's thoughts were racing. Was this the fate in store for her? All the more reason to get out. Quickly.

'Does Zak know about this?' She kept her voice down.

'He does what he can to help me,' Armajit whispered. 'I'm so glad he's here. If there was just the two of us… ' her voice trailed off.

'Oh, Armajit.' Nikki didn't know what else to say. She knew she should tell her to go to the police, but she knew she wouldn't. 'You'll be safe at the temple,' she added lamely.

'Yes.' Armajit managed a smile.

'If you see my mom, say hello for me.'

'I will.' She patted Nikki's hand. 'You're a good

girl. Try to be a good wife.' She gazed into her eyes for a full second, and Nikki got the message. She longed to tell her what she was planning, but daren't. She was frightened, but she was going to do it, no matter what the repercussions might be. She tried to smile and ignore her heart, which was doing its best to bash its way out of her chest.

'I'll do my best,' she mumbled.

'It's better that way,' Armajit said quietly. 'I'll go and get ready, and put on a brave face.'

'You shouldn't have to.'

'Yes. I do.'

Nikki didn't sleep well that night, despite having had several drinks in a grotty pub Zak had insisted on taking her to. He was still spark out when she got up for work the next day, so she shoved some clothes into a carrier bag, as she had been doing every day. The locker she had at work was nearly full now, but there was still some room in the boot of her car. She was longing to get her keys to the flat in Lichfield.

Eventually the phone call came from the estate agent, telling her she could come in to finalise the arrangements. When she put the receiver down, she felt like jumping to her feet and punching the air, but she controlled herself. Stuart was sitting opposite her, and Vic was floating about as well.

'Anything?' Stuart asked.

'No, that was personal,' she said quietly. I could do with getting off a bit earlier today. What you up to?'

'He's got me looking into these car thefts.' Stuart sighed. He lowered his voice for the next comment. 'It's only because he doesn't want to do it. The Super's on his back.'

'Found anything?'

'Not really. They're all high-end cars. Probably being stolen to order and shipped off abroad. That's what I'm looking at. Find out which port it might be.'

'Sounds a bit of a long shot.' Nikki frowned.

'I know. Just doing as I'm told.'

'Yes. Often easier that way,' she said, her mind going back to her mother-in-law. When she glanced up, she noticed that Stuart was looking at her.

'Everything alright?' he asked quietly.

She nodded and smiled. 'Getting better by the minute.'

'Go if you want. I'll cover for you.'

'Thanks, Stuart.' She was already on her feet.

She collected her keys after signing some papers, and went straight to the flat. After she had emptied the boot of her car, she felt better. There was no furniture, but she could sort that out later. For now, she had a sleeping bag she had borrowed from Frankie. Once she had sorted out her clothes, she supposed she had better go back to Walsall to collect the rest of her possessions. There wasn't too much to move now, but she would need to be careful.

The sinking feeling in her stomach returned as she approached the house. Zak's vehicle wasn't outside, which cheered her up somewhat. She went inside, hoping that maybe everyone was out. Could she get that lucky?

No. Armajit was in the kitchen, brewing up one of her huge pots of curry, which weren't a patch on Nikki's mom's.

'Hello, Norinda, you're early today.' Armajit looked surprised to see her.

'A bit, yes. Where is everyone?'

'Rahul's out, and Zak has gone to the airport.'

'What for?'

'He's going to Dubai, something to do with work. Didn't he tell you?'

'No.' Nikki gritted her teeth. He didn't.'

'Oh.' Armajit stirred the pot. 'Hungry?'

'Not just now, got a few things to do.'

Nikki went upstairs and bagged up the rest of her things. Then she went downstairs, put her keys on the hall table, and left the house.

For ever.

CHAPTER TWENTY

Stuart walked into Brodewell Police Station with a worried frown on his face. On two occasions recently he had found Nikki close to tears, and didn't know what to do about it. He sighed and tried to get on with his work. Vic had still got him chasing stolen cars.

Across the room, the phone rang. Nikki wasn't at her desk, so he went over to answer it. A male voice started to gabble.

'CID office,' Stuart said, in an attempt to slow it down.

'I want to speak to Nikki.'

'She's not here at the moment.'

'Don't give me that, I know she's there.' The tone of the voice had changed to something a little more threatening. 'Put her on. Now.'

'I can assure you, sir, that she really isn't in the office.

If you give me your name and number, I'll get her to call you back.'

There was what sounded like a snarl, then the line went dead. Stuart stared at the receiver for a second, then replaced it. Alarm bells were going off. His instincts were telling him that this was the cause of Nikki's upsets.

A few minutes later she came back into the office, clutching her usual mug. She didn't say anything, so neither did he. As he went back to the file on his desk, he heard her open a drawer and get out a bottle of water. She glanced across the room, so he pretended to concentrate on his papers. Out of the corner of his eye, he saw her open the bottle. Something was poured into the mug, and the lid of the bottle replaced. Stuart frowned. What on earth was she doing?

Nikki's phone rang again but she didn't react. She buried her nose in the tea, and ignored the ringing.

'I'll get that, shall I?' Stuart offered.

'Oh.' Nikki suddenly seemed to wake up. 'No, it's alright, I'll do it.'

'Put it on speakerphone.'

She didn't answer, but picked up the phone. Stuart could see that her hands were shaking. A second later she hung up, and went back to her coffee, or whatever it was. Stuart inwardly sighed. How could he help her if she wouldn't talk to him?

He was just about to ask her what was wrong when Vic walked into the room.

'Both hard at it, are we?' He actually sounded cheerful for once.

'Yes, Guv,' Nikki muttered.

'Good.' Vic was smiling. 'Getting things organised for the retirement do. Don't forget. It's this Saturday and we're going to be there, suited and booted.'

'Yes, Guv.' Stuart almost groaned.

'Yeah, I know.' Vic caught the tone of his voice. 'I don't like it any more than you do, but it's got to be done.' He turned to Nikki. 'You all ready?'

'Yes, Guv. Of course, Guv.'

'Gawd, you sound worse than he does.'

'These do's are boring.' Stuart said.

'I know, son. But we're going. No choice.'

'I know, Guv.'

'It'll soon be over.' Vic smiled. 'Might even be fun. Okay, carry on. I'm going to Tamworth. Fatso's orders.'

When he had gone, Stuart closed the office door.

'Okay.' He looked at Nikki. 'What's going on?'

'What do you mean?'

'The phone calls.'

'Oh, it's nothing.'

'Nikki, don't give me that. Is someone threatening you?'

She hung her head and seemed to be searching for the right words.

'It's personal,' she eventually said.

'So it might be, but it's affecting your work.' Stuart tried to sound stern. 'You should tell the Guv about it.'

'I'd rather not. Like I said, it's personal.'

'Okay. But from now on, your calls are coming through me. I'll organise it.'

She hesitated, then said. 'Thank you.'

'I'm going for a coffee. If the phone rings again, ignore it.'

She nodded as he left the office.

Stuart didn't go to the kitchen. Instead he headed for the Forensic Manager's office, to ask if Frankie was around. He was in luck. She was outside in the van.

'I wonder if you can help me,' he said when he found her. 'I think Nikki's in trouble.'

Frankie eyed him warily. 'What sort of trouble?'

'That's what I'm trying to find out. She's been having phone calls, and they're upsetting her. I want to help, before the Guv finds out. I think she'd be better talking to me.'

'Yes.' Frankie pulled her face this way and that, as if she was trying to decide what to say. Then she smiled nervously. 'She's left her husband. His family are trying to get her to go back.'

'Oh, God.' Stuart put his hand to his head.

He and Frankie looked at each other in understanding.

'Is Nikki somewhere safe?' Stuart's heart was in his mouth. The poor girl must be terrified.

Frankie nodded. 'They don't know where she is. I'm the only one who does, and no, I'm not going to tell you. I've told her to take some leave, she's owed some. Keep her head down for a while.'

'What can I do?'

'I don't know. Watch out for her? There isn't much either of us can do. She's got balls, I'll give her that.'

'She certainly has,' Stuart murmured.

'We've swopped cars for a while. Until she can get hers changed.'

'But that could put you in danger.'

'I can handle myself.' She didn't look as sure as she sounded. 'And anyway, she's my friend.'

'I'm her friend too. Well, I'm trying to be. She's in a right state.'

'I know.' She looked at the floor, seeming embarrassed. Then she looked up at him. 'Anyway, I'd better get on. And whatever you've heard, it didn't come from me. Alright?'

'I won't say anything.'

'Try to get her to talk to you. She's trying to handle all this herself, and I don't think she can. She needs all the friends she can get.'

'Yes.' Stuart nodded. 'She does.'

He went back to the office filled with renewed determination. He contacted the switchboard and told them to remove Nikki's extension number until he told them otherwise. Then he decided to try to be firm with her.

'Right then,' he began. 'You'd better start talking. I can see there's something wrong, and even though Shorty's an arsehole, it won't take him long to realise either, so you've got a choice. You can either tell me, or you'll have to tell him.'

'I can handle it.'

'No, you can't. You're a nervous wreck. You can't work properly with one eye over your shoulder all the time.'

Nikki bowed her head over her desk, and Stuart suspected she might be crying.

'Nikki, please.' His voice was softer now. 'I'm trying to help you. If you need protection, I'll arrange it.'

She tried to speak, but it came out all garbled. Stuart longed to put his arm around her shoulder, but what if Vic walked in? That was the main reason he wanted Nikki to talk. So that they could sort something out before he came breezing back into the building.

Eventually Nikki calmed down and began to whisper. She confirmed what Frankie had said but, like her, didn't go into detail. The calls were coming from her father-in-law, who was far from a sympathetic man. He wanted her to go back to Zak. Appearances were all he was worried about.

'I don't know how far he'll go with it,' Nikki ended by saying.

'All we can do is try to keep you safe.'

'I'm changing my car at the weekend, and staying with a friend. I should be safe enough for now.'

'Has Zak rung you?'

'Only once.' She tried to smile. I told him it was over, and he seemed to accept it. I think we both got married to keep our parents happy, but it's no use if we're not. Might as well end it now.'

'I'm sorry, Nikki.'

'We all make mistakes. It's not the end of the world.'

Now she sounded more like her normal self, although Stuart knew she was putting a brave face on things. Now all they had to do was stop Vic from finding out.

Vic didn't come back to the office for the rest of the day, so they weren't disturbed by him. Stuart and Nikki didn't speak much, but she managed a little smile as she said goodnight to him at the end of the afternoon. He was dying to ask where she was going, but knew she wouldn't tell him anything. He sighed, then decided it was safer that way. Two more phone calls had come through, but when the caller heard Stuart's voice again, they rang off. It seemed father-in-law was slowly getting the message.

All Stuart could do was hope so.

CHAPTER TWENTY-ONE

The next morning caused some hilarity in the CID office. Vic was half an hour late arriving, and when he did, no one spoke. Stuart glanced across at Nikki and suppressed a smile.

'Morning, Guv.' Stuart knew he had to say something.

'Yeah, whatever.' Vic winced. 'Tell you what, there's some rough buggers in Tamworth.'

'Oh. Is that where–?'

'Yeah. Do us a favour someone. Fetch me a black coffee.'

'I'll go,' Nikki said. Stuart could tell she was trying not to laugh.

Vic didn't speak again until she had gone.

'I'm gonna look a right mess at the Chief Superintendent's bash.'

'What happened?' Stuart was having trouble holding back his own laughter. That was one hell of a shiner around the Guv's right eye. Left-handed, was he?'

'Oh, very funny. Ow. Yeah, I suppose he must have been.'

'Pub?'

'I don't spend all my time in pubs, you know.' He tried to scowl but it obviously hurt, so he gave up. 'But yeah, it was. I went over there about these cars. Thought a few pubs might give me some info.'

'Well, you must have rattled somebody's cage.'

'Stupid prat thought I was after his bird. Said I was looking at her funny.'

'Never,' Stuart couldn't resist saying.

'Bog off.'

Now Stuart did laugh, he couldn't hold it back any longer. Vic glared at him.

'Sorry, Guv,' he spluttered after a while.

'So am I, son. I dunno what she's going to say.' He raised his eyes to the ceiling.

'You don't have to see her today, do you?'

'I ain't worried about today. Wot about Saturday?'

'Yeah, you've got a point there. Make-up?'

'Fuck off. I ain't no fairy.'

The thought of Vic trying to cover his bruises with concealer set Stuart off again. This time he had the sort of giggles that just won't stop no matter what anyone does. Nikki came back with the coffee, and handed it to Vic. He snatched it from her, went into his office, and slammed the door behind him.

'Stuart,' she said quietly.

'Ca – can't help it.' He nearly choked on his own words.

'Come on.' She grabbed his arm.

Stuart let himself be led into an empty interview room, where he sat and chortled for quite some time. Nikki stood by the door with her arms folded over her chest, waiting in vain for him to stop. Every time he did, he looked at her and started again. Eventually he was exhausted and his stomach was aching. He had laughed himself out, and sat with his head in his hands. He felt worn out.

After a few hours everything settled down, and they had got used to the sight of Vic's black eye. Stuart had to admit he was right about Saturday. Police would be there from all over the county, and the sight of DCI Hardcastle sporting a shiner was bound to cause some speculation. Maybe his suggestion of hiding it with make-up wasn't such a bad one after all.

As he thought about this, the Super came into his mind. In Stuart's opinion she should know about the problems Nikki was having. Whether Vic would agree was another matter. In the afternoon, he decided to tackle him about it. He took a deep breath and knocked on his door.

'Keep out of it,' he was told, after he had explained what was going on. He wanted to do this quietly, before Nikki came back from the kitchen.

'She's frightened, Guv, and I don't blame her for being.'

'You're getting too fond of her, son. Leave it. Let her sort her own problems out.'

'Well, I think she needs protection. She could be in danger.'

'Cobblers. Anyway, she should have thought about that before she left. What do you expect me to do about it?'

Stuart could tell that he didn't want to know, but he persisted.

'I think the Super should know about this. She's got the resources to protect her officers.'

'No. This is a personal problem, and it's nobody's business but the person concerned. We can't go round poking our noses into other people's lives. How would you like it if I did that to you?'
Stuart had to admit he had a point there. He wouldn't like it at all if someone invaded his highly valued privacy.

'Well, there you are then. Keep yer nose out. It'll all settle down in a week or so. She'll be fine.'

When Stuart went home, he thought over what had been said throughout the day. He knew the Guv thought he was right, but he couldn't bear the thought of Nikki being in danger. In the morning, he arranged to see the Superintendent.

He knocked on her office door, convincing himself he was doing the right thing. She didn't say much, but she did listen attentively. Stuart told her everything.

'Your concern is very commendable, Stuart, but really the report should come from the individual involved. We can't go around interfering in other people's lives.'

'But I feel that Nikki could be in real danger. Surely we owe it to our colleagues to offer them protection?'

'Yes. You are correct there, but there are certain protocols we have to observe. Detective Constable Singh should come to me herself. Such issues should remain confidential.'

'I understand that, ma'am, but there must be something we can do. I'm really worried about her.'

'I can see that.' She smiled. 'What does himself have to say about all this?'

'Nothing. I don't think he wants to know.'

'So, you've gone over his head to approach me?'

'Er, yes, ma'am.'

'Oh dear,' she muttered.

Stuart's heart sank at her words.

'I did try to talk to him, but he told me not to get involved. None of my business.'

'He's quite right, actually, but as I said, your concern is commendable. We should help and support each other as best we can. Morale is low enough as it is.'

While she had been talking, Superintendent Lowe had opened a drawer and removed a slim folder. Stuart wondered what was going on. She flicked through it, apparently idly, until she found what she wanted.

'I have to pop out for a moment,' she surprised him by saying. 'Please, stay where you are. I shan't be long.'

She left the large office and the door clicked shut behind her. Stuart stared at the open file on her desk. Had she left it there on purpose for him to read? Whose was it? Dare he?

He dare.

He left his seat and went around the other side of the desk. The file was on Vic, and Stuart found himself reading it avidly. Once he started, he couldn't stop. His eyes widened as he absorbed what was on the page, and his hands were shaking when he resumed his seat. He told himself to calm down and act normally when she came back, vaguely wondering where the information had come from.

'Wow,' he murmured.

CHAPTER TWENTY-TWO

Eventually the day dawned that Vic had been dreading: the Chief Superintendent's retirement party. It was to be held at a hotel in Stafford which had a large function room that the police used for such occasions. Birthdays mainly, and the obligatory Christmas do, which were usually great fun. Retirement bashes were a different thing altogether, especially when they were on a Saturday: ruining everybody's plans.

He went into work in the morning, to take his mind off what was threatening to be a long evening. There had been complaints from higher up about the lack of information on crime figures. When he started looking at them, he could understand why, he was way behind on his paperwork.

'Why can't she do this?' he muttered, glancing up to the ceiling. 'I wouldn't mind her job. Swanning about with her nose in the air all day.'

He knew he hadn't got the hang of this particular Superintendent yet, whom had suddenly appeared on the scene less than six months ago. Restructuring, he had been told but he didn't believe a word of that. Maybe he should try harder to get up the ladder himself, but he didn't really fancy it. It seemed that the further up a person went, the more political things got, and Vic was a copper. His mission in life was catching criminals, not dancing around in ever decreasing diplomatic circles. He guessed there would be some of that going on tonight, and winced at the thought.

When he got home, the first thing he did was pour himself two fingers of whisky. He downed it in one.

'Right.' He put the glass down. 'Better find some decent clothes.'

This didn't take long. He didn't have many clothes; he kept and wore old favourites from years back. This was a throwback to his formative years, living in Tipton, the youngest of four sons. But – he did have one good suit – which came out on occasions such as this. He smiled as he imagined his brothers' reaction to seeing him in it, and mentally stuck two fingers up to them.

'It's just me and you, kid,' he said to his second glass of Scotch, a few minutes later, in the kitchen. He held it up and toasted himself. A few more of these, and he would be ready to face the world.

A taxi took him to Stafford and he made sure he was a few minutes late, as he didn't want to be the first one to arrive. As it was, he ran into Superintendent Lowe just inside the entrance, who was obviously on meet and greet duty.

'Victor,' she said with a smile. He wondered whether he should shake her hand, but none was forthcoming.

'Ma'am,' he answered, politely for once. 'All raring to go, are we?'

'People are arriving. He's not here yet, he's coming at half past.' There isn't an R in past either, Vic wanted to say. 'Didn't want to be in an empty room.'

'Who does?' Vic laughed, itching to get past her to get to the bar.

'We'll have to do something about that eye.' She wasn't smiling any more. Vic mumbled something that neither of them understood as she reached for her handbag. 'I have just the thing. I have to use this to cover up the chicken pox scars on my face.'

Vic squirmed as he saw the concealer stick in her hand; he was going to turn into a fairy after all. He had no choice but to stand still and let her work her magic on him. Eventually she seemed satisfied.

'That's much better.' She smiled again now. 'I must say, you scrub up very well.'

'So do you, ma'am.' She had on a long green gown, which suited her rather large frame. He thought he should say something nice. Perhaps then he could get away from her. 'You look quite lovely in that dress.'

'Why, thank you, kind sir.' She looked somewhat taken aback.

'See you later, for a dance, maybe?'

'Maybe.'

Phew, he was walking past her, he had escaped

'Some party,' he muttered as he moved towards the bar, noticing that Stuart was already here. He would be, he was a stickler for punctuality. He was a nice lad, if a bit soft. He had only just made Sergeant, so Vic hadn't had long to work on him. He would be okay once Vic had toughened him up a bit.

There was a queue at the bar. The guests were arriving in droves now, it was just after seven o'clock. Vic guessed there would be some sort of speech and presentation ceremony in an hour or so, then things could really get going. It would be even better once the great man had gone home, as usually happened at these events. Then people could enjoy themselves.

'Evening, Guv,' Stuart greeted him once he had fought his way through the throng. Eventually he got served. With two double whiskies.

'Bleedin' 'ell,' he complained. 'Need more bar staff.'

'Good turn-out, isn't it?' Stuart was saying. 'Must be a popular bloke.'

'That's got nothing to do with it.' Vic fought his way, quite rudely, to the back of the room. He didn't like crowds. He didn't trust them. 'You been to one of these before?' Stuart shook his head. 'Be alright in a couple of hours, when everyone's loosened up a bit.'

'So basically, it's just an excuse for a booze-up?'

'Yer learning, son.' Vic smiled. 'Yer getting there.'

Vic sensed that Stuart wasn't listening to him, and followed his gaze towards the main doors. Even he drew his breath in at what he saw. Frankie Baxter and Nikki Singh were making one hell of an entrance. They both looked fantastic. Frankie in a long, red glittery dress, with ribbons threaded through her thick rebellious hair, and Nikki in a beautiful silver and blue number with definite

Indian undertones. Her long almost black hair was in soft ringlets that framed her small face perfectly. Vic was impressed. These two scrubbed up very well indeed, and he felt something stirring inside his trousers.

'Wow,' Stuart breathed, 'look at those two.'

'Yeah,' Vic agreed. 'Things are looking up alright.'

Nikki walked straight up to Stuart, but Vic hardly noticed. He was busy staring at Frankie. He had never realised how good looking she was before tonight.

Vic sent Stuart to get a round in, and they were halfway down their drinks when someone got onto the stage and asked for everyone's attention. The room took a while to quieten down, but eventually there was silence. The Chief Superintendent was ushered to his place to give a speech, which thankfully was quite short. The buffet was opened, and when the word went round that he had gone home, everyone could relax.

Stuart asked Nikki if she wanted to dance. She blushed, then said yes. Vic watched them go, with a frown on his face.

'Ah, here you are,' Joanne Lowe's voice interrupted his thoughts.

'Ma'am.' Where had she come from?

'I believe we arranged a dance?' She was smiling at him.

'Yes, of course, ma'am,' Vic almost stuttered. It seemed there was no way he could get out of it. Stuart and Nikki had seen them, and were trying not to laugh. 'Right away, ma'am.'

'Come along, then.'

141

Vic did his best to manoeuvre her into the middle of the throng, hoping that no one had noticed them. When he began to shuffle around the floor with his amply built partner, he felt as if he had gone deaf. His head was level with her boobs, which was making things awkward for him. She was leading him in the smooch dance, and he had no choice but to follow. Frankie let out one of her laughs. Vic cringed in embarrassment.

Eventually the Super let him go, with a small clumsy curtsey and a beaming smile. He mumbled something, then moved away, heaving a massive sigh of relief. He didn't go back to the table. Instead, he headed for the bar.

He stood some distance away, watching Stuart and Nikki, who were wrapped in each other's arms and looking very cosy. Why did things like that never happen to him?

It seemed like it was time to go home.

CHAPTER TWENTY-THREE

On the very same Saturday, Connie was bored and didn't really know what to do with herself. There was only one cure for that, she knew from experience. She took a deep breath, then set out to clean the house from top to bottom. She had got as far as the bathroom when her phone rang. Glad of an excuse to have a break, she threw down the cleaning cloth and rushed to answer it.

'Hallo,' she said cheerfully.

Silence. She repeated the greeting. Still nothing.

'Bugger you, then.' She hung up.

She hated calls like that, they were unnerving. She decided it was either a cold call from outside the UK, or a recorded message that hadn't switched itself on, and went back to cleaning the shower. Half an hour later, it rang again. She didn't hurry this time.

She picked up the phone, and saw Clive's name

on the screen, so swiped the green button. She hadn't had any contact with him for a couple of days, and had missed him.

'Clive, darling, how are you?'

'Better now. Sorry I haven't been in touch. Had an issue with one of my properties, it's taken me a while to sort it out.'

'Bad?'

'Yeah, burst water pipe. The place is a right mess, but I've got someone on it. It'll be okay. Anyway, what are you doing?'

'Oh, exciting stuff. Housework.'

'Want an excuse not to do it?'

'You naughty boy.'

He laughed. 'Actually, I was thinking of going for a drive. Maybe to the marina at Riversholme. I hear they've built some new stuff up there.'

'Okay. How long will you be?'

'Twenty minutes or so. See you in a bit.'

Connie finished what she had been doing, then went to get changed. Her mood had improved dramatically since hearing Clive's voice. She was becoming very fond of him, and had started saving money towards getting a divorce from Andrew. There was no way she was going back to him now. That was another lifetime ago.

She was ready and waiting in her small living room when her phone rang again. It was the unknown number once more. Connie hesitated, then decided to make sure.

'Hallo.'

'Hi there,' a male voice that she didn't recognise

spoke quickly. 'I'm not sure I've got the right number. Are you Connie Ferguson?'

Her heart nearly stopped at the mention of her married name. What was she going to say? Had Andrew found her? She tried to think but her mind had stalled.

'No, I'm not,' she managed to say. 'You've got the wrong number.'

The voice was asking what her name was, so she ended the call as fast as she could, with shaking hands.

'Oh my God,' she said aloud, then buried her face in her hands. 'Andrew's found me!'

She was still shaking when Clive arrived. He seemed to have taken ages to turn up.

'Connie, God, what's wrong?' he asked when she finally managed to get the front door open. 'You look terrified.'

'Get in, quickly.' The words came out in a rush. She looked out of the door and up and down the street. She was getting more scared by the minute.

'What's happened?' He looked really worried.

'I've had a strange phone call.' She closed the door and joined him on the settee. 'Well, two of them. Och, I don't know what to do.'

Clive put his arms around her and pulled her towards him. She blurted out the details, everything she could remember, then lay in his arms as if she was absolutely exhausted.

'It might be nothing.' She didn't believe that for a second, but realised he was trying to comfort her and calm her down. 'Was it Andrew on the phone?'

'No, I didn't know the voice.'

'So it could have been genuine.'

'Who would be looking for me? Who knows I'm here?' She was still in a panic.

'Connie, it's a mobile. You could be anywhere.'

'You think I'm overreacting.' Her voice was dull. He didn't believe her.

'It could be just a coincidence, but I can understand why you're scared.'

'I don't want him back in my life, I couldn't stand that.'

'Come on. Let's go for that drive. I'll buy you a coffee at the marina. Or something stronger, if you prefer.'

'Oh, Clive.' She kissed him, long and hard. 'I'm so glad you're here. I always want you here.'

'Come on, bit of fresh air'll do you good.'

It didn't take long to drive to the marina, and Connie felt a bit better once she was out of the house. They walked past the rows of narrow boats lined up like soldiers, some of them plugged into the electrical supply. A new build pub stood majestically in the right-hand corner, The Water Wheel. It was busy, so they moved on to read the menu outside the Thai restaurant and look around the new shops, selling clothes and wine. The butcher and baker got their attention too. Clive was virtually licking his lips at the selection of well-presented meats.

'I'll have that coffee now, I think.' Connie smiled up at him. They were standing outside the coffee shop containing a tantalising deli counter. 'We can sit outside if you like. It's warm enough.'

'Cappuccino?'

'Yes, please. I'll find a seat.'

She chose one overlooking the boats, and sighed. She felt a lot more relaxed now, and realised that Clive had been right. She was being paranoid. There was no way Andrew could have found her. She was a long way from Glasgow now.

Clive joined her a few minutes later, and told her the drinks were on the way.

'It's nice here,' she said with a smile. 'We should come here more often.'

'I thought you were a city girl?'

'Och.' She laughed. 'I like the villages too. Hawksmere in particular.'

'Has Hawksmere got any special attraction?' She could tell that Clive was taking the mickey.

'Yes.' She leaned towards him. 'You, you fool.'

Clive laughed now. 'Well, thank you, kind lady.'

A waitress brought two coffees out on a tray, and placed them on the table. Clive blushed and Connie wondered what he was thinking. He didn't say anything until the waitress was back inside.

'Would you ever consider getting married again?' he said quietly.

Connie's insides did a summersault. Was this a proposal? She wasn't sure what to say, in case it wasn't.

'Maybe.' She hesitated. 'Although I'm still married to Andrew.'

'You don't have to be.'

She nodded. 'I'm putting money on one side to pay for a divorce. I've been to see a solicitor, so I know how much it costs.'

'I'll pay for it, Connie.'

'You can't do that.' She was surprised, but pleased.

'Of course I can. I want us to be together. Permanently.' He smiled. 'Would you like that?'

'You know I would,' she whispered. Then her mind went back onto more practical matters. 'I'll go to see the solicitor again. Get things going.'

'How long were you and he - ? You know... '

'Only just over a year. Once I found out what he was really like, I knew I had to leave.' She tried to smile. 'It's right what they say. You don't really know what a person is like until you live with them.'

'So come and live with me. See if you can put up with me full-time.'

'Alright. I'll give that a try, but let's take it slowly.'

'Okay. No rush. We've got plenty of time. And in the meantime, why don't you come and stay with me for the rest of the weekend?'

I'd like that.' *I'll feel safer with you.*

'That's settled, then. Change of scene'll do you good.'

'You are such a lovely man, Clive.'

Connie felt safer already. She knew no harm could come to her while he was around. With him, she totally forgot she had an unwanted husband lurking around in the background.

Until she got home from work on Monday.

She was unlocking her front door when she felt a presence behind her. She turned around quickly, and gasped.

'Hello Connie,' a soft Glasgow accent purred in her ear. 'Long time, no see.'

CHAPTER TWENTY-FOUR

Connie stared at her husband in horror. This soon changed to terror as he pushed her inside the house.

'We need to talk,' he snarled as he slammed the door behind her.

Connie was dying to ask the obvious question, but it hardly mattered now. Her priority was to get rid of him. As quickly as she could.

'Nice place.' He nodded approvingly. 'Put the kettle on, there's a love.'

'What do you want, Andrew?'

'What I've always wanted. You.'

'It's over.'

'Not for me. Come on, make us a cup of tea. We can be civilised about this.'

You? Civilised?

Connie didn't know what to do. Maybe if she

humoured him, she could get him to leave. Now more than ever she was glad she had Clive in her life. Clive, yes. What would her husband's reaction be to him? She could only imagine. She knew only too well how violent Andrew could be.

He sat on the settee and made himself comfortable. Connie sighed and went through to the kitchen on the back of the house. As the kettle boiled, she glanced at the drawer that contained her knives. No, she wouldn't risk that again. She needed to find a more subtle way to defend herself this time.

She made two mugs of tea, and took them to the table in front of where Andrew was sitting. She sat down in the armchair a few feet away, feeling nervous. This wouldn't be the first time he had thrown a hot drink over her. So far he was behaving himself, and he seemed to be sober. Sometimes it was difficult to tell. He was good at hiding it.

'So,' he said. 'You're working at another gym. You shouldn't have done that.'

She stared at him in silence.

'That's how I found you. All I had to do was ring round. It's taken me a while, but I enjoyed the chase.'

Her heart sank. *I should have known.*

'Changed your name to Mackenzie, I see.' He picked up his mug, looked at it for a few seconds, then took a sip. 'That's something else you shouldn't have done. You're still married to me.'

'Well, even you should have worked out by now that I don't want to be.'

'And you should know by now that I don't give a shit about what you want.' He smiled, and she tried not to cower. He was being far too charming and polite, and it was unnerving her. This wasn't like him at all.

'Oh, yes.' She gave a nervous laugh. 'I know that alright.'

'So, it's quite simple. You're coming back to Glasgow with me.'

'So you can bash hell out of me whenever you feel like it? I don't think so, Andrew.'

'If you behaved yourself, that wouldn't happen, it's your own fault. You should learn to be a better wife.'

'I tried, I really did.' He was trying to make her feel guilty. Again. She felt like crying, but he would take great pleasure in that. She needed to stay strong. And get him the hell out of her house. Her sanctuary.

'All you need to calm you down is a couple of bairns.' He grinned. 'We can start on it right now. This settee is comfortable enough.'

'No!'

'Strange how you can get so much feeling into that word, but not the one yes. Why do you think that is?' He leaned forward. 'That's the trouble with you. Always coming up with the wrong answers.'

'Andrew, please. Just go.'

'No.' He said the word as forcefully as she just had.

This is getting us nowhere. What am I going to do?

'The only way I'm leaving this house is with you, so be a good girl. Get a bag of things together, and we'll be off.'

Connie stood up, not knowing what else to do. She was wondering if she could make her escape through the back door, or even an upstairs window. She should have done it when she went to make the tea, but her mind hadn't been working properly then. Andrew must have sensed that, as this time he followed her as she walked towards the kitchen. Connie was beginning to feel frightened. He had gone very quiet, and that was always a bad sign.

'Ah, the kitchen,' he said quietly. 'You going to try the trick with the knife again?'

'No,' she said, equally quietly. 'I've learned my lesson on that one.'

'See, you can be a good girl when you try. You'll never get the better of me, Connie. I'll make quite sure of that.'

'Yes.' She sighed. 'I know.'

'So, upstairs and pack a bag. Either before or after we've had some fun.'

'Oh, no.' She almost laughed. 'There's no way that's going to happen.'

'You are such a slow learner.' He grabbed hold of her arm and swung her around to face him. 'You're mine. You'll always be mine.'

'I don't want to be with you.' Her voice was high with fear.

'I know,' he hissed, 'and I don't care.'

Connie struggled, but he was far too strong for her. He slapped her across the face, and it stung. She gasped and he reached in to kiss her. She squealed in protest, but that just made him hold her tighter.

She kneed him in the groin, but only made partial contact.

His mouth released hers. Then she saw his eyes, and shuddered. She had never seen such madness in them before. Usually when he attacked her, he was in total control, but this time was different. Connie was petrified. She knew she had stepped over some sort of invisible line, and that whatever was about to happen next was going to be a hundred times worse than anything that had gone before.

'You think you can beat me?' His lips turned into a snarl as he whispered the words, his eyes never leaving hers. His gaze seemed to be burrowing into her very soul. 'You think you can win?'

Connie said nothing. She couldn't. Then she flinched as he began to laugh. It was the most horrible sound she had ever heard. Suddenly, she realised she was walking backwards towards the fridge-freezer. He still had hold of her arm, and his grip was so hard it was going numb.

The laugher abruptly stopped as he turned her round. He was almost gentle in his movement, until he wrenched her arm he was holding halfway up her back. She screamed as she felt something give way in her shoulder. Then the pain hit her, and she thought she was going to faint.

'Let's make a start on those bairns, shall we?' he said, in a very matter of fact voice.

'No, Andrew, please God, no!' Connie shouted as loud as she could, praying that her next-door neighbour might hear her.

'Oh, yes,' he purred in her ear. 'You've said no to me for the last time, Connie. Very definitely the last time.'

Oh, my God, somebody help me, please.

She felt him groping around behind her. Her trousers and panties were being slid down over her hips. She began to cry, she couldn't stop herself. She was shaking with both fear and the pain from her shoulder.

She felt her clothes fall to her ankles. Andrew was forcing her legs apart, and she tried to struggle. He grunted in frustration, her clothes were hindering him. Then he growled. She had heard him make that noise before, and it always came before something very bad.

Connie stiffened her entire body as his hand left her legs and moved up to grab her hair. He pulled her head back slowly, then smashed it into the front of the white fridge. Her blood splattered across it, and she knew her nose was broken. She tried to cry out, but he was rubbing her face against the fridge door.

As she tasted her own blood in her mouth, he freed one of her ankles from her clothes. She hardly noticed.

'A kiss for you, Connie,' he said in a very soft voice. 'Scottish special. A nice big Glasgow kiss.'

He swung her around with her uninjured arm, and smiled at her. Almost affectionately, she thought.

She knew he was going to kill her.

Connie screamed as loudly as she could, despite the fact she was having trouble breathing. She could feel her heart pounding, and pain seemed to throb through her entire body. This was worse than anything he had done before. And it wasn't over yet.

Andrew drew his right fist back, and Connie tried to hide her face. She knew what was coming, and when it did, she was sure she felt her jaw bone shatter.

'You're mine,' Andrew snarled. 'How many times do I have to tell you? This time I'll make sure. By the time

I've finished with you, no man will even look at you.' He leaned in closer. 'But I will.'

Connie screamed again, shouting for help. Andrew laughed. She tried to pull away from him, knowing it was useless. She thought her upper arm was going to explode, his grip on it was so tight. She stumbled over her clothes, which were still attached to her right ankle. This threw Andrew off balance.

The two of them fell, as if in slow motion, away from the fridge-freezer towards the granite work tops. Connie's head made direct contact with the end corner, but she didn't see it coming. She slid to the floor.

She was dead before she hit it.

Andrew landed more or less on top of her, letting go of her arm as he went. A pool of blood began to spread across the tiled floor, and he stared at it in disbelief.

'Och, Lord, what have you done?' he groaned. 'You stupid woman. What did you do that for?'

He didn't touch her. His survival instincts were kicking in, and he had had plenty of dealings with the police. He knew how they worked, what they looked for.

He stood looking at her for a full minute. The he checked his clothes for blood. There didn't appear to be any, he was impressed with himself.

He smiled and left the house.

He walked calmly down the road, as if nothing had happened. Anyone seeing him wouldn't give him a second glance.

CHAPTER TWENTY-FIVE

'Is that the bloke who killed his wife?'

Clive heard this comment as he waited at the bar in the Red Lion. It had come from a woman sitting behind him, and he cringed as he heard it. Phil had warned him that people would talk, but he thought she could have done so a little quieter.

'Don't think they were married,' the man with her replied. Anyway, he couldn't have done. He'd be locked up if he had.'

'Dunno how he's got the nerve to show his face.'

Clive paid for his pint, and looked round for somewhere quiet to go and drink it. He was willing Phil to hurry up and arrive. They had arranged to meet here sooner than their usual early doors, and Clive was already feeling uncomfortable. He glanced at the couple sitting near the fireplace and realised he didn't know them. They obviously knew who he was. Phil had been right: bad news did travel fast.

He looked up at the clock behind the bar: ten to four. He was a bit early. The woman threw him a death stare as he turned towards the front window, but he tried to ignore her. Instead he took his pint of lager outside onto the pavement. There were two bench tables there, so he sat at one of them.

'Pub full, or something?' Phil's very welcome voice broke into his dark thoughts a few minutes later.

'Nah,' Clive lied. 'Fancied a bit of fresh air.'

'Going to the gym has given you some good habits.'

'Not the gym. The people you meet there.'

Phil gave him a cheery knowing smile, then went to fetch a drink. He was soon back, sitting opposite Clive.

'It is busy in there. Loads of people I don't know.'

'They seem to know me alright,' Clive muttered. 'Bit more finger pointing going on.'

'Ah.' Phil took a swig of his beer. 'Well, it is a village.'

'Yeah, but if they're going to talk about me, you'd think they could get their facts straight.'

'Gossips never do. What they don't know, they make up.'

'Especially round here.' Clive tried to laugh, but didn't really succeed. 'Good job you're the only one who knows about Connie.'

'It'll all die down after a while.'

'Suppose so. Comes to something when I don't feel welcome in my local. I was thinking of trying the Kings Arms.'

157

'Is Connie coming over later?' Clive nodded. 'Thought that's why you'd come out early. Suits me. Michelle's been out shopping all day. Again.'

'She must miss Birmingham.'

'Yeah, she does, she's told me.'

'Villages don't suit everybody. I ain't too keen on this one at the moment. Bad enough the police thinking I'm a murderer without this lot starting.'

'Tell you what, shall we drive over to Aldermarsh?' Phil suggested. 'The White Hart'll be quiet at this time of day.'

'Yeah, go on, then.' Clive drained his glass. 'Pissed off with this place.'

It only took a few minutes to get to Aldermarsh, and Clive began to feel better. He only knew a few people in this village, and none of them seemed to be interested enough in him to discuss what had happened.

He followed Phil into the White Hart, and stood by as he chatted to the barman, who was also the landlord. He remembered the last time he had been in here, just after Debs had died. He had virtually had the place to himself. It was a bit busier today.

They got their drinks and sat in the large bay window, watching the world go by. A white Maserati pulled onto the car park. Clive and Phil glanced at each other then back at the car enviously. The owner of it soon walked into the pub. Before long he was in conversation with the landlord, telling him all about the car and where he had taken his lady friend in it. Phil was trying not to laugh. The landlord was looking bored stiff as he was forced to listen to one shaggy dog story after another.

'And you think you've got problems,' Phil muttered to his friend.

'Yeah.' Clive laughed.

'What time's Connie coming?'

'Another hour or so. She's going to ring me before she leaves. Don't want her catching me in the pub.'

'Won't she let you have a drink?' Phil looked surprised.

'It's not that. Me and her aren't common knowledge yet. Don't want people talking about her as well as me. I'll get a Chinese takeaway later. After we've had a bottle of wine.'

'All sounds very cosy. Dunno what I'm doing. Depends on what time madam decides to come home. Dunno what she's up to half the time. Suppose that's part of the attraction.'

'Mm,' was all Clive was prepared to say.

They heard the click of the back door opening down the corridor, but couldn't see who was coming in. The owner of the Maserati obviously could. His eyes widened, he drained his glass and made a hasty exit out of the front door.

Clive and Phil looked at one another, then both shrugged their shoulders. Phil glanced up at the new arrival and sucked in his breath between his teeth. He nudged Clive gently and muttered.

'Don't fancy yours much.'

Clive looked towards the back of the room and frowned. He could see what Phil meant. The woman was tall and slim, with very short hair, and was what his mother would have called a lemon sucker. She didn't look happy at all. She looked down her nose at the three people in front of her, then put her hands on her hips.

'Has my husband been in?'

The landlord smirked. Then he frowned and tried to look serious.

'Not today, darlin'.'

'His car's across the road.' She glared at him accusingly.

'There's something on in the Methodist Hall.'

'Oh, yes? As if!'

With that, she returned the way she had come.

The landlord let out a titter before he came out from behind the bar to collect up the few empty glasses that were scattered around.

'Having another?' Phil asked. He was already halfway to his feet.

'What's the time?' Clive reached for his phone. 'Bloody hell, it's after seven.'

'Must have been having fun.'

'Must have.' Clive hadn't realised it was so late. 'Strange Connie hasn't rung by now.'

'Phone reception ain't too good round here,'

'Think I'll go home. There's no problem there,' Clive decided. If he drank much more beer, he wouldn't have room for a Chinese.

'Okay, mate. Another time.'

'Yeah. Catch you later.'

Clive left the pub by the back door, noting that Phil was heading for the bar again. Clive didn't blame him. He could tell he was worried about his domestic situation.

He went home and sat in the living room for a while. When it got to eight o'clock, he was worried. Connie should definitely have rung by now, even if it was to say she had been delayed. He picked up the landline and dialled her number. It rang. And rang. Clive frowned. It wasn't like her not to answer.

Five minutes later, he tried again. Still nothing. Then his imagination went into overdrive. Had Andrew found her? She had told him that her husband was violent. Had something happened to her?

'Connie,' he shrieked as he reached for his car keys.

CHAPTER TWENTY-SIX

Clive drove to Burton in a blind panic, all sorts of horrific scenarios going through his mind. This only got worse when he reached her house. As he pulled up outside, he could see that the front door was partly open.

'Oh my God, he's found her.'

Clive rushed from his car and into the house. The living room looked the same as usual, except for the two mugs of cold tea on the coffee table. Clive made sure he didn't touch them as he scanned his wide eyes around the room. His heart was beating a lot faster than it should have been, and he could feel his pulse throbbing in his neck. Andrew must have taken her. He could be doing God only know what to her at this very minute.

'What am I going to do?'

He headed for the kitchen: perhaps that would hold a clue. As he entered it, he stopped dead in his tracks.

Connie was lying on the floor in a pool of blood. He could hardly recognise her face. It had been beaten to a pulp.

Clive screamed. He thought he was going to faint. He grasped the door frame and let it support him as he stared at Connie. He could hardly breathe as he took in the sight of her. Here was his woman, with all the life drained out of her. The woman he was going to spend his life with. The woman he loved.

He wanted to take her into his arms. Try to bring her back to life. Plead with her to wake up. Murmur something soft into her ear. A sob took what breath he had left away. Connie was dead, but he couldn't take that knowledge in.

He reached out to touch her, then stopped himself. He shouldn't touch anything. Nothing at all. He would have to call the police, and let them take over.

He heard a noise behind him, but it barely registered. Then a male voice spoke, and he felt like he had jumped out of his skin, three metres into the air.

'Wha – what?' Clive stuttered. He hadn't heard the words.

'I said.' Clive turned to be confronted by a young uniformed police constable. 'What's going on here, then?'

'I –' Clive looked back at Connie. He was sure he felt his heart break as he stared at the mess on the floor. Suddenly, he couldn't see properly. Something was in his eyes, and he didn't realise it was tears. 'I don't know.'

He sank to his knees, the life draining out of him.

'I don't know, I don't understand.' He reached out his hand. 'Connie – Connie!'

'Who's he?' an older voice asked. When he received a shrug of the shoulders from his colleague, he said. 'Get him away from there, and shut the door.'

Clive was half led and half manhandled towards the settee. The two police officers had a brief discussion, then the older one came back to Clive.

'Now then, sir. Your name, please.'

Clive put his head into his hands for a moment. He could hear the other policeman on the phone as he was walking towards the front door. Eventually Clive tried to pull himself together and told the officer all he knew, which wasn't much. How he had met Connie, how he was planning to marry her. The two strange phone calls she had received. Somebody calling her by her married name. He ended by saying that she had been very afraid.

'So, she was calling herself Mackenzie, but that isn't her real name?'

'No, maiden name probably, I don't know. Her married name was Ferguson. Her husband is called Andrew, he's from Glasgow. They both are.'

'Did Ms Mackenzie let you in?'

'No. She was supposed to ring me, and when she didn't, I just knew something was wrong. I drove over here and the front door was open. I came in and found –' He waved towards the kitchen. Then he thought of something. 'How did you get here so quickly?'

'Someone called us, a neighbour, I would think.' The younger officer was back now. He spoke quietly to the other man, but Clive heard the word forensics mentioned.

'Good. Take Mr Morrison's details, then start on house to house. We'll get to the bottom of this.'

'What's the point of that?' Clive wailed. 'What can that do?'

The policemen looked at each other, and the younger one grimaced. The other one answered.

'Police procedure, sir. All very routine.'

'Are you going to arrest me?'

'Did you kill her?'

'Of course not.' Clive burst into tears now. 'I loved her. We were going to get married.'

'But she wasn't divorced?'

'Not yet, but she would have been.'

'Ring this in to Brodewell.' The officer instructed his partner. 'They'll need to find the husband. History of violence, you say?'

Clive nodded.

'Okay. You'd better come with us now. We can't do any more here.'

Clive choked on his own breath. This was like something out of a bad dream. Connie was dead, and now he was going to be alone.

Alone. He could hardly deal with the concept. Until this evening he had thought he would never be on his own ever again. He had spent most of his life in that lonely state, and it seemed that this was only going to continue. Somebody was trying to tell him something. And he had no choice but to listen.

The police escorted him from Connie's house, and his breath caught in his throat. What was he going to do now?

His life was over.

165

CHAPTER TWENTY-SEVEN

On Monday morning, Brodewell Police Station was buzzing with gossip. Quite a few people had seen DCI Hardcastle chatting to Frankie and getting drunk together. Hands had wandered, then they had both disappeared. The muckrakers made the rest up, as usual.

Stuart and Nikki had missed the entire incident. They had been on the dance floor when Frankie made her apparent move on Vic. While whatever was going on, they had been holding each other close, and gazing into each other's eyes. This had led to the inevitable action. Snogging.

At the time Stuart hadn't realised what a risk they had taken. Nikki might have left Zak, but she was still married to him. Stuart had old-fashioned values, and took them seriously. They had both been drunk but that was no excuse. Now, in the cold light of a sober Monday morning, he knew he and Nikki needed to talk. But he didn't regret anything he had done.

He doubted whether his boss would be able to say the same.

It seemed as though everyone in the station was having the same thought. As Stuart walked through the front entrance, he could hear Pete, the uniformed sergeant discussing the Guv with two young officers. They were all laughing about what had happened, and a few crude comments were exchanged. Stuart went on his way, glad it wasn't him that was being torn to pieces. He told himself to be very careful. If Vic even had the slightest inkling about him and Nikki, he would never hear the end of it.

Stuart walked past the Forensics Manager's office, and was relieved to see it was empty. He wondered where Frankie was, and if anything really had happened. If it had, he guessed she would be pretty embarrassed. Or maybe she didn't even remember? She wouldn't stand a chance of using that as an excuse. There were far too many people around who would fill her in on every last detail, real or imaginary.

And enjoy doing it. Very much.

What a mess. Wonder how long it'll take for all this to die down?

With this thought very much on his mind, he found his way to the CID office. Nikki had just arrived, and was hanging up her jacket. She smiled at him nervously as she went to her desk.

'Is he in?' Stuart nodded towards Vic's office.

'Not seen him,' she replied. 'Stuart –'

The phone rang, and they both froze. Stuart answered it, on speakerphone.

'Ah, Stuart.' He recognised the Super's voice. 'Can you locate DCI Hardcastle and ask him to come and see me?'

'Certainly, ma'am.'

She rang off with no further comment. Stuart twitched his lips.

'Wonder what she wants?'

'No idea,' Stuart answered. 'Hope it's nothing about the other night.' The words were out of his mouth before he had a chance to stop them.

'Yes. About that…'

'We need to talk,' he said quietly, 'but not here. When he's seeing her, we'll go out somewhere. I'll leave him a note.'

'On enquiries?' He nodded, and she laughed. 'He'll never fall for that. It's the oldest trick in the book.'

Stuart wrote a Post-it note and placed it on Vic's phone. Then they left. Nikki followed him out of the building and onto car park.

'Stuart,' she called after him. 'Where are we going?'

'Let's get some distance between us and the station. Let all the gossip die down.'

'I heard some on the way in.'

'So did I.'

They had reached his car now. Stuart unlocked it, and Nikki slid into the passenger seat.

'That's mine over there.' She pointed. 'That red one. Still getting used to it.'

'How are things?'

'I feel safer now I've got a different car. I stayed at Frankie's for the weekend, but I've got my own place. I'm getting used to that now too.'

'Think his dad'll carry on trying to get you to go back?'

'He'll get the message eventually, I suppose. I just hope Armajit is alright.' She noted the blank look on Stuart's face. 'Zak's mom. He hits her.'

'Oh.'

'I think that's why Zak hasn't left home, which is all very well for his mom. It was no good for us.'

'Will you go back?' Stuart's heart was in his mouth as he asked the question. If she said yes, he thought it was about to break.

'No way. Marriage isn't for me.' She glanced across at him, then added. 'Not with him, anyway.'

'Let's get out of here.' Stuart's throat had just gone very dry. 'Before they start talking about us.'

He drove to Lichfield and took her to Beacon Park. It was peaceful there. The day was sunny so they wandered around for a while under the tall, well-established trees until they reached the boating lake. The only activity was a few swans gliding around, and three Canadian geese who seemed to be keeping out of their way.

'I like Lichfield. Been here since I transferred.'

'Why didn't you stay in Bristol?' Nikki asked.

'No room for another sergeant.'

'That seems to happen a lot.' She smiled up at him. 'Let's not talk about work. Enjoy the sunshine.'

'Fancy an ice cream?' he asked, as he noticed the van

by one of the pedestrian entrances. Nikki nodded, and headed for the nearest bench.

'Takes me back, this,' Stuart said when he had nearly finished. 'Me and my sister used to go to the docks and watch the ships, and we always had an ice cream on the way. Her idea really. She loved the ships.'

'Is she still in Bristol?'

'At uni.' He nodded. 'She's the clever one in the family. My folks weren't exactly over the moon when I joined the police.'

'Neither were mine.' She threw her empty stick in a nearby bin. 'Mom said it was no job for a good Sikh girl. I told her I was English. Through and through.'

'And you are. Very definitely.'

'Stuart.' She looked at him properly now. 'About the other night.'

'Sorry,' he mumbled, not sure what she meant.

'No, don't be sorry, I'm not. Unless you really do regret it?'

'No.' He tried to smile. 'I don't.'

'Oh good.' She leaned towards him and he put his arm around her shoulder. She snuggled closer to him, and he felt his heartbeat increasing. 'This just feels so right,' she murmured.

'Yes.' Stuart realised it did. She was so close to him now he thought his body was going to explode. She looked up at him and he couldn't stop himself from kissing her. Over and over again.

Later they walked quickly back towards the city centre. The three spires on the cathedral loomed over them as they passed Minster Pool and headed towards the market place. Round the corner from Dr Johnson's birthplace was a row of shops. One of them was a coffee house. It was busy, but they managed to find a seat.

'I'll get these,' Nikki insisted. 'Latte, cappuccino or black?'

'Cappuccino.' He said as he sat down. 'Thanks, Nikki.'

When she came back carrying a brown tray, Stuart thought he ought to get onto the serious stuff.

'If we're going to be seeing each other,' he said as he ripped open a packet of sugar, 'we'd better keep it quiet. If he finds out, we'll never hear the end of it.'

'Yes, I know. He's not very keen on me, although he does his best to hide it.' She stirred the chocolate sprinkles into her coffee.

'I don't think it's personal. I did, but not now.'

'What do you mean?'

'I went to see the Super, about the phone calls you were getting.' Nikki stared at him, her mouth falling open. 'She wasn't much help, but she went out of the office for a few minutes, and left a file open on her desk.'

'Did you look at it?'

'Is the Pope Catholic?' He laughed. 'Of course I did. Now I think she did it deliberately. It was interesting reading.'

'Go on. You can't stop now.'

Stuart could see she was bursting with curiosity. 'He had a son. He was nearly three and was taken ill. They took him to the hospital, and an Asian doctor looked at him. He wanted to keep the kid in, but

Shorty refused. Said he didn't know what he was talking about.'

'And?'

'The child died two days later.'

Nikki didn't speak straight away. She digested the information first. 'So,' she began slowly, 'he blamed the doctor.'

'Or himself.'

'Crikey,' she muttered. 'This explains a few things. Seeing me every day must be reminding him.'

'Maybe. But he still shouldn't take it out on you.'

'Easier than taking the blame himself.'

'I suppose so.' Stuart reached for some more sugar. 'Now we know why the Super puts up with him. She must know everyone's secrets.'

'I hope she doesn't find out about ours.'

'Rather her than him.'

'Yes, you're right there.'

They finished their drinks, and walked back to the car. As they re-entered the park, Stuart put his arm around Nikki. They strolled to his Ford Fiesta slowly, both enjoying being together and alone. But not too alone. Stuart didn't think she was ready for that yet. He wasn't sure he was either.

'I'm living in Lichfield now,' she said as they reached his car. 'One bedroomed flat on Boley Park. Nice and anonymous.'

'Not far from me, then.' He smiled at her. 'We'll have to meet up in The Turnpike for a drink.'

'I'd like that, Stuart.'

As he opened the car door, his phone began to ring.

'Oh no,' he groaned, 'it's the Guv.'

'Where the 'ell are you?' Vic bawled down the phone. 'Is Nikki with you?'

'Er – yes, Guv.'

'You'd better get yer arse back 'ere, pronto. While you've been out swanning around, there's been another murder. It's Clive Morrison again.'

CHAPTER TWENTY-EIGHT

Vic scowled as Stuart and Nikki walked into the office, both looking a bit guilty. He didn't have time to wonder what was going on between them, if anything. Perhaps they had been looking for Frankie Baxter, who hadn't been seen all day. Even the Forensics Manager had made some comment about it.

'What's happened, Guv?' Stuart asked, while Nikki went quietly to her desk.

'I've had Burton on the phone. There's been a murder in a terraced house near the hospital, and they found a man at the scene. When they put his name into the computer, it came up that we'd had dealings with him, so they've passed it on to us.' Vic clenched his fists. 'I knew there was something about that bloke. Said we hadn't heard the last of him, d'ain't I?'

'Who, Guv?' Stuart was looking puzzled.

'Clive bloody Morrison.' The words came out between Vic's gritted teeth.

'What's happened?' Nikki asked.

'That new woman he had on the go, the Scottish one. Someone's done her in, and it sounded messy.' Vic almost smiled, but thought he hadn't better. This was hardly the time to start gloating over his gut instincts being right. 'A neighbour heard her yelling and screaming, and called the police. When they arrived, the woman was dead in the kitchen, and our favourite geezer was standing in the doorway. Said he'd just arrived.'

'Where is he now?'

'Still at Burton, they're sending him over tomorrow.' Vic did smile now. 'And I can't wait to get me 'ands on 'im.'

Stuart glanced at Nikki, and this didn't go unnoticed by Vic. Yeah, Stuart was probably right, he shouldn't see him on his own. The mood he was in, he was likely to overdo it.

'I want you at the interview.' He stared straight at Nikki. 'You did okay at the last one. You got him to open up. Do it again when I give you the nod.'

'Yes, Guv,' Nikki mumbled, her eyes widening in surprise.

'In the meantime, have a look for an Andrew Ferguson, lives in Glasgow,' Vic said to her. 'Seems this woman was married to him, and according to Morrison, he has a history of violence. Need to eliminate him.'

'Or arrest him,' Stuart said quietly.

'Nah, it's Morrison.' Vic was sure about that. He'd had a niggling feeling about the man since his first encounter with him, and it hadn't gone away. Over the years, he had learned to trust his instincts. Coppers nose, people called it, and it had solved many a crime in the past. He couldn't ignore it, his gut wouldn't let him. He was going to use it to pick holes in whatever alibi Clive threw at him.

When he arrived, Clive was taken straight to an interview room.

'Come on, Nikki.' Vic was looking forward to this. 'Let's go and see wot the lying bastard has to say.'

Vic caught her rolling her eyes at Stuart as they left, and also noticed him wink back at her. He was going to have to keep an eye on these two. They seemed to have become very friendly all of a sudden.

When they got to the interview room, Vic took control. He plonked himself down opposite Clive, and gave him a twisted sort of smile. He had to admit, he looked a mess. His hair was all over the place, as if he had been running his hands through it, his face was blotchy and his eyes were red. Seemed like this one had upset him. Nikki sat next to Vic in silence, but he was very aware of her presence. Probably because she smelled really nice today.

'Right then, Mr Morrison.' Clive didn't react to his voice. 'Can you tell me where you were yesterday afternoon?'

'I've already told them at Burton,' Clive said, staring at the wall.

'Yeah, well, you're at Brodewell now. I'd like you to tell me.'

Clive sighed, and it sounded as though it had come up from his shoes. He rubbed his eyes and sighed again.

'I went to the Red Lion just before four o'clock.' His voice sounded weary, as if he was reciting a poem he had been forced to learn. 'Got a pint, took it outside, then my mate Phil turned up.'

'The Red Lion in Hawksmere?' Clive nodded. 'Did anyone else see you?'

'Yeah, it was busy. The bar staff all know me, it's my local. And some woman was going on about me being the bloke that murdered his – girlfriend.'

Vic nodded. This all sounded plausible so far.

'And then?' he prompted.

'Didn't like the atmosphere in there, so we went to Aldermarsh. To the White Hart. It was nearly half past seven when I left there. Phil stayed.'

'Did anyone see you in there?'

'The landlord, he was behind the bar. The only other person was some bloke with a Maserati. I don't know him. And a woman came in, don't know her either.'

'Check on that,' Vic muttered to Nikki.

'I didn't kill Connie,' Clive suddenly shouted, making them both jump. 'I wanted to marry her.'

He put his head in his hands, and started to cry. Vic didn't know what to do, he was embarrassed now. He nodded at Nikki.

'Would you like a cup of tea, Mr Morrison?' was all she could think of to say.

'Connie,' Clive wailed. 'All I want is Connie.'

'Think we'd better leave him to calm down for a while,' Nikki muttered.

'It all started on Saturday.' Clive was suddenly quiet. 'I rang her and she was in a panic. She'd had two

177

funny phone calls, and was scared her husband had found her.'

'They were still married?' Vic noted the surprise in Nikki's voice.

'Yes, but she'd left him. He used to knock her about, but she said he'd told her he'd never let her go. She'd been so careful, changed her name and everything. But he found her. He did this to her.'

Vic had to admit, that sounded plausible as well.

'What happened after you rang her?' he asked.

'I went to her house, tried to calm her down. She came to mine for the rest of the weekend, then I took her to work on Monday.'

'At the gym?' Nikki said.

Well remembered, I'm impressed.

'Yes.' Clive nodded. 'She finishes there at four.'

'So, she'd have got home at what? About half past?'

'Around then. She goes on the bus usually.'

'Okay,' Vic murmured. 'And the police arrived at seven-fifty-five. That's the time frame we've got to look at.'

'Is that it, Guv?'

'Yeah.' Vic stood up. 'Okay, Mr Morrison, thank you very much. You can go now.'

'Is there anyone we can call to come and stay with you?'

'No, thanks all the same.' Clive smiled at Nikki. 'I don't have any family. Phil'll keep an eye on me, I'm sure. Him and his girlfriend.'

'I'm very sorry for your loss, Mr Morrison,.' Nikki said gently. 'Take care of yourself.'

Clive's eyes were brimming with tears again as he left the police station.

'Mm.' Vic looked at Nikki after he had gone. 'What d'ya think?'

'It wasn't him,' she said, as they left the interview room.

'No,' Vic said thoughtfully. 'I really don't think it was.'

Bollocks!

CHAPTER TWENTY-NINE

Back in the CID office, Stuart was waiting for them. He had a sheet of paper in his hand, and everyone knew what it was.

'PM report on Connie Mackenzie, Guv.'

Anything interesting?'

'Yes. DNA results on the semen found. Belongs to one Andrew Ferguson, well known to Glasgow police.'

'The husband,' Nikki murmured.

'Yeah. Seems Mr Morrison was right. He did find her.'

'He's got a record as long as your arm.' Stuart smiled. 'Now all we've got to do is find him.'

'Got Glasgow on it?'

'Of course, Guv.' Stuart was annoyed at the suggestion that he wouldn't have. He wondered about Vic sometimes. 'Do you still want me to check out Phil Bateman?'

'Yeah, might as well find out what he knows.'

'Okay.' Stuart couldn't see the point, but decided it was easier to keep his thoughts to himself. Vic disappeared into his own office, looking as though he was on some sort of mission.

'Do you think he would really go back to Glasgow?'

Stuart didn't answer for a second. He was still staring at the office door.

'Eh?' He remembered that Nikki was there. 'Well – I wouldn't.'

'Nor me.' She sighed. 'That means he could be anywhere.'

'Great.' She wasn't doing anything to improve his mood. 'Want to come with me to see Phil Bateman?'

She looked at the office door now, and nodded.

Stuart drove to Hawksmere and pulled up on the Red Lion car park.

'Check in here first. Clive Morrison was supposed to be here yesterday at four o'clock.'

The person behind the bar confirmed that he and Phil had drunk one pint and then left. No, he didn't know where they had gone.

'Aldermarsh?' Nikki asked as they walked to the car.

'That's what Morrison said.'

'You okay, Stuart?'

'Yeah, it's just the Guv. Sometimes he treats me as though I haven't even got a single brain cell. It pisses me off sometimes.'

'How do you think I feel?' Nikki said quietly.

'Sorry, Nikki. You get it much worse than I do. Like I said, you ought to report him. The Super'll back you up.'

'I like working in Brodewell, I want to stay there. If I report him, he'll make my life hell and I'll have to go somewhere else. I don't want to do that.'

He glanced across at her and smiled. 'I don't want you to go either.'

'That's settled, then.'

After they had paid a short visit to the White Hart, they returned to Hawksmere. Phil Bateman lived on the opposite side of the village to Clive, but his house was just as impressive. It was mock Tudor with lots of false chimneys, and looked out of place with the mixture of modern and thatched houses they had passed to get to it. It stood in two acres of land on the edge of Hawksmere.

As they approached, they could see two cars were outside.

'The girlfriend must be here,' Stuart murmured. 'Michelle, is it?'

Nikki checked her notebook, then nodded. She rang the doorbell, which played a tune she knew but couldn't put a name to. A woman answered it.

'DS Young, DC Singh, Brodewell CID.'

'You'd better come in. Phil's in the lounge.'

She was a tall slim attractive woman with a rather sullen face. She pointed the way, then walked off into the kitchen and closed the door behind her. Stuart and Nikki exchanged a glance before they walked into the lounge.

'Good afternoon, Mr Bateman,' Stuart began. 'Nothing to worry about, just checking a few facts.'

'What's all this about?' Phil was looking puzzled.

'Oh,' Nikki said. 'Has Clive Morrison been in touch with you?'

'Saw him yesterday, we went for a drink.'

'What time did you last see him?' Stuart took over.

'He went home about half seven. What's all this about?'

'Do you know a Connie Mackenzie?' Phil nodded. 'How do you know her?'

'She works at the gym on the way into Burton. I've been going there for a while, and I talked Clive into joining. He wanted to lose some weight and get fit.'

'So that's the only way you both know her?'

'Sort of. Why you asking about her? Has something happened?'

'I'm afraid so, sir,' Nikki said.

'Oh God, is she alright?'

No one answered right away. They were both looking at Phil.

'Clive was seeing her. It was going on before Debs died, but he kept it quiet. You know what people are like for gossip, especially in a place like this. What's happened to her?'

'She's been murdered, sir.' Stuart thought he might as well come straight to the point. 'Yesterday afternoon, while you were both at the White Hart.'

'Oh my God.' Phil gripped the arm of the settee. Stuart could almost see his thoughts swirling around in his head. 'Oh God, Clive'll be in bits. He and Connie were planning to get married.'

A crashing noise came from the other side of the door. It sounded as if Michelle had dropped a glass.

Stuart had forgotten she was there. Phil looked up in alarm.

'Shell?' he called. 'What you doing?'

'Nothing.' She sounded a tad panicky. 'Just dropped something.'

'Okay.' He lowered his voice as he continued, apparently to himself. 'Thought you were in the kitchen.'

So did I. Stuart looked towards the door. The entrance to the kitchen was several metres away and the noise had been too loud to have come from there. *Interesting.*

'We're sorry to have brought you bad news, sir,' Nikki was saying as Stuart stared at the living room door. 'I think we've covered everything, haven't we?'

Stuart nodded, bringing his attention back to the job in hand. Clive's alibi had been well and truly confirmed, but he had a feeling the Guv wouldn't be too happy about it. 'Yes,' he said. 'Thank you for your help, Mr Bateman.'

'No worries.' Phil tried to smile as he stood up to show them out. 'Think I'd better ring Clive.'

Stuart paid particular attention to the wooden flooring in the hall as they left the house. There was no sign of Michelle and the kitchen door was closed. He nudged Nikki and glanced down. She did the same, but said nothing. They said goodbye and walked to the car.

'Did you see it?'

'Yes.' Nikki nodded. 'She didn't do that in the kitchen. She must have been listening at the door.'

'Seen that trick in old films,' Stuart agreed. 'Glass against a wall or door. But what made her drop it?'

'It was when Mr Bateman mentioned Clive getting married.'

'Why would that upset her?'

'Maybe she's got a thing for him. Stranger things have happened. She might even have killed his girlfriend.'

'Her?' Stuart laughed. 'I shouldn't think so.'

He unlocked the car door as he dismissed the thought, but it went over in his mind as they drove back to Brodewell, and by the time they got there he had made a decision. It wouldn't do any harm to look into her background. She definitely seemed to be hiding something.

CHAPTER THIRTY

In the privacy of his office, Vic was enjoying a drink of Vimto in his Stoke City Football mug. He would have preferred coffee, but was sick of the stuff that was in the kitchen. He wished they would install a machine instead, but had been told they couldn't afford it. He was tempted to pay for one himself.

His computer pinged and he sighed. Better have a look, he supposed. It was an email from Glasgow police, and contained several attachments. He opened the first one. It was a picture of Andrew Ferguson.

'Mm,' he murmured as he looked at it. 'Good looking bloke. Bet he's broken a few hearts, as well as other things.'

Vic was disappointed he didn't look like a nasty bastard. He had had visions of someone covered in tattoos and snarling all over the place. His imagination ran away with him sometimes, and he knew only too well that villains didn't really look like that. They looked like Andrew Ferguson, perfectly normal and respectable, smiling at the camera while wearing an Armani suit.

He printed off the image, then started on the other information. It was a summary of the man's police record, and seemed to go on forever.

'Who's been a busy boy, then?' Vic took another slurp from the mug. 'I'd like to get me 'ands on you. Now, where the bleedin' 'ell are you?'

Glasgow had no sightings of him to report, and Vic wasn't surprised. He was hardly likely to go back to his old stamping ground in a hurry, not if he had any sense anyway. Vic tried to think. Where would he go to hide?

Somewhere anonymous. Loads of people. Get lost in the crowds.

'London.' He paused. 'Gawd, I hope not. I don't want to deal with them. Birmingham, yeah, he could get there on a train easy enough.'

Ignoring the fact that he could have got a train to London just as simply, Vic went through to the main office to speak to the others.

'Load of stuff's just come through from Glasgow. They've circulated Andrew Ferguson on the national computers there and here.' He placed the photo of the man on Stuart's desk. 'Good looking geezer, the sort of bloke people'd remember.'

'Especially women,' Nikki murmured.

'We've got a trace on his car,' Stuart added, 'although he's probably dumped it by now.'

'Anything on his phone?'

Stuart shook his head. 'He's no stranger to the police, he'll be being careful.'

'He'll slip up sooner or later.' Vic was sure of that. 'All we can do now is start going through all the information.'

'Great,' Stuart managed to hold back a groan. 'Now all we've got to do is find him.'

★ ★ ★

Andrew Ferguson looked out of the grimy window down onto the street. A woman wearing a black headscarf was pushing a buggy along the pavement. It was quiet at the moment, so he knew he should stay put. Later he would venture out to find something to eat, probably from another takeaway. Once the heat had died down, he might be able to move on. Get a bit closer to home.

This place is a dump, but at least they didn't ask any questions. I should be safe enough here for a while.

He looked around the scruffy room and sighed. The only good thing he could say about it was that it was clean. The sheets only had one hole in them and the towel was thin, nearly threadbare, but he wasn't in a position to complain. He had searched the second city for a place like this. Somewhere where the police were unlikely to look for him. He knew they would check all the normal hotels, but this was a back street B & B which probably wasn't even registered. He hadn't seen any of the other residents, but imagined them as a load of dossers. He needed to keep his head down in this awful place. He would be alright as long as he kept his temper under control.

His temper, yes. It had caused him many problems in the past, but he had never thought that was his fault. The private school his parents had sent him to had only served to reinforce his belief that he was better than anyone else. He had always known he was special, destined for higher things, power and control. The school had taught him how to speak properly, put his class distinctions behind him and go out and get what he wanted. He had left there even more smug and conceited than when he had arrived.

I am of the elite, all the others are stupid. People like Connie. God, she was really stupid. All she had to do was obey my orders, but she couldn't even do that. If she'd kept still and behaved, she'd still be alive. It's her own fault she died, and now the police are going to be after me. I'm in this dump because of her, but I can't stay here forever. Need to get closer to home, go and hide in the Highlands somewhere. Until they forget about her and leave me alone. Shouldn't take long, she was just another brainless woman. Good body though, I'll give her that.

He sat on the creaky bed and tried the television again. It worked when it felt like it, and he had been monitoring the news channels to see if he had been featured on them. So far there was nothing, but he could have missed it. He was sure he would have had a mention, him being so very important.

Local newspapers, have I been relegated to those? Need to find out. If my face is plastered all over them, it'll make things awkward.

His stomach was rumbling as he left the building. He needed food and cash to buy it with, but he daren't use a cash machine round here. He turned his collar up and kept his head down as he headed for the city centre and its midday crowds.

★ ★ ★

Back in Brodewell, Vic was still ploughing his way through Ferguson's file and was getting angrier by the minute. He had never come across such a prolific con artist and swindler before. This bloke was the Leonardo da Vinci of crime, and there wasn't one twist or turn on an angle that he had missed. It was almost admirable, and Vic would have had some respect for it if he hadn't beaten so many people up along the way. Now he had progressed to murder, and that told Vic one important thing. The geezer was a madman, and had to be caught before he did it again.

Too bloody quiet round here, like something's going to happen. And when it does, I gotta be ready.

He left his desk and checked his jacket pockets. Yes, there were a few things he could do with, and he wondered if the Super would let him check out a hand gun. Probably not. With a sigh he went in search of some handcuffs. Ferguson was clever, and Vic was determined he wasn't going to get caught out by him.

The CID office was quiet as well, and Vic didn't like it one bit. The phone rang and he froze. This was it, he just knew it. Nikki answered it and sure enough, her eyes widened.

'Confirmed sighting of Andrew Ferguson,' she said, while still holding the receiver. 'Entering New Street Station on foot.'

'Tell them to keep an eye on him.' Vic's eyes were on fire. He was looking forward to this. 'I'm on my way.'

CHAPTER THIRTY-ONE

Vic hated going to Birmingham, but this he was convinced he would enjoy. One of the PC's was driving him to the city with the siren blaring and all lights flashing, and Vic was taken back to his youth. He hadn't done this for years, and was loving every minute of it.

Gene Hunt, eat yer heart out! This thing'll tear the arse of yer Audi any day of the week.

Vic would never admit it, but that man was a hero of his. That was one cop show he liked. When policemen didn't have to work with one hand tied behind their backs. When rules could be bent or broken, and not many questions were asked. Ah, the good old days.

He was brought back roughly to the here and now as the car screamed up to the main entrance of New Street Station. They had ripped through the traffic, which had mostly leapt out of the way, ignoring every red light. The siren had been turned off half a mile before they got to the station, and a radio report had said that Ferguson was looking at the departures board. On it were several trains heading north.

The young police officer who had spotted him met Vic near the main entrance, and seemed overawed by the whole business. Ferguson was being monitored by the CCTV cameras and two station staff were watching his every move. He wouldn't be able to fart without them knowing about it.

Vic turned to the cheery PC who had brought him here. Another wannabe Jeremy Clarkson from the way he had been driving; there seemed to be a few of them about.

'Can I stay, sir?' PC Comer asked. 'I'd like to help.'

'Sure, why not?' Vic answered. 'Can't have too much help.'

He turned to his new companion and introduced himself. PC Whitfield of West Midlands Police seemed to know his way around the rebuilt station, and Vic was glad. He had felt lost since the moment he had walked in. Now it looked more like a shopping mall than anything else, with areas marked off in different colours. He hadn't liked the old system much, but at least he had been able to find his way around. At the moment, he felt as if he was in the middle of Chicago.

'Right,' Vic said to both of them. 'Yer with me.' He suddenly noticed something in PC Whitfield's hand. 'Wot the 'ell is that?'

PC Whitfield grinned at him. 'Electric scooter,

they're brill. They've been using them at the airport for a while, and the station thought they'd give 'em a go. Dead useful if you're in a hurry.'

'Sounds ruddy barmy to me.'

'No, they're great, sir,' PC Comer said. 'I had one when I was a kid. All you do is put your foot on there, and do this.'

PC Whitfield demonstrated and whizzed around in a small circle. When he came back, he handed the small machine to PC Comer, who looked delighted.

'You got a name, son?' Vic asked him.

'Richard, sir.'

'Right, you and speed demon here get going. I think I'll stick to walking.'

Andrew Ferguson had stopped looking at the departures display and was on the move. He was heading for a large cabinet of sandwiches and drinks. Nobody paid any attention to the mirrored surface behind the neatly stacked plastic triangles.

The police had a clear view of him, but no one was close to him. Two officers slid up to him, each one on a scooter, one on each side. The small machines were virtually silent. As they drew alongside, ready to grab him, Ferguson bent both arms then jabbed outwards with his elbows. Both officers went flying.

'That's what you call grab and go,' Ferguson said as he reached for a cheese and ham sandwich. He stuffed it in his jacket pocket, snatched up one of the scooters and threw it across the floor. A passer-by tripped over it and let out a yell. Ferguson picked up the other one and sped off. In the direction of the shops.

'Like you said,' Vic's voice was heavy on the sarcasm. 'Useful if yer in a hurry. Shit, look at him go.'

His companion was on his radio, his voice panicky. Vic sighed. This was turning into something out of the Blues Brothers, only on a smaller scale.

'Why me?' Vic wailed. 'Why do I get all the weird stuff?'

'I've twisted my ankle,' the passer-by was shouting. Vic took no notice as he went over to get the scooter. The injured person looked at him in amazement as he totally ignored him and put a foot onto the machine. Vic swore as it whisked him away.

'Really.' The man stared after him. 'What kind of language was that?'

Vic felt pretty stupid on what looked like a kids' scooter, but he had to admit it was fast. Certainly quicker than he could run. Younger and fitter police officers seemed to be everywhere all of a sudden, all going after Ferguson, who was laughing. He glanced over his shoulder every now and then, and if taunting everyone to catch him. This was one occasion Vic thought he could rise to.

He was heading towards a stand containing books, and Ferguson was in front of him. Vic yelled at him to stop, but he was having none of it. The manager of the shop looked on in horror, and she screamed as Ferguson slammed into the stand and sent paperbacks flying everywhere. The wheel of the scooter was jammed for a second, then Ferguson got it free and was off.

Towards a crowd of people entering the station. One of whom was a family, happily clutching packets of food from outside.

'Oh, no,' Vic groaned. 'There's gonna be shit flying everywhere.'

The first thing that whizzed past his ear was cardboard containing skinny fries, which the little girl had let go of when Ferguson had driven between her and her mother. Her brother laughed as the fries hit the floor and a scooter behind Vic skidded on them. A person landed with a slippery thud, and Vic carried on regardless. He still had Ferguson in his sights, and he was damned if he was going to let him get away again.

Chicken nuggets were the next casualty as Ferguson caught the woman's arm as she was trying to pull her children towards her, for safety. The lid of the box flew open, and the rest of the contents went flying. Vic bent his head to dodge them, but got some of the lemonade on its speedy way out of a plastic cup. The ice from it caught several few people unawares.

'Aw, Mom,' the boy bawled. 'You've lost my happy toy.'

'Never mind, lad,' Vic said as he went past the enormous bull that had been the mascot for the recent Commonwealth Games.

Out of the corner of his eye, Vic noticed two things. Ferguson was heading towards the entrance gates of one of the platforms, and someone he recognised was sailing alongside him with a big daft grin on his face. It was Richard, the maniac who had driven him here.

'Wot the –?'

'Hi, sir.' Richard looked over his shoulder at the gang who were behind him. 'Up here, we've nearly got him.'

Vic glanced back too, and soon decided he had better

get out of the way. A dark blue swarm was heading his way and was about to engulf him, like a hoard of rampaging ancient Britons. He headed sideways towards Greggs, hoping he wasn't about to get covered in sausages and pastry.

Somehow Ferguson had managed to get the scooter over the platform gate by riding up a large suitcase that was being wheeled towards it. The woman pulling it screamed as he went into the air over her head. The security man's mouth fell open in astonishment as what seemed like a ski jumper flew past him. Ferguson landed on the other side and sped towards the escalator.

Vic watched as everything happened at once. The station staff were yelling at each other. Ferguson was riding around in circles, obviously wondering where he could go to escape the police. The passengers down on the platform knew something was going on, and the people on the escalators had eyes wide in disbelief as they wondered what the hell was happening.

The escalators suddenly stopped moving after one of the staff switched them off, and everyone was told to stay where they were.

'Open the gates,' Richard shouted, 'let us through.'

This statement caused panic but the station staff took over, doing their utmost to calm people down. The ones on the platform could see what was going on, and were taking an interest in the proceedings. A fair few of them were laughing and filming what was going on, no doubt eager to share their experience later on Facebook.

Ferguson was swearing and almost spitting in frustration. He had realised there was no escape and was looking absolutely furious. The platform barriers opened and the police streamed through. Vic went after them.

Ferguson stood still as they approached, knowing there was nothing he could do. Vic was at the back, but even from there he could see the look of disdain on the Scotsman's face. The officers quickly surrounded him.

Vic walked up to Ferguson and gently took the scooter from him. He looked into his eyes and nearly shuddered at the hate and anger he saw there.

'Andrew Ferguson,' he said quietly. 'Guess wot? You're nicked.'

CHAPTER THIRTY-TWO

Vic was sitting in the Birmingham police station waiting for Andrew Ferguson to be processed through the system. PC Comer was with him, having a quiet conversation with PC Whitfield. They were discussing gadgets, and seemed to have a lot in common. It seemed a friendship had been struck up, and the last thing Vic heard was them arranging to meet up at some point.

'Richard.' He thought he should break this up, it was hardly work talk. 'We should be ready to go back soon.'

'Yes, sir.' He smiled at his new mate. 'Catch you later, Mark.'

Vic's instincts were proved right as the custody officer came walking towards him. He didn't look very cheerful.

'DCI Hardcastle?' Vic nodded. 'He's all yours now, but I have to warn you, he's being very uncooperative.'

'Is he now?' Vic smirked. 'We'll see about that.'

'He's said no comment to everything he's been asked. Seems to think he's above all us lot.'

'Yeah, I've read his file. Went to some posh school wot taught him he's better than everyone else. But he hasn't dealt with me yet.'

'Best of luck.'

Back at Brodewell, Ferguson was put into an interview room and Vic went to fetch Stuart. Before they returned, he told him what the custody officer had said.

'Seems he wants his own lawyer and won't say anything till he gets here. He's got him off serious charges before. Probably thinks he's going to get off again, but if he does, he's got another think coming.'

'He's never killed anyone before.'

'No. But he's done just about everything else.' Vic growled.

'You alright, Guv?'

'Can't stop thinking about the way he looked at me on the station platform,' Vic said quietly. 'The look in his eyes, it was – evil.'

'Mm.' Stuart tried to smile, but failed. 'So, when's this lawyer getting here?'

'He's flying down from Glasgow, should be here any time now.'

Soon afterwards the four of them were sitting in Interview Room One, and Vic was trying not to lose his temper. All they had got out of Ferguson so far was his name, address and age. The same as in Birmingham.

'Your wife, Connie Mackenzie –' Vic began again.

'Ferguson.' The man glared at him. 'Get your facts straight.'

'How long were you married?'

'Irrelevant.'

'You were separated from your wife –'

'No,' Ferguson interrupted him. 'I was never separated from her. Ever.'

'She left you?' Stuart suggested.

'She belongs to me. I came to take her home.'

'Even though she didn't want to go back?'

'What's that got to do with anything?'

Vic glanced at Stuart. They could see the confusion on Ferguson's face. Even the lawyer looked surprised.

'So.' Vic took over again. 'You came down from Glasgow to look for your wife.'

Ferguson nodded. 'It wasn't difficult to find her. She tried to cover her tracks, but she isn't clever enough to fool me. No one is.'

'So, you found her and went to her house.' Vic's temper was coming up again. 'And then you killed her.'

'I must object to this line of questioning,' the lawyer sounded indignant. 'My client is –'

'Your client is under arrest for murder,' Vic hissed. He nearly added the word 'mush' on the end, but remembered that the interview was being recorded. There was a chance it might be played in court, when this bastard finally got to trial.

It's up to you to prove that,' the lawyer as good as hissed back.

'We have your fingerprints in her house,' Vic said to Ferguson, after taking a deep breath. 'And DNA evidence from bodily fluids.'

'So I visited her home.' Ferguson looked very calm. 'So what? I am her husband.'

He threw a look at his lawyer that seemed to say, 'Honestly, these people!' The lawyer smiled back, looking like a poised cobra that was about to strike its latest victim. Vic was confused. The lawyer had been given all the facts, so why was he looking so smug?

'Your semen was found at the scene,' Vic persisted.

'So we had sex.' Ferguson rolled his eyes. 'Don't husbands and wives do that?'

'Your wife had left you, and was in a new relationship.'

'No!' Ferguson shouted, and made everyone jump. His demeanour had changed completely, in an instant. The look he had given Vic at New Street Station was back in his eyes. 'Connie's mine. And mine alone.'

The lawyer put his hand on Ferguson's arm, but he threw him off. Vic saw his chance.

'Your wife had left you,' he repeated, 'because of your previous violence towards her. We have evidence of several untreated fractured bones, and hospital reports of contusions consistent with a beating.'

'She was a very clumsy woman, always falling and walking into things.'

'Such as your fists?'

Stuart cleared his throat as a warning to Vic. For once, he listened.

'Your wife was found in the kitchen of her house, having sustained a heavy beating. The post mortem showed a broken jaw and nose, and a dislocated shoulder. And severe internal damage.'

'So? You can't prove that I did any of that.'

'Your previous history will count against you. There are several police statements made by your wife that you were violent towards her.'

'The trouble with women.' Ferguson was examining the fingernails on his right hand. 'Is that they never know when they're well off. All they have to do is do as they're told, then they can have a good life. Connie was like that, always doing the wrong thing. She needed steering in the right direction sometimes.'

'You mean, she needed to be disciplined?' Vic's eyes were shining. They were getting somewhere now.

'Exactly. You know, you're not as stupid as you look.'

The lawyer was looking uncomfortable now and was trying to attract Ferguson's attention, without success.

'People of the elite, such as myself, have a right to be in control of any situation. Marriage is no different. I am the master and she is the minion. It's as simple as that.' Ferguson smiled. Vic clenched his fists. 'People should do my bidding. That's what they're there for.'

'You do realise this interview is being recorded,' the lawyer said quietly.

'I should think so too,' Ferguson said. 'My words are important. Everyone should listen to me. I can show them the way. The right way to live, and the right way to serve me.'

This bloke's completely off his trolley.

'Don't say any more.' The lawyer was barely audible. 'Stick to the plan.'

'I don't need it. I am a superior being. Nothing can touch me.'

The lawyer gave Vic and Stuart a pleading look and all they could do was respond. Stuart terminated the interview, ignoring Ferguson's demands to continuing listening to his lecture on the Homo Superior. Vic was grinning on the inside, and jumping for joy. Ferguson had given himself away, and was now heading for psychiatric reports and the funny farm.

One less villain on the streets.

CHAPTER THIRTY-THREE

'What are we going to do about Clive?'

Phil didn't like the way Michelle was staring at him, as though he had just landed on earth from another planet. Eventually she answered him.

'What you asking me for?'

'Thought you might have some ideas.'

She snorted and turned her attention back to Facebook.

'You haven't really got any friends, have you?'

'Of course I have,' she said, a little too quickly. 'Loads of them.'

I meant real ones.'

Michelle glared at him, and he knew he had hit a nerve. He chewed at his bottom lip, wishing he could take back his words. He had never seen her cry, but she looked close to it now.

'Want a drink?' he asked. He didn't know what else to say.

'Yeah,' she muttered. A second later she put down her phone. 'No. Let's go out. I'm fed up of sitting around in here.'

'Nothing any good on the telly anyway.'

'There never is.' She stood up. 'And I won't make any friends stuck in the house, will I?'

'I'm sorry, Michelle. I shouldn't have said that.'

'No, you shouldn't, but you're right. The only friends I've got are in Birmingham. Never made any here.'

Phil could see that she was upset and winced. He was aware there was a lot about her that he knew nothing about. He promised himself he would tread more carefully in future.

'Come on, then,' she sounded irritable.

Neither of them spoke on the short drive to the Red Lion. Phil parked at the back of the pub, frowning at the two youths who were hanging about looking shifty. He didn't know them and wondered what they were doing here. Most of the younger people went to the pubs in Aldermarsh.

The Red Lion was busy, so Michelle couldn't sit in her usual spot by the fireplace. They stood together at the bar and as he ordered their drinks, she looked around to see if there were any spare seats.

'Going over there,' she said as she nudged his elbow. 'Say hello to Clive.'

'Okay.'

Phil watched her as she headed towards his best friend. He saw her speak, but Clive didn't respond. He had changed completely since Connie had been murdered. He had withdrawn into himself. Phil hadn't seen him smile or laugh for weeks. Suddenly he reminded Phil of Michelle half an hour ago. Lost and lonely.

He got the drinks and went to join them. Clive looked up at him and tried to smile.

'How ya going, Clive?'

'Oh, you know. Slowly.'

'Yeah. Suppose so.'

'One good thing,' Clive said. 'The gossip seems to have died down. Only the occasional finger pointing at me now.'

'Probably found someone else to rip to pieces.' Phil laughed.

'Yeah.' Michelle sounded as though she really meant it. 'This village is like that.'

'I suppose they all are.' Clive sounded serious too. 'Small community. Everyone knows everyone.'

Phil glanced at Michelle, who turned away. Perhaps she was right not to get involved with village life. Maybe she had something to hide. This thought made him frown. Just what was it about Birmingham that kept dragging her back there?

'We ought to do something,' Phil said without thinking. 'Away from here.'

'Why don't we go to the cinema at Riversholme Marina?' Michelle amazed the pair of them by saying. 'And go for a meal in the Thai restaurant afterwards?'

'Hey, that's not a bad idea.'

'The last time I saw Connie was up there,' Clive said quietly.

'Oh hell, Clive,' Phil muttered.

'Sorry, Clive. I didn't know,' Michelle added.

Clive didn't say anything for a while, which only added to Phil's embarrassment. Michelle was looking uncomfortable as well.

'No,' Clive eventually spoke. 'That's a good idea. We'll do it in her memory. I can't hide from it forever.'

'You sure, Clive?'

'Positive, Phil. Bloody good idea.'

'I'll find out what's on,' Michelle offered.

Phil was impressed. This was the friendliest he had ever seen her be. He wondered how long it would last, then decided to enjoy it while it did.

'Have you heard what happened in Aldermarsh at the weekend?' Phil heard a man on the next table say. He assumed he was speaking to him.

'Oh, that was so funny.' His wife laughed.

'No,' Phil answered.

'You know the field on the edge of the village that belongs to the geezer with the double-barrelled name?'

'The bloke that owns lots of land round here? With the stuck-up wife?'

'Yeah, that's the one. He was getting it ready for the church fete. Anyway, the night before the main event, a gang of travellers arrived. Parked all over the field. Caravans and horses everywhere.'

Phil laughed, and even Clive smiled. Michelle was looking bored. That hadn't lasted long. Typical.

'Of course, geezer was having none of that. Do you know what he did?'

'No idea.'

Michelle was reaching for her phone again. Phil was annoyed with her. Couldn't she leave the damned thing alone? He was going to have to get hold of it and find out exactly what was on there. She lived on the bloody thing.

'He got hold of a muck spreader from Riversholme. Paid the driver to go up to the field and aim the thing over the hedge. The travellers copped the lot. Made more mess than they ever could. They soon buggered off.'

The man's wife was laughing, and it seemed to be infectious. Phil had a picture of the scene in his mind's eye and started to titter. Michelle glanced at him and rolled her eyes towards the ceiling.

'Must had been a pretty smelly fete,' Phil managed to say, in between giggles.

'They postponed it. Wonder why?'

The man started laughing now, and Phil was in full flow. Then Clive started, nearly choking on his lager. He put it down and wiped his left eye.

'I wish I'd seen that,' he said.

'So do I.' Phil had to put his beer down too. 'I can just imagine it. Oh boy, those travellers'll never come back round here.'

Clive was laughing so hard he was nearly in tears. Phil was the same, and everyone who had heard the story were also in fits of giggles. Even Michelle managed a smile.

'That is a classic,' Clive said when he had calmed down a bit. 'Never a dull moment in a village.'

'See, Michelle,' Phil couldn't resist saying, 'look what you've been missing. Village life, you can't beat it. I bet things like that don't happen in Birmingham.'

'No.' She didn't look impressed. 'They've got more important things to worry about. And places that are open all night.'

'Well, I know where I'd rather be.' Phil was definite about that. 'Give me Hawksmere any day of the week.'

'Huh,' was all she had to say.

'Thanks, you two,' Clive said after a minute or two. 'I thought I'd never laugh again. I feel better for it.'

'Life does go on,' Phil said quietly.

'And you've got us,' Michelle amazed him by adding.

'Yeah.' Clive nodded. 'It's at times like these you need friends. And when you find out who your real ones are.'

'We'll always be here,' Phil said. 'Want another pint?'

Clive nodded again, so he went to fetch another round.

'There's a comedy on at the cinema,' Michelle told him when he came back. 'Clive says he fancies that. I can book the tickets online.'

You do that. Might as well get something useful out of that bloody phone of yours.'

Michelle stuck her tongue out at him as he handed her his credit card.

Yet again.

CHAPTER THIRTY-FOUR

Stuart wasn't a naturally curious person, but there was something about Michelle Clark that had fired his imagination. He had heard about coppers nose, they all had, but he had never felt it before. Despite the fact he had other work to do that was far more important, he was glued to his computer screen looking into the woman's background. What he had found so far wasn't particularly interesting, but he was sure there was something hidden in her past that would prove to be relevant.

'It's here somewhere, I know it,' he muttered to the screen.

'Stuart?'

Nikki's voice reminded him of where he was, and he looked up.

'That girlfriend of Phil Bateman. Don't you think there's something funny about her?'

'She wasn't particularly friendly, but that's not a crime. A lot of people aren't very keen on the police turning up at their houses.'

'She reacted strongly to hearing about Clive Morrison getting married.'

'That's not a crime either.' Nikki looked sideways at him. 'We're supposed to be collating all the information on Andrew Ferguson, and there's a lot of it. There's a lot of copying to be done as well.'

'Yeah, I know. I've given some of it to Ella in the front office. She offered to help.'

'Only coz she fancies you.' Nikki looked annoyed. 'You shouldn't take advantage of the uniform staff. They've got enough to do.'

'Basically, we haven't got enough staff.'

'Yeah, well, there's nothing we can do about that. There's been cutbacks everywhere. We should be concentrating on getting Andrew Ferguson to trial, and making it stick.'

Stuart didn't answer. He knew she was right, and he had to admit he felt a bit guilty for wasting valuable time on an unconnected matter.

'Come on, then.' Nikki almost smiled. 'What have you found out?'

Stuart did smile, he was dying to tell someone. Nikki was usually perceptive. Maybe she would spot something odd amongst all the bits and pieces.

'Age forty-seven, born in Castle Vale. Her mother still lives in the same tower block. The area was an aeroplane factory during World War Two, but it was redeveloped in the nineteen sixties. Soon got a reputation for trouble.

Father deceased, ten years ago. There's a sister knocking about somewhere, but I haven't been able to find her.'

'Not much to go on so far. Has she got a record?'

Nikki was trying to look patient, but Stuart could tell she thought all this was a complete waste of time.

'One arrest when she was seventeen. She worked in the Jewellery Quarter in Birmingham, and two diamond rings went missing. They were never found and nothing was proved, but it probably was her. Later she had several jobs in nightclubs, posh selective ones. One of them got closed down for prostitution. She seems like a money grabber who doesn't much care what she has to do to get it.'

'That isn't a crime either,' Nikki pointed out. 'There are plenty of men who'll pay for female company.'

'Phil Bateman's got money, loads of it. I bet that's why she's taken up with him. Clive Morrison isn't too shabby either. Perhaps she's playing both of them.'

'You've been looking at Phil Bateman's finances? That's not part of any investigation.' She was looking annoyed again.

'I was curious.'

Stuart's spirits were sliding down into his shoes. She was right. He was wasting his time. And everyone else's.

'We haven't got time to be curious. All you've found out is that she's not a very nice person, and that's not a crime either.'

'There's something, I know there is.'

'Well, it seems like the only thing you can get on her is being a prostitute, but that's got nothing to do with any of our cases.'

'She owns three properties.' Stuart sounded more hopeful than he intended to.

'So what?' Nikki gave a near hysterical laugh born out of obvious exasperation. 'Unless you can get her for living off immoral earnings or tax evasion, give it up.'

'Mm.' Stuart was thinking. 'I'll stay behind tonight and do a bit more digging.'

'Oh, Stuart.' Nikki flounced out of the room.

'Woops,' he muttered.

As he turned back to the computer, he heard a laugh come from down the corridor, and knew it was Frankie. He hadn't seen much of her lately but it seemed she had come out of hiding now. He guessed Nikki would stop for a chat with her, so he should be safe for a while.

'Still at it?' Nikki said when she came back ten minutes later, carrying two coffees. 'Here.' She put one down beside him. 'That should keep you going.'

She rolled her eyes and tutted as she went back to her desk. Stuart ignored her. Some quiet rattling came from her keyboard, but he ignored that too. His guilt only grew as the afternoon wore on, but at least Vic didn't disturb either of them. He seemed to be busy in his own office, apart from a short meeting with the Super at three o'clock.

'So,' Nikki said after a while, 'what time do you think you'll be back tonight?'

'No idea.' He wasn't really listening.

'Okay.' She paused. 'I'll go out with Frankie then, shall I?'

'Fine.'

He heard the 'huh' that came from across the room, but didn't react to it. He was digging into Michelle's finances now, and carried on long into the evening. He finally got home at half past ten, ate a ping meal and crashed into bed.

'You been here all night?' Nikki asked as she arrived for work the next day.

'Of course,' he lied with a smile. 'Dedication to duty.'

'Bloody stupidity, more like,' she muttered. 'Come on then, let's hear it. What else have you found out?'

'Well, it's a bit of a coincidence that car thefts from villages have increased dramatically since she moved to Aldermarsh. Three in the last month. One from there, and two from Riversholme.'

'And this has led you where?' She was trying not to smile.

'Of the three properties she owns, only two are rented out. Seems she liked to keep one as a bolthole, and after what else I've found out, I can't say I blame her. A while back one of the other two was rented by a known associate of one Tony King.'

'Who?' Nikki's face was blank.

'Well known criminal around Birmingham, been at it for years. And,' he paused, as if waiting for a drumroll, 'he likes cars. He's got a Ferrari, a yellow one, and I'd bet my pension he didn't get that through legitimate means.'

'Can you prove any of this?'

'Er, well -'

I'll take that as a no.' She sighed as she turned to her computer screen.

'Wait a minute, there's more, and this is the really interesting bit.' Nikki didn't look at him. She was opening up a file on Andrew Ferguson. 'One thing I can prove is a link between Michelle Clark and Tony King, a strong one.'

'Oh, yeah?'

'Yes. When they were both in their twenties, they were married. Still might be for all I know.'

Nikki stared at him, her eyes wide with interest now.

'Hell,' she breathed. 'I wonder if Phil Bateman knows about this?'

CHAPTER THIRTY-FIVE

Two days later Phil and Michelle met up at Clive's house, and Phil drove them to Riversholme, less than five miles away. It was bigger than Hawksmere or Aldermarsh, so had more facilities. The marina had been built about ten years ago, but additions had been made to it since. The cinema was quite a new extra, which was proving popular. It made a change from sitting in the village hall at Aldermarsh. They showed films there, but the place was old and draughty. There were plans to give it a makeover but everyone was still waiting. It would probably be sometime, never.

'Why is this place called Riversholme?' Michelle showed a rare bit of curiosity into things local. 'There isn't even a river here. Just this old smelly canal.'

'It's not smelly,' Phil protested. 'They've cleaned it up a lot since they built the marina.'

'I think the River Trent used to come through here years ago,' Clive added. 'Apparently rivers do that. They move around.'

'Who told you that? Google?'

Phil wondered why Michelle's comment sounded like an accusation. He sighed. She was on the defensive again.

'Yeah,' Clive chuckled. 'Think so.'

'You ought to know enough about Google.' Phil couldn't help himself as he looked at Michelle. 'Should be your bestest ever buddy, the amount of time you spend on that phone.'

'Piss off.'

He had been expecting this reply. Usually he just laughed it off, but on this occasion, he didn't find it funny.

'Bollocks,' he hissed at her.

'If you two are going to have a domestic, I think I'll go and look in the butcher's shop.' Clive looked embarrassed. He began to walk away before anyone had a chance to answer.

'Can't you be nice to someone for once in your life?' Phil was getting angry now. 'Especially to my best friend whose just lost his woman. We're supposed to be cheering him up.'

She muttered something that he didn't catch. He glared at her.

'Sorry,' she said it again, louder this time.

'I should damn well think so. Think about someone else other than yourself for a change. You're not in Birmingham now.'

'Don't I know it.' She sounded sullen.

'Well, if the place is so fantastic, why don't you piss off back there?' He glared at her again. 'You chose to come and live in a village, but all you ever do is moan about it. Make your bloody mind up, Michelle.'

She looked at the floor.

'I tell you one thing, if you keep on like this, upsetting my best mate and winding me up, then we're through. Then you'll have to go back to your precious Birmingham.'

'I can't,' she cried out.

'Oh yeah? And why not? Have you pissed everyone off there as well?'

She looked up at him, the beginnings of tears in her eyes. Then she nodded. 'Sort of,' she said quietly.

'I can believe that.' He was feeling a bit guilty now. He hadn't meant to make her cry, but she was getting on his nerves. 'Come on, out with it. What've you done?'

'What do you mean?' She was looking nervous now.

'Why did you leave there, Michelle? And why can't you go back?'

She didn't say anything for a while. Phil could almost see the thoughts going around in her brain as she tried to find the right words. Just what had she been involved in?

'I got tangled up with the wrong people.' Phil could hardly hear her. 'Dangerous people. Criminals. I came here to get away from them.'

'But you keep going back.'

He looked at her as sternly as he could manage, waiting for her reply.

'I've still got family there,' she said quietly. 'My folks are pretty old now. They don't understand. I've lived what they would call a bad life.'

She dropped her eyes to the floor, as if frightened of his reaction.

'So, you're trying to protect them?'

She nodded. 'I've got a sister as well. She's been a good girl. I'm the bad one in the family.'

'God, Michelle. Why didn't you tell me this before?' Phil could hardly believe his ears.

'There's nothing you can do,' she mumbled.

'Of course there is. There must be something I can do to help. You shouldn't be dealing with all this on your own.'

'It's my problem. They're my family.'

'I'm going to help, and there's nothing you can do to stop me.' He was determined about that. 'We'll talk about this when we get home. We've brought Clive out to cheer him up, so let's do just that. Give us a smile, and I'll go and find him.'

She looked up at him, her bottom lip quivering.

'I'm sorry,' she just about managed to say before the tears started to flow.

'Oh, come here.' He gathered her up into his arms. He could feel her shaking as he held her. He murmured something into her mass of blonde hair, and eventually she nodded.

Clive was on his way back from the butcher's shop, all smiles.

'They've got some fantastic stuff in there,' he said, apparently ignoring the scene of tenderness in front of him. 'I'm going to come back up here and have a good stock up. What time does the film start?'

That question brought Phil back to reality, and he let Michelle go.

'You got the tickets?' he asked her.

'Sure.' She reached into the large bag. Phil was amazed she could ever find anything in there, but she pulled out three pieces of paper folded together. 'We'd better be going in.'

Michelle walked off towards the cinema, but Phil hung back.

Sorry about that,' he murmured to his friend.

'Don't worry about it. These things happen.'

'Thanks, Clive.'

'Come on. Let's have a good laugh and remember the good times.'

'No point in doing anything else, is there?' Phil smiled.

The film was extremely funny, and all three of them were in tears long before the end of it. Phil suspected that Michelle's weren't everything to do with the content of the movie, but he didn't say anything to her. When it finished, they all dried their eyes and joined the queue to leave. The Thai restaurant was only a few steps away and as they walked there slowly, Phil glanced over at the many narrow boats. It was getting dark now and all the lights from them were twinkling in the twilight. That reminded him of something.

'I think I've heard they have a Christmas market up here every year. Never been to it.'

'It's a great setting to have one.' Clive nodded. 'Sounds good. We'll have to have a look at that.'

'Fancy it, Michelle?' Phil looked at her. She looked more cheerful now. 'You can spend loads of money on stuff you don't need.'

'Like I usually do, you mean?' she said it with a smile.

'You buy whatever you want,' he said quietly.

'I might come back here with Clive, and have a look in this butcher's shop.'

'Yeah. They've got chicken parcels wrapped in bacon and stuffed with Cumberland sausage. And beef ones with garlic and red wine. Gawd, the thought of them is making me hungry.'

Phil laughed. 'Come on, it's food time. Let's see what this Thai place has got. See if we can find you a great big steak.'

The restaurant was busy, but they were shown to their table straight away. Michelle opted for noodles. Clive surprised Phil by going for a chicken dish, and Phil had the red curry. They shared a bottle of white wine and sipped this as they waited for their order to arrive.

'This place is nice,' Michelle said as she looked around. 'You wouldn't think you could find places like this in the middle of nowhere.'

Phil had a comment about Birmingham on the tip of his tongue, but wisely bit it back. When the food came it was quickly demolished. Then they all sat back and finished off the second bottle of wine.

'That film was really good,' Clive said as he ran a hand over his very full stomach. 'We'll have to do this again.'

'Yeah.' Phil smiled. 'It's like everything's getting back to normal. That can't be a bad thing.'

'Mm,' Clive agreed. 'I had some good news yesterday. That horrible inspector came round to see me. Said the police wouldn't be bothering me anymore.'

'They got someone? For - ?'

Clive nodded. 'Her husband. He's been charged with murder. Open and shut case.'

'Oh, Clive, that's brilliant news.' Michelle sounded a bit too enthusiastic, Phil thought. Then again, she had drunk several large glasses of wine.

The waiter brought complimentary drinks to finish off the meal, once the table had been cleared. Phil picked his up, and cleared his throat.

'This has been a wonderful evening, and I've got some news too.'

Clive looked up in curiosity.

'Here's to the future,' Phil continued. 'Michelle and me are going to get married. Aren't we, babe?'

Phil reached over to kiss her. As he did so, he missed the expression of horror on Clive's face.

CHAPTER THIRTY-SIX

Vic sat in the Superintendent's office, trying not to squirm in his seat. So far. she hadn't had a good word to say about anything. He knew he had caught her on one of her rare off days. She was usually very level headed and virtually unflappable. But not today. After a while, he found out why.

'I've had the new Chief Constable on the phone. Again.' She sighed. 'He's turning into a right –' She stopped abruptly.

Pain in the arse?

'– stickler for detail.'

'Yes, ma'am.'

'Very much of a stickler, actually.'

'He's doing yer head in,' Vic couldn't stop himself from saying.

'Something like that, yes. Actually, you might be able to help me with him.'

'Oh, ar?' Vic couldn't keep the sarcasm out of his voice.

'Mm,' she hummed. 'His niece lives in Riversholme, and she's fairly certain she's had her car stolen.'

'What d'ya mean, fairly certain? She either has or she hasn't.'

'It's not as simple as that. Actually… '

If she says that one more time, I'm going to ram it down her big fat throat. Get to the point, woman.

'It's all rather silly really,' she continued.

'No kidding,' Vic muttered.

'She went on holiday to South Africa for three months.' The Super hesitated, as though she was waiting for another sarcastic comment. Vic had one on the tip of his tongue, but wisely kept it to himself. 'As they have a Bentley, they decided to put it into storage for the duration of the holiday. For safety, you understand.'

'Of course, ma'am. Sounds like a good idea. Actually.' Vic was sniggering inside his mind.

'They found a website that purported to be based in Tamworth. I understand one has come up in the car theft investigation.'

Ah!

Now she had Vic's full attention.

'Yes, I thought you might find that interesting. Anyway, it was offering long term car storage, so they put in their details, and got a reply virtually straight away.'

'Sounds very efficient, ma'am.'

She really was going all round the Wrekin today, even more so than usual. What was it with women, he wondered? Why did they have to turn the simplest thing into a three-act play? His wife had been exactly the same, and she had got on his nerves as well.

'Yes, that's what they thought. The car was collected on the appointed date, with an assurance that it would be returned the day after they returned from their extended holiday.'

'Only it wasn't?'

'That's correct. All attempts to contact the company failed. Money for three months' storage was taken from their credit card, which they have now cancelled, to be on the safe side.'

'Is this website still operating?' Vic's eyes were gleaming. She really had got him interested now. So far, his investigations into the car thefts had got nowhere, but now he had a lead. Maybe he could get this issue off his books once and for all, and concentrate on the really important issues. Two murders.

'It appears to be.'

'Good. What do you want me to do?'

'I want you to visit her. And take DC Singh with you.'

'Jigsaw?' he said, without thinking. The Super was looking down her nose at him. 'Oh, yeah, I mean DC Singh.'

'Yes, I've heard about your treatment of Nikki. Really Victor, you shouldn't call her names like that.'

'It's only a laugh, ma'am. I call her that coz she's a puzzle to me. Everyone's got a nickname.'

Vic did squirm now. He hated being called by his full name, especially when people added Frankenstein on the end of it. Still, that was better than some of the other things he had been called over the years.

'Even you, I understand. And myself, I'm quite sure.'
She didn't look amused by the thought.

'Oh, I don't mean anything by it, ma'am. Just a bit of banter.'

'It's got to stop, Vic. Right now.'

'Yes, ma'am,' he muttered sullenly.

'I know you had a problem with one particular Asian, but that's by the by. There are not all the same, as you seem to think. Nikki Singh is a very bright young woman, and as we don't have many staff from the ethnic minorities, she is to be nurtured. We need more like her.'

Bleedin' 'ell.

Vic almost spoke aloud. He managed to stop himself just in time.

'I've already had one complaint about you on this issue. I don't want any more. Understand?'

She was glaring at him. Vic swallowed hard. She looked as if she meant business, so he didn't answer back. He shuffled in his seat, and her gaze didn't waver. He was more than a little relieved when she eventually looked away.

'Do you understand?' she repeated.

'Yes, ma'am. I understand completely.'

As he spoke, he imagined his hands round Nikki's throat. So, she had complained to the Super, eh? He'd get her for that.

'And before you go off doing something stupid, I have to tell you that it wasn't Nikki who came to me. Apparently she is far too loyal to do that. You're very lucky to have her in your department. Look after her from here on in.'

'Yes, ma'am.'

Three bags full, ma'am. Whatever you bleedin' well say, ma'am.

'Anyway.' She seemed to relent now. 'We're straying from the point.'

'Yes, ma'am.'

'As I said, I want you, and Nikki to visit the Chief Constable's niece. I have all the details here.'

She handed him a sheet of paper with a barely concealed smirk. Vic noticed it, and wondered what was coming next. His eyes widened as he read the note.

'Precious? Is that her name?'

'Yes. She's of West Indian origin, as is the Chief Constable.'

'But – but –'

'But nothing. His family left Trinidad quite some years ago and have assimilated into our society. Really Victor, you must do something about this xenophobic attitude of yours. We are a multiracial and multicultural country now.'

'Maybe so, ma'am.' Vic was bristling with anger. 'But that doesn't mean I have to like it.'

'True, but in our job, we have to accept it. We have no choice. It's part of who we are. Remember that.' Her voice softened a little. 'Please. Try to remember that.'

'Yes, ma'am,' he said. Very quietly.

'Good.' She stood up, smiling now. 'I must say, it was a very good turn out for the former Chief Superintendent's retirement do. And I enjoyed our little dance.'

'So did I, ma'am,' he lied, and fought back a grimace at the memory. She was holding the door open for him to leave, and he could hardly get through it quickly enough.

He marched back to his office with his head full of dark thoughts about Riversholme. He hated villages. He never knew what he was going to find in them. Why did he have to waste his time on something so trivial when he still had a murderer to catch? He didn't understand the political manoeuvrings that went on in the higher ranks.

Stuart looked up as he walked in.

'Guv, the Super has just rung down. There's something she forgot to tell you.'

'Wot?'

Stuart winced but continued. 'She's bringing someone in to help with the paperwork on Andrew Ferguson. We need to build a solid case to take to court, she said.'

'Ar, we do,' Vic agreed. 'Any idea who it is?'

'That PC you keep going on about in Lichfield. Hazel Johnson.'

Vic smiled. He had met Hazel a few times, and made no secret of the fact that he fancied her. It would be good to have a bit of glamour about the place.

'Good, bring it on. I'll enjoy having her round the place.'

CHAPTER THIRTY-SEVEN

Nikki was on her way to the kitchen while the Guv was out of his office. She had heard that Frankie was in the building, and she hadn't seen her for a while. She walked past the office where the Forensic supplies were stored, hoping to catch sight of her.

'Hiya, kiddo,' a Manchester accent purred in her ear. 'And where do you think you're off to?'

'Kitchen,' Nikki said, in a similar tone. 'I'm on the trail of an elusive cup of tea and a vicious piece of chocolate cake. Wanna come help me?'

Frankie let out one of her laughs, and the whole station must have heard it. 'You got the handcuffs?'

'You got enough evidence bags?'

'Sure thing, kiddo, let's go. They don't stand no chance of getting away from us.'

Nikki linked her arm through Frankie's and they went on their way.

The kitchen was quiet, so they could have the only table to themselves. Nikki went to the kettle, wondering how to start a conversation which didn't involve what had happened at the retirement do. A couple of PC's were just leaving, looking over at them and talking in whispers. It seemed the gossip hadn't quite died down yet.

'How are things with you?' Frankie asked when the drinks were on the table.

'Not so bad. Settling into my flat.'

'Cor, that cake looks good.' Frankie's eyes lit up. 'Can't resist a good bit of chocolate.'

'Nor me. It's the only cake I ever eat.'

I read somewhere that it's a substitute for sex.' Frankie laughed, and everyone winced. 'Must be why I'm eating more of it lately.' She looked sideways at Nikki. 'What's your excuse?'

Nikki laughed nervously. 'Have you heard from Paul?' she said instead.

'Yeah. He's been to see the girls, but it didn't go very well. Don't know if he's coming again.' Frankie stood up. 'It's no good. I can't sit here watching you eat that.'

Soon she had a piece in front of her too, liberated from the communal fridge. While she had been fetching it, Nikki had been thinking. The last thing she wanted to mention was sex, but Frankie had dived straight in. Lately it seemed to be the only thing she wanted to talk about. Nikki was trying to think of another conversation starter.

'Your mom okay?'

'Yeah, she's fine,' Frankie said, picking up the fork and attacking the cake. 'Mmm.'

'Mine's alright too, although she says she misses me. She goes to the temple a lot just for the company. Doesn't see anyone otherwise.'

'She not got any English friends?'

'No. Different generation,' Nikki sighed. 'We're miles apart sometimes.'

'How's Stuart?'

Nikki wasn't sure what to say. Frankie's eyes were gleaming again. So far Nikki hadn't told her – or anyone else – that she was seeing Stuart. The last thing she wanted was to be the subject of station gossip. Fortunately, the two PCs had gone.

'Still working on the two murders. We've got someone coming over from Lichfield to help us on the one. Paperwork.'

'Know who it is?'

'Hazel Johnson, she's a PC. Quite young, I think.'

'We'll have to make up a threesome.' Frankie hesitated, then laughed. 'Hey.' She leaned across the table. 'You ever done that?'

'No, I haven't.' Nikki was shocked. This was hardly work talk. 'Eat your cake.'

As soon as she could, Nikki went back to the safety of the office. Frankie had embarrassed her, and she was wondering if she should see her again. Ever since she had met her, she had always spoken her mind, but today had been way over the top. She had heard Frankie described as a bad influence, and was now thinking that maybe those people had been right.

She hadn't been at her desk for long when their uniformed sergeant came to the door, accompanied by a young woman with long blonde hair.

'Hi, Pete.' Stuart smiled up at him. 'Is this our new recruit?'

'PC Hazel Johnson from Lichfield,' he replied. 'Reporting for duty.'

'Thanks. We'll take it from here.'

'Best of luck.' Pete patted her on the shoulder, then walked away. She looked nervous, as if she had never seen the inside of a CID office before.

'Hello,' Nikki said, to break the awkward silence which was developing. 'I'm Nikki, DC Singh.'

'And I'm DS Young,' Stuart added.

'Will I be working in here?' Hazel asked. She looked scared to death. The fact that she was in uniform made her look as though she didn't belong, and she seemed very conscious of it. Stuart stood up and walked towards her, so Nikki stayed where she was.

'No,' he tried to reassure her. 'There isn't really room in here.'

Nikki nearly pointed out that there was a spare desk pushed up against the far wall. It was only being used to pile junk onto. She kept quiet. It would be difficult to work normally with a stranger in the room, and then there was the Guv. If anyone was going to frighten the life out of her, it would be him. Better to put as much distance between them as possible.

'Yes, we've got another office down the corridor,' she said with a smile. 'Shall I take her to meet Ella?'

'Yes.' Stuart nodded. 'She'll look after you.'

Hazel looked relieved as Nikki took her towards the front of the building where all the officers were in uniform. She looked more comfortable amongst them. The other office was busy, but up the corner sat Ella, another PC. The one Stuart had conned into doing his copying. That's how it seemed to Nikki anyway.

Once the introductions were over, Ella set about finding Hazel somewhere to sit, close to her. Nikki explained about Andrew Ferguson, trying to ignore the look of shock on Hazel's face.

'The priority with this is to build as strong a case against him as we can,' she ended by saying. 'There's a lot of copying to get through, to be sent over to the MCT. It's a boring job, but it's important. This is one nasty bloke we need to keep in prison for as long as we can.'

'I understand.' Hazel nodded. 'Where do I start?'

'I'll talk you through where we've got to.' Ella smiled at her. 'Glad to have you on board, Hazel. You're going to be a big help.'

'I'll do my best,' Hazel promised.

'Any problems, you know where I am,' Nikki said as she left them to it.

'Thanks,' Hazel called after her.

'She seems like a nice girl,' Nikki said to Stuart when she returned.

'Too nice for him to get his claws into.' Stuart nodded towards Vic's door. 'He's back, by the way.'

'Okay.' Nikki grimaced as she went back to her desk. 'What you up to?'

'He's got me on cars again.'

'Best of luck.'

'Yeah.' Stuart threw a death stare at the door.

Nikki couldn't concentrate for the rest of the day. Stuart commented on it later, when they were in his flat.

'It's Frankie,' she eventually told him. I mean, she's always a bit over the top, but today was weird. I'm wondering if she's alright.'

'What d'you mean, weird?'

'Everything I talked about got turned round into sex. That's not normal, surely? It's like she's cracking up. Heading for a breakdown, or something.'

'You'd better keep an eye on her.'

'Yes. I think I better had.'

CHAPTER THIRTY-EIGHT

The room Frankie was working in was unbelievably hot. Inside her paper scene suit she was melting. Her hair was glued to her head, and she could feel sweat running down her back. It was almost enough to take her mind off the sight in front of her.

Frankie had attended suicides before, but never one as peculiar as this. She was at a three-storey town house in Brodewell and was standing in the bedroom of a young man. A definitely deceased young man. He had been certified as such less than an hour ago, but there could have been no doubt about it anyway.

He was about twenty and was lying on his back on top of a green double duvet. A plastic bag was tied over his head, and the bed and floor were littered with pornographic magazines. Some sort of sex game gone wrong, the attending doctor had decided, and Frankie agreed. She didn't even really know what she was doing here. Still, she went about her business, collecting samples of various unpleasant substances. He could have been murdered, she supposed. The bag over his head did look to have been tied very tightly.

She was just filling in the last exhibit label when her eyes landed on one of the magazines on the floor. It was open at the page of a very well-endowed man in his thirties.

Cor, that's a big one. Reminds me of Paul.

On the opposite page was a picture of him and a woman with her mouth open. Now there was no sign of the big one.

Crikey, where did all that go?

Frankie shook her head to get rid of the thoughts. She had shocked herself, thinking of things like that when this poor lad was lying dead in front of her. What was she doing? She should get her mind back on the job.

On the job, oh yes. God, what's the matter with me? Hurry up and get out of here. I'm going doolally.

The doctor had long gone and she was alone in the room with the corpse. She wondered what his name was, and whether he had a girlfriend. Whatever he had been doing he was now here alone. Frankie felt sorry for him. No one should have to die alone.

She finished up and put all the evidence bags into a plastic box. All she wanted to do now was go home and have a long warm shower. Deaths like this upset her, especially when the people were young.

Poor lad.

She felt tears coming to her eyes and knew she had to get out of here. But before she left, she picked up the magazine she had been looking at. She put it in the box, feeling shifty, like some sort of pervert. She went to the van and drove away.

Back at Brodewell police station she logged all the exhibits, rolled the magazine up and stuffed it into her handbag. Then she went home to get changed.

That night she went to bed early and took the magazine with her. She had drunk a bottle of wine beforehand. This was getting to be a regular thing, and she knew she shouldn't be doing it. On more than one occasion she had woken up with the mother of all hangovers, not exactly the best thing to have when she had to concentrate on her work. Then again, she had been doing it for so long she could do it in her sleep.

That night she did exactly that. Over the years she had been involved in some horrific cases, and they all came into her dreams. There was the man who had lain undiscovered for over a week, his stomach eaten away by bacteria and his house full of flies. There was the woman who had drowned and left in the river for several days. The bloated body that was recovered from the water was unrecognisable. Shootings, stabbings, the list went on and on…

Frankie woke up at three in the morning, thrashing about in her bed hardly able to breathe. The young man she had attended yesterday had risen up with a snarl and was trying to strangle her. She cried out, then burst into tears.

A few minutes later her mother tapped on her door, then came into the bedroom.

'Are you alright, love?' she asked, without putting the light on.

'Yeah, yeah, I'm fine,' Frankie lied.

'You had another one of those dreams?'

'Yeah. It was nothing.'

'You ought to pack that job in. It's getting to you.'

'I know.'

Frankie reached for the bedside light, then remembered the magazine. She shoved it under her pillow so that her mum wouldn't see it. What had she been doing, bringing that home? She had two young daughters. She hadn't even looked at it. She had been so drunk that she had gone straight off to sleep.

'I think I overdid the wine a bit,' she admitted to her mother. 'Don't let me buy any more.'

'You need to do something to relax. I have to sometimes as well.'

Frankie knew that. She understood that her mum still missed her husband. Frankie missed him too, he had been a good man. He had been a firefighter, and had been killed in the line of duty. That had been the official story anyway. His breathing equipment had failed while out on a shout. Frankie felt as though her own was failing her at the moment. She lay back on her pillows and tried to pull herself together.

'How do you cope with it, Mum? Being on your own?'

'You just do,' her mum said quietly. 'You have to.'

Frankie sighed.

'It gets better as time goes on, and anyway, you're still young. You might find someone else.'

'I dunno.'

'It's too late for me. There'll never be anyone else.'

'You can't say that, Mum. You're not exactly ancient.'

'No. No one'll ever be able to take the place of your dad.'

Frankie didn't answer. Mum seemed determined about it, and if she had made up her mind, no one would ever change it. That was the only thing they had in common. Unbelievable stubbornness.

'Would you like a cup of hot chocolate?' Mum eventually asked.

'No thanks.' For some reason, the mention of chocolate reminded Frankie of sex. 'I'll try and get back to sleep. I feel better now.'

'If these dreams carry on, you should go and see a doctor.'

'Maybe.' Frankie had been thinking about this. But what would her manager say? She didn't want anyone suggesting that she wasn't up to the job anymore. Just imagine what that arsehole Hardcastle would say when he found out.

Frankie eventually went back to sleep, her thoughts full of the inspector. Fortunately, she didn't have any more nightmares that night.

The next day was a rest day. When she woke halfway through the morning, she retrieved the magazine from under her pillow and leafed through it. It wasn't hard porn, just enough to suggest and titillate. She went through it twice, knowing she had to get it out of the house in case thirteen-year-old Rosie got her hands on it. She was getting to the age where she was asking more and more questions, and Frankie didn't want to explain such things as erections or oral sex. Not yet. She had no idea how much either of her daughters knew. The subject wasn't really discussed.

Mum never talked to me about it much. I wish she had really, but I know it's difficult. I want my girls to stay children for as long as they can.

She lingered on the page she had looked at in that awful bedroom yesterday. Vague memories of the Chief Superintendent's retirement do were surfacing, and she wished they wouldn't. She didn't remember all the details of that Saturday evening. The bits she did recall, she wished she hadn't. She had made an exhibition of herself, she did know that. It had ended with her grabbing hold of Vic and dragging him off to the toilets. She cringed. How could she have done that? With him of all people?

'I'm not right, I know that much,' she whispered to her reflection in the mirror. 'And I've got to get rid of this.'

She rolled up the magazine and put it back into her handbag, still not knowing why she had taken it in the first place. She had a shower and got dressed slowly. By the time she went downstairs, she had made a decision.

She was going to see the FMO, Force Medical Officer. She knew there was a problem somewhere, and she also knew that things wouldn't be right until she found out what it was.

CHAPTER THIRTY-NINE

The next day Vic and Nikki left Brodewell to go to see the Chief Constable's niece. After a while, they drove through Lichfield onto the A38 and then turned off into Riversholme. It was bigger than the other two villages, and seemed more like a small town. Nikki followed the instructions from the rather snappy sounding voice on the satnav, and soon they were pulling up outside a large detached house that looked as though it had had a lot of money spent on it.

'Somebody's doing alright for themselves,' Vic muttered as he got out of the passenger seat.

'What we doing here, Guv?'

'You'll see.'

The front door was opened by a very attractive young woman in her thirties. Vic introduced the two of them, showed her his warrant card, and they were ushered into the house.

'Now then, Miss –'

'Oh, call me Precious, everyone does. Tea? Coffee?'

'No, ta. Now, about this car . . .'

'Yes. Please, come through to the lounge.'

As he followed, Vic sized her up. She had obviously been to a posh school, her accent told him that. It riled him that some people could have that advantage when all the kids he had grown up with in Tipton had no chance of bettering themselves. He had joined the police to get out of there, but he knew that most of his classmates hadn't been so lucky.

He and Nikki were waved into comfortable armchairs, and he noticed that Nikki was looking all around herself and taking in every detail. She looked ill at ease in the large room. Or maybe she was jealous.

'Right then.' Vic decided to get straight to the point. He didn't want to hang around here for any longer than was necessary. 'What's the name of this website you used?'

Precious smiled, and showed a set of perfect white teeth.

'I've got it up here, on my laptop.'

'Nikki, take a look at it, will you?'

'Of course, Guv.'

He watched as Nikki went over to the table in the corner and sat down in front of the computer. Vic watched her closely as she studied the screen. At one point her eyes widened, as though she had recognised something, but she made no comment.

'Have I been scammed?' Precious asked after a while.

'I would guess so.' Nikki nodded. 'It all looks genuine, but there's a few things about it that I don't like.'

'Such as?' Vic reminded her that he was there.

'There's no physical address for this company and no phone number either, just an email address.'

'I didn't notice that.' Precious looked annoyed with herself.

'Plus, they only seem to want to deal with high-end cars. The drop-down box only has those in it.'

Vic was nodding. He had noticed that too, and had thought it was suspicious. It was as good as saying that ordinary cars weren't good enough for them.

'I did see that,' Precious said, 'but I thought that was good. Even my husband said so. They specialise in certain cars, so we thought that meant they knew what they were doing.'

'Oh, I think they do.' Vic laughed, earning a sharp glance from his hostess. 'What happened after you booked it in?'

'I put in our card details, and the day before we went away, two men came to collect it.'

'They arrived in a car?' She nodded. 'Can you remember anything about it?'

'Only that it was blue.'

'Big? Small?'

'Quite big. Nothing flashy. Nothing stood out about it.'

'Figures,' Nikki muttered.

'Yes.' Vic had heard her. 'They wouldn't want to draw attention to themselves. The men. What did they look like?'

'One of them was Asian, the other white. In their late twenties, early thirties, I'd say.'

'Local accents?'

'I don't really know what the local accent is like.' Precious smiled nervously. 'We haven't been here long, and we don't go into the village much. We came here from Oxfordshire.'

'Ah,' Vic said, as though that explained everything. 'These men. Would you recognise them again?'

'Oh, I don't think so, Inspector. I didn't really take any notice. My husband dealt with them.'

'Maybe he could remember something. Is he here?'

'No, he's at work. He's a lecturer at Derby University.'

'I'd like to speak to him.'

'I can arrange that.' Precious nodded. 'I'll get him to ring you, if you like.'

'Yeah.' Vic handed her his card. 'You do that.' He turned to Nikki. 'Finished on there now?'

'Yes, Guv. All done.'

'Anything useful?'

'Yes. There's a few things I can look into.'

'Good.' He stood up. 'We'll be off, then.'

Nikki drove them both back to Brodewell, and neither of them spoke much on the way. When they got back to the office, Vic left his door open so he could hear what she had to say to Stuart.

'We've been to Riversholme. The new Chief Constable's niece has had her car stolen through a website.'

'Careless of her.'

'I think I recognise it.' Nikki lowered her voice. 'Just

245

before I left Zak, I found him messing around on the computer. He said he was building a website to do with his work. From what I saw of it, which wasn't much, it looked very similar to this one.'

'What is his work?' Stuart sounded interested. So was Vic. He had no idea about any of this.

'I don't know, he never talked about it. Not long afterwards, he went off to Dubai.'

'Give me his full name. I'll see what I can find out.'

Vic was nodding. He needed to find something on this case so that he could get it off his books. He had better things to do than chase all-round the district after stolen cars.

The next day, he overheard Stuart and Nikki talking again, and was disappointed at the outcome. Stuart had dug into Zak's background, but had come up with nothing conclusive.

'I'm sure he's up to something,' Vic heard him say. 'There's money going to Dubai on a regular basis, but it's only small amounts. Not enough to get the money squad interested. Does he go to Dubai a lot?'

'I don't know. Possibly. Before we got married, he told me he did a lot of foreign travel. He's only been the once in the three months we were married.'

'I'll keep an eye on it, coz I've got a feeling about this. Something about it feels dodgy somehow. Can't explain it.'

'Okay, Stuart. I don't mind what you do. He's not my problem anymore.'

Vic looked round sharply as his phone rang. Hoping it wasn't the Super, he answered it.

'Good morning,' a cultured voice greeted him. 'My name is Darren Armstrong. I believe you spoke to my wife Precious yesterday.'

'Yes sir, I did.'

'I've thought of something that may be of interest to you. We have CCTV outside our house.'

Vic sat to attention. Evidence at last?

'Really?' he said hopefully.

'It works off a motion sensor. Saves trawling through loads of recordings. I've checked through it, and we actually have film of the two men who came to collect the car. I thought you might like to see it.'

'I certainly would.' Vic's heart was racing.

'I'm in all day today, if you'd like to come round.'

'I'll be there in an hour.'

Vic's eyes were gleaming as he came off the phone, and reached for his jacket.

Right,' he said, to the empty room. 'Gotcha, ya bastards!'

CHAPTER FORTY

Stuart stared after Vic as he flew out of his office towards the door to the corridor. He shouted something as he went.

'What did he say?' Nikki asked as Vic almost skidded around the corner to the right.

'I think it was CCTV at Riversholme. Mean anything to you?'

'Yes, the car theft. The Chief Constable's niece.'

'He'll have the Super on his back if he doesn't sort that out soon. Seeing as it's the Chief Constable's niece.'

'You're not wrong there,' Nikki laughed.

An hour later Vic was back, with a disc in his hand.

'Alright, Guv?'

'Yes, son.' Vic smiled. 'Got 'em banged to rights, all we got to do is identify them. Mr Johnstone did me a copy. 'Ere, bung it in the machine, and we'll all 'ave a look.'

Stuart led the way to the front office to do just that. Ella smiled at him and Hazel looked up at them hopefully. Vic ignored them both. The footage didn't take long to view. It was just as Precious had said. Two young men, one white and one Asian.

'Right,' Vic said loudly when they had finished. 'I want one of you lot to find these two scrotes. Any volunteers?'

Hazel raised her hand with no hesitation.

'Not you, darlin'. You concentrate on the paperwork, that's why you're here.' She blushed and put her hand down again. She looked a bit annoyed as well. 'Yeah, I know,' Vic said as he noticed her reaction. 'It's a shit job, but someone's got to do it.'

'Yes, sir,' she mumbled.

'I'll do it, sir,' Ella spoke up. She was talking to Vic but was looking at Stuart. This didn't go unnoticed by anyone.

'Good.' Vic stood up and winked at Stuart. 'Come on, then. Let's all get back to it.'

'Yes, Guv.' Stuart and Nikki spoke at the same time as they followed him. It sounded like a mutual groan.

Vic went off to fetch a coffee. Nikki touched Stuart's arm when they got back to their office.

'We've got a problem,' she said quietly. Stuart's face was full of questions. 'The Asian guy on that recording. It's Zak.'

'Are you sure?' Stuart asked, realising how stupid he must sound. Nikki nodded. 'Did you know he was involved with this?'

'Of course not,' she snapped at him, then added,

with a heavy note of sarcasm. 'Now, if you don't mind, some of us have got work to do. Real work.'

Stuart stiffened. He had been on the verge of apologising to her for his insensitivity, but now it seemed as though she had thrown down a challenge. She was having a dig at him over Michelle Clark, and his bruised male pride wasn't going to take that lying down.

'Of course.' His voice sounded cold, even to him. 'I shall leave you alone to get on with it.'

'Fine.' That seemed like the last word on the subject.

Silence ruled in the CID room, and after a while, Stuart was feeling even more uncomfortable that he was at the start. He felt Vic's presence, so buried his head in the file on his screen as the man himself breezed into the room. He slowed his step, and wrinkled his brow. Stuart waited for the inevitable non-witty comment.

Which didn't come.

He could feel Vic's eyes on him, but didn't look up. Out of the corner of his eye, he saw him glance at Nikki, but she did the same. Vic made a strange little herumping noise, shrugged his shoulders, and carried on into his office. He closed the door firmly behind him, sending a waft of coffee their way.

Stuart let out a quiet breath of relief, then began to really read the file in front of him. The rattling coming from Nikki's keyboard seemed to be getting louder and louder as the silence continued. After a while, it sounded like a machine gun.

A knock came on the door and Stuart looked up in almost alarm. It opened and in came Ella, with some papers in her hand.

'Hi, Stuart.' She gave him a bright smile, winced slightly, then walked up to his desk. 'Thought you'd need these.'

Nikki glanced over at them, trying not to look interested, but not really succeeding. Ella handed Stuart two photographs. The men from the CCTV footage.

'Yeah, thanks, Ella. We'll soon find out who they are.'

'This dark haired one's a good-looking bloke.' There was almost a chuckle in Ella's voice.

Now it was Nikki's turn to stiffen.

'How are you getting on with Hazel?' Stuart had decided to keep her here for a while, to wind Nikki up.

'Okay, I suppose, but she isn't too keen on all the paperwork. I hear a lot of sighing.'

'Keep her on it. That's why she was brought over here. We need all the help we can get.'

'Right. Anything else you need, you know where I am.'

'Might keep you to that.'

Stuart smiled at her as she turned to leave. He heard the quiet ' huh.' that had just come from across the room.

He heard movement in Vic's office, so collected up all the papers and put them back into the file he was compiling on Michelle Clark. Most of it was interesting reading, but not much of it was relevant to any case they were on. He was dying to talk to someone about it. He was sure Nikki was wrong, and Michelle was involved in something illegal.

The door opened and Vic leaned against the frame doing a very bad impersonation of some fifties film star. Stuart wondered what he wanted.

'Any luck on the scrotes yet?'

'On it now, Guv,' Stuart lied. 'Nothing on the Asian. He doesn't seem to have a record.'

'You know him?' He directed the question to Nikki. Her eyes widened for a second. Stuart winced.

'I don't know every Asian on the planet, Guv.'

'No, I suppose not.' Vic laughed. 'There are rather a lot of you, aren't there?'

Nikki went back to her work with a very stony face.

'Right, then.' Vic reached for the door handle.

'There is something I'd like to talk to you about, Guv. If you've got a minute.'

'Yeah, come in. You can help me drink this lousy coffee.'

Stuart gathered up the file and held it close to his chest, with a smile on his face. He caught a glimpse of Nikki's as he went through the door. She looked worried, but Stuart had no idea why. In his haste to prove his theory right about Michelle Clark, he had forgotten all about Zak.

'Wot you got there, then?'

Hey, they don't call him Super Dick for nothing.

Since the retirement do, this had become the latest nickname. No one could say the police didn't have a sense of humour.

'I've been digging into the background of witnesses in the Hawksmere case,' Stuart began. He knew he would have to get to the point quickly, before Vic lost interest. 'One of them has got links to Tony King.'

Vic looked up sharply, his eyes starting to shine.

'Sit yerself down, son. And tell me all about it.'

Stuart did just that, and wasn't too surprised when Vic left shortly afterwards to go and talk to the Super. He was soon back, but what he had to say filled Stuart with alarm.

'You know when this wedding is?'

'Yes, Guv. It's all over Facebook. Next Wednesday.'

'Right. Fatso's decided we need someone in there undercover. I'd like it to be one of us, but they've all seen us, so,' he hesitated slightly. 'It's going to be Hazel Johnson.'

'Guv, she's only a PC. She hasn't got any experience.' Stuart was appalled.

'She's keen though, and there's only one way to get experience.'

She'll mess it up, Stuart wanted to say but he knew he would be wasting his time. The decision had already been made, and the Super was notorious for not changing her mind on anything.

'What's she going in as?' he asked instead.

'Waitress. She'll be able to move around. Watch and listen. That's all she needs to do. Don't see how she can cock it up.'

'Suppose not.' Stuart knew he sounded uncertain.

'It's happening anyway, Fatso's organising it now. Blondie'll be glad of a change of duties, I expect. Everyone hates paperwork.'

Especially you. Anyway, looks like she's teacher's pet. Might as well save my breath.

Yes, Guv.' He sighed.

'I'll go and give her the good news.' Vic smiled as he stood up. Stuart could read his mind. He thought he was earning a few brownie points with Hazel. Stuart thought he was wasting his time. He couldn't imagine her fancying anyone as rough and ready as the Guv, but if he wanted to make a fool of himself, Stuart wasn't going to stop him.

He went back to his desk. He was glad to have passed the information on, but wasn't happy about the outcome.

'Okay?' Nikki asked quietly.

'Oh, another of his hair brained schemes.' Stuart wasn't paying attention to her. He was thinking of all the things that could go wrong. 'I've told him what I've found on Michelle Clark.'

'Oh, not that again.'

Stuart's temper flared. He was sick of her running him down.

'Yes, that again. He was very interested, and so was the Super. I was right and you were wrong. Fancy thinking that Michelle Clark could fancy Clive, how stupid.' Nikki was staring at him, her mouth falling open. 'She's getting married on Wednesday. To Phil Bateman.'

CHAPTER FORTY-ONE

For a Wednesday lunchtime the Red Lion was busy. People were ordering food before the kitchen even opened at twelve. Clive had arrived a few minutes early in order to give himself some Dutch courage. He was determined to have another go at talking Phil out of what was going to happen in just over an hour's time.

Clive felt more than a little conspicuous standing in the pub in grey top hat and tails. He had the hat in his hand. He was frightened to put it down in case he forgot it. There was a man holding a pint of Guinness at the bar next to him, so he moved. He had visions of beer stains all over his hired suit.

He was about to order a second pint when Phil walked in, dressed in an identical suit to his own. He looked harassed but managed a smile when he saw his friend.

'You look like you need to calm down.'

'Do I ever,' Phil replied. 'We stopped up late last night talking and drinking. Should have gone to bed earlier.'

'Come on. Let's find somewhere to sit, away from this lot.' Clive grabbed the two pints from off the bar. The man with the Guinness was becoming a little too animated for his liking.

'Don't want to crease my trousers.'

'Sod yer trousers. No one's going to be looking at you.'

They found a couple of seats up the corner, well away from the diners. Phil put his head in his hands and let out what sounded like a full lungful of air.

'Deep breaths,' Clive suggested. 'Might be a good idea for both of us.'

'You nervous as well?'

'Only in that I think you might be doing the wrong thing.'

'At the moment I think you're right.' Phil tried to laugh. 'I never knew getting married could be so stressful.'

'Wouldn't know,' Clive said quietly. All of a sudden his thoughts were full of Connie.

'Michelle's banned me from the bedroom so she can get ready. Glad to get out of the house to be honest.'

'She gonna be wearing white?' Clive had to hold back a smile as he spoke. If anyone was less suited to a traditional wedding dress, it had to be Michelle.

'Don't know, she hasn't said anything about it.'

If ever she does I'm not going to be able to keep my face straight. Oh, I really wish he wasn't doing this.

'Get that beer down you. Hair of the dog and all that.'

'Yeah, it might liven me up.'

'It's going to be a long day.' Clive suspected as much anyway. He hesitated, then added. 'It's not too late to change your mind, you know.'

'I can't do that to her. She needs me.'

'She doesn't come across as needing anyone.'

'You don't know her like I do.' Phil looked serious. 'She hasn't had an easy life.'

'Suppose so,' Clive didn't know what else to say.

'She asked her parents to come today, but they said no. That shows you what sort of a family they are.'

'I think Michelle's always been able to look after herself.'

'Just as well, ain't it?'

Phil got stuck into his pint and was soon wanting another one. Clive fetched two more. When he took them back, Phil was looking at his phone.

'Better go after this one,' he decided.

'Yeah, I reckon.' Clive nodded.

The wedding venue was only a few miles away, roughly halfway between Hawksmere and Aldermarsh. It was an old manor house that nobody could afford, set in large well maintained gardens, and had been converted to hold meetings, weddings and conferences. The eatery had a good reputation, so Clive could understand why they had opted for the place.

They finished their drinks in virtual silence. There was nothing more Clive could say to make this wedding not happen. If it had been anyone other than Michelle, he would have been happy for his friend.

257

'Come on, then,' Phil said after he had drained his glass. 'Let's get this show on the road.'

Clive stayed where he was.

'Clive, come on. What's the matter with you?'

'Eh? Oh, sorry, Phil. I was thinking about Connie.'

'Oh.'

Clive sat quietly for a moment, then told himself to snap out of it. The past was past and there was nothing he could do about it.

'Yes.' He stood up. 'Let's get you married and see you live happily ever after.'

'I hope so.'

So do I, but I can't see it happening. Not with her.

Clive stood up and grimaced as he put on the hat. Phil had already done the same, so at least he wasn't the only one who looked like an overdressed penguin. Several people wished Phil well as they left the pub and walked to Clive's car.

'How's Michelle getting there?'

'Her sister's picking her up. At least she's got enough about her to come.'

'What's she like?' Clive hardly dare ask.

'Never met her, but Michelle says she's nothing like her.'

Thank God for that.

Clive tried to smile as he unlocked the car doors. Phil was going through with this and there was nothing do to stop him.

The civil ceremony was short. Clive spent most of it trying not to laugh, as Michelle had indeed turned up in a full-length white wedding dress complete with veil.

He didn't know how she had got the nerve. Afterwards they moved into the main hall for the reception

The few tables which had been laid very decoratively looked lost in the large room. It seemed as though Phil had invited everyone he could think of as he didn't have much in the way of family. Michelle appeared to have even less.

Each table sat six people. Clive found himself being directed to the one in the middle and grimaced as he realised he would be sitting next to Michelle, with Phil on the other side of her. Now he wished Phil hadn't asked him to be best man. Still, Michelle was unlikely to take much notice of him. He wished she would keep still. She had on too much perfume, and her veil wacked him in the face every time she moved. Phil seemed to be having the same trouble.

'Why don't you take that damned thing off now?' Clive heard him say. 'It's getting in the way of everyone.'

'Oh, sorry.' Her voice was full of derision.

As she was fiddling with the veil, a woman walked up to the table, smiled, and sat down next to Phil. She held out her hand to him. The man with her remained standing.

'Hi, I'm Kirsty. Michelle's sister.'

'Pleased to meet you. I'm Phil, but then I suppose you know that.'

'This is my boyfriend, I hope you don't mind me bringing him, but he wanted to come. He loves weddings.'

'No probs.'

She looked up at the tall man who looked as though he was trying not to laugh. 'Sit down, Tony.'

Michelle froze. Clive noticed but nobody else seemed to. He was intrigued, so kept his attention on her. She got the veil off and sat staring at the man across the table from her. Her expression was a cross between shock and disbelief.

'Hello everyone,' Tony said, still smirking.

Strained small talk began as waiters came round pouring wine. Michelle didn't seem to know where to look for the best, and Clive's imagination was going into overdrive. He was convinced these two knew each other but were trying to hide it. Tony looked perfectly relaxed, so he was doing a better job of it than her. Clive was all ears and eyes. This wedding reception promised to be entertaining.

The three-course meal seemed to go on forever. Conversation was in short supply, and what bit there was felt awkward and stilted. Tony smiled all the way through, and Michelle looked uncomfortable. Clive couldn't understand it. Was he the only one who could see they had history? Why had he come?

What was he going to do?

CHAPTER FORTY-TWO

Eventually the meal was over and people were free to leave their tables. Most of them were heading for the bar. Clive could do with a pint himself, but he didn't want to miss anything.

Music started and Phil did the traditional thing by asking Michelle for a dance. She couldn't get to her feet quickly enough.

'Maybe I can have a dance with you later?' Tony called after her as she walked away, hand in hand with her new husband. Even Kirsty noticed the death stare she gave him.

'Don't think she likes you,' she said.

'From what you've told me, she doesn't seem to like anyone.'

'Yeah, well, she isn't much like me.'

'Yeah.' Tony laughed. 'You're a sweetie.'

Kirsty blushed. Clive thought it was time he made a move.

When he had got his pint, he watched the proceedings with amusement. Tony was kissing Kirsty in between making her laugh, and Michelle had her face hidden on Phil's shoulder. Clive's curiosity was burning a hole in his brain. He had to find out what was going on.

Phil and Michelle finished their dance, and he led her back to the table. She had a face like thunder as she sat down. Clive saw Phil hold out his hand to Kirsty and say something. She looked surprised, but stood up and followed him onto the dance floor.

Michelle and Tony exchanged a few words, then she shot to her feet and headed towards the open French windows. Tony went after her. Clive followed him at what he thought was a safe distance.

Once outside, he could hear them arguing, so moved as close as he dare. Fortunately, there were plenty of trees and shrubs for him to hide behind.

'You really are a bastard,' he heard Michelle say. 'What are you doing here?'

'I had to have a look at lover boy, seeing as you've chosen him over me. He doesn't look up to much.'

'He was a professional rugby player, so you hadn't better start anything.'

Clive frowned. There was more to this than he had thought.

Oh, I won't do that.' Tony laughed. 'Not on this occasion anyway. I'll let you have your happy day first.'

'It's not very happy with you here,' she snapped. 'And what are you doing with my sister? How did she get involved with an evil bastard like you?'

'There's something to be said for keeping it in the family. Actually, I sought her out. She led me straight to your new life.'

'You –'

'Yeah, I know, I'm a nasty shit. I've heard it all before, but there's fuck all you can do about it.'

'I could tell Phil – and his mate. I'm sure between them they could sort you out. I know where you live as well, you know.'

'Watch your step, Michelle.' He sounded angry. 'You wouldn't want anything happening to your sister - now would you?'

'You wouldn't dare,' she breathed.

'Oh, wouldn't I?' he hissed back. 'She's really quite sweet, your sister. Not much good in bed, but then she hasn't had as much practice as you. That's the best thing about you, you're a good fuck, very inventive. And we can carry on with that once you've got this crap out of the way. Keep the dress, we'll use that.'

Clive's mouth fell open in shock. This was worse than he had ever suspected.

'No way.' Michelle sounded very definite.

'Oh yes, Michelle. Any way I say, any time I say. You want to hang on to lover boy, don't you? Seeing as you're so in love.' Michelle glared at him. 'That's a load of bollocks. The only thing you've ever been in love with is money. I suppose he's got loads of it?'

'As least his is legit, not like yours.'

'So what? The police'll never get me, I'm far too clever for that.'

Clive had heard enough. More than enough. Time to make a hasty and discreet exit.

★ ★ ★

Hazel was still excited. She could hardly believe she had landed an undercover job in CID. It certainly made a welcome break from the boring paperwork she had been ploughing through for the last week or so. She felt like 007 as she moved around the room dressed as a waitress. It was only a small wedding, so it wasn't easy to blend in, but she had her instructions. Collect glasses inside and in the garden, empty ashtrays, keep the place clean and tidy. And keep her ears and eyes open. She had been shown several photos of people of interest to the police, and one of them was here. Some guy by the name of Tony King.

After an hour, Hazel decided that this job was boring as well. At least one of the waiters was easy on the eye, and had flirted with her once or twice. She was looking forward to running into him again. It was time to do the rounds again, so she went outside, carrying a deep plastic tray.

'Going to be busy for a while,' she heard Tony King say. He was on the phone, so she hovered. 'No, the stuff's going out in two days' time. Three container loads. Need you to sort the paperwork.'

Not more bloody paperwork. God, it's everywhere.

Easy on the eye was heading her way again, with a cheeky smile on his face. Hazel smiled back at him, and was so busy gawping at him that she wasn't really listening to Tony any more.

'Yeah, Portsmouth.' He laughed. 'Yeah, last lot went from Thamesport. Keep changing it, keep everyone guessing. Yeah, yeah, okay. Speak to you soon.'

Hazel told herself to remember those two place names as easy on the eye took her hand and led her into the bushes...

★ ★ ★

Back inside, Phil and Kirsty had returned to the table; neither of them looked very happy. Clive had to walk past them to get to the bar. Kirsty took another drink from the wine in front of her. 'Where's Tony?' she asked.

'Here.'

He had appeared in front of her. Michelle was nowhere in sight.

'Where have you been?' Her bottom lip was quivering. 'I don't know anyone here.'

'It's alright, bab. I only went to the loo.' Tony avoided everyone's eyes. 'Come on, let's have a dance.'

Phil looked after them as they walked away. 'Who is that bloke?' he asked Clive, who had returned with another drink.

'I dunno, but he was outside just now, talking to Michelle.'

'What's she doing out there?'

Clive didn't know how to answer that question. He was watching Tony and Kirsty, who had reached the dance floor but weren't doing any dancing.

'Looks like those two are having a row.'

'Not surprised.' Phil laughed. 'I will have a pint. Fed up of all this wine.'

'I'll go,' Clive offered. Michelle was on her way back, so he knew there was likely to be another argument in a minute. He took his time at the bar and let a couple of people get served in front of him. Phil and Michelle were sitting side by side but didn't appear to be talking at all. Clive considered that she had rather a lot of explaining to do. He sighed. Earlier he had had the feeling that this was going to be a long day and now he knew he was right. It was only halfway through the afternoon but he'd had enough already.

He took Phil's pint over to him, then went back outside. The gardens were beautiful, and looking at them made him feel better. He was still wondering what to do. He should say something, but this was Phil's wedding day. He didn't want to go down in history as the one who had ruined it.

Phil appeared and sat down beside him. Clive looked up in surprise.

'Getting lonely in there,' he said. 'Kirsty and her fella have gone, and Michelle's gone to get changed.'

'Sorry Phil, I got thinking. Lost track of time.'

'It's alright, mate, I understand. This could have been you and Connie.'

'I wish it was.'

'Yeah.' Phil hesitated. 'If you had got married, would you have changed your will?'

'I suppose so. Hadn't thought about it.' Clive did so now, briefly. 'Yeah, I reckon.'

'I've already done mine. Thought I might as well get it out of the way before I forgot.'

'It's a bit soon, Phil. I mean, you hardly know her.' Clive was horrified. Now he was going to have to say something.

'I know enough.' Phil sounded very sure.

'I don't think you do,' Clive began. 'She was outside earlier, talking to her sister's boyfriend. They were an item, those two. Probably still are.'

'Whatever happened before I met her is nothing to do with me. It doesn't matter, it's in the past. She's my wife now.'

'Well.' Clive was bristling with anger. 'I hope you'll be very happy with the lying, cheating cow. She couldn't wait to get her claws into you. You've been a fool. She's only after your money, and now you've handed it all over to her. Congratulations to the pair of you!'

CHAPTER FORTY-THREE

The day after the wedding, Stuart went to work with a heavy heart. The previous evening, he had invited Nikki round to his flat but she had turned down the offer. The excuse she had given was very flimsy, and he suspected she was avoiding him. He remembered getting a bit annoyed with her the other day, but he thought she was overreacting. He had been right to investigate Michelle Clark, and now that had been proved. Nikki was being a sore loser, so he had decided to let her stew for a while. There wasn't much else he could do.

Another woman had been giving him grief too. His mother had rung earlier and he had sent her to voice mail. He hadn't listened to it yet. His mum could make the slightest thing into a major crisis, and he wasn't in the mood for her yet.

When he got to the office, Nikki was already at her desk. She answered his 'good morning' quietly and barely glanced at him. He sighed. Seemed like she and his mother were on the same wavelength.

Vic arrived a few minutes later, and hovered in the doorway to his own office.

'Get PC Johnson in here.' Now Nikki looked up in curiosity. 'Debriefing, tell her.'

'Yes, Guv.' Stuart picked up the phone as Vic disappeared. He could feel Nikki's eyes burning into him. 'Phil Bateman got married to that Michelle yesterday. Hazel went in as a waitress to nose around.'

'Whose idea was that?' She sounded annoyed again.

'Not sure,' he said as he dialled the front office, feeling as though the whole female population were ganging up on him.

'I could have done that job.'

'Both the Batemans have seen you,' Stuart pointed out.

'They wouldn't remember me.'

'Nikki.' Stuart smiled. 'I'm sure they would.'

He got a half smile for his efforts. She was coming round slowly.

Neither of them said anything as Hazel walked into the room without knocking, and marched straight up to Vic's door. She reached for the handle, then remembered her manners.

'Come in, Hazel.' They heard him call.

Hazel did as she was told, but didn't shut the door properly. Stuart and Nikki heard every word of the conversation between them. It started off calmly enough, but after a while Vic's voice got louder. Stuart could tell he was losing his rag.

'So, which port was it?' he asked, for the third time.

'I – I'm trying to think.' Hazel sounded a bit panicky. She obviously didn't know.

'You were supposed to be watching and listening. Wot were you doing, eyeing some lad up instead?' Vic had got the hard edge to his voice, which meant trouble. Stuart and Nikki exchanged glances.

'It was Portsmouth.' She sounded confident, then it slipped. 'Or it might have been the other Port one. Had port in it.'

'Best of three, Hazel. Thamesport, Portsmouth or Portbury. Make your choice.' Now he shouted. 'And get it right.'

'Not Thamesport, the word was at the beginning.'

'So.' He seemed to be trying to control his frustration. 'You can't remember. You'll never get into CID at this rate, girl. I said it was a mistake to put you in undercover and now because of your incompetence, we're going to have to check both those ports. All you've done is cause us more work. Now get out of my sight and back to wot you're supposed to be doing. Let's see if you can get that right.' There was a slight hesitation. 'Go!'

Stuart put his head down as Hazel left, in a huff and in a hurry. He could hear Vic cursing and banging things around. A few minutes later, he joined them.

'That was another of Fatso's stupid ideas,' he said as he perched on the corner of Stuart's desk. He waved towards the door. 'Tony King turned up at the wedding, and she overheard a phone call he made, about three containers going out, but she can't remember where from.'

'I might be able to help with Portbury. I'm going down to visit my folks this weekend, and my dad works at the docks, in admin.'

'Brilliant.' Vic looked a bit happier now. 'Can you do Portsmouth?' He looked at Nikki, who nodded. He looked back at Stuart. 'Forgot you came from Bristol.'

'I do my best to as well.' Stuart laughed, but there was a lot of truth in his comment. He hadn't been back there since he had come to Brodewell.

''Course, you could just ring your dad.'

'I won't get anything out of him over the phone.' Stuart was sure about that. 'Take him out for a drink would be better.'

'He's your dad.' Vic shrugged his shoulders.

'It'll kill two birds with one stone.' Stuart was surprised how confident he sounded. 'I haven't seen him for ages.'

'Check it out anyway,' Vic instructed. 'If Tony King's involved with these car thefts, then I want to know about it. It'd be one in the eye for West Midlands if we could get him on something. He's been getting away with murder for years.'

'Literally?' Stuart asked.

'Probably.' Vic laughed as he slid off the desk. 'Oh,' he added as he walked towards his office. 'Both of you, keep away from Miss Marple. Bad news, that one.'

'He's not wrong,' Stuart said, after he had gone.

'Mm,' was Nikki's only comment. 'You really going to Bristol this weekend?'

'I wasn't, but I will. Mum rang earlier but I haven't listened to the message yet. It'll get it out of the way, and Dad might know something.' He looked at her closer now. 'Why?'

'I haven't seen my mom for a while either. I'll give her a ring.'

Later, Stuart listened to the voice mail, and winced when she said his father hadn't been well lately. Fear struck at his chest. He had been diagnosed with a heart condition several years ago.

'They've put him on some different tablets,' his mum was saying, and he relaxed a little. She was no doubt exaggerating again. When she started moaning about his sister, he switched the message off. Then he rang her, and told her he was coming.

Only a couple of days, Stuart?'

'That's all I can manage at the moment,' he lied. 'We've got a lot on at work.'

'Oh, that awful job of yours.' She sounded annoyed. 'I knew we should never have let you join the police. Especially when there was a perfectly good job waiting for you at the docks.'

'I never wanted to work at the docks,' Stuart explained. For the forty millionth time.

Eventually he got her off the phone. He doubted his father was as ill as she was making out, but he didn't want to run the risk of not seeing him, just in case. They had never been exactly a close family, but there were the only one he had.

The next day, Stuart went to the train station straight from work, with the holdall he had packed earlier. It was nearly seven-thirty when he got to his old home, an ordinary semi-detached in a quiet suburb.

He took a deep breath as he rang the doorbell, anticipating the onslaught of questions and complaints from his mother. He was pleasantly surprised when his father answered the door with a cheery, 'Hello, Son.'

'Hi, Dad.' Stuart smiled. 'How are you?'

'Fine.'

'Mum said –'

'Yeah, she would, wouldn't she?' Dad rolled his eyes towards the ceiling. 'Welcome to the madhouse.'

Over the weekend, Stuart realised his dad had been right. His mother seemed to have turned into an even bigger drama queen since he had left. He wasn't the slightest bit sorry to get back to Lichfield. The first thing he did was ring Nikki to ask if they could meet.

I'm sorry, Stuart, I can't. I've got Frankie with me.' She sounded worried. 'She's been diagnosed with PSTD and suspended from work. She's got to go for counselling.'

Stuart's heart fell, that was the last thing he wanted to hear. It seemed that nothing was going right for him lately. When he came off the phone, he decided he needed a beer and went to the fridge.

Empty.

'Bugger,' he groaned.

CHAPTER FORTY-FOUR

On Saturday morning, Nikki drove to Walsall. She had rung her mom to say she was coming and had been talked into staying the night. She knew she would be fed as if she hadn't eaten for months, and was likely to be sent home with all sorts of goodies too.

What she wasn't expecting was a message from Zak.

'He wants to speak to you.'

'I'm not going back to him.'

'I don't think it's about that,' Mom said quietly. 'I think it's about Armajit. He worries about his mom. He's a good lad in a lot of ways.'

'Oh.' Nikki wondered if her mother knew about that situation. One glance at her told Nikki that she did. Whether she would admit it was another matter.

'He said, will you go to the house.'

'No.' Nikki shook her head firmly. 'I'll meet him somewhere public. I'd better ring him, I suppose.'

On the walk into Walsall later, she went over her plan, such as it was. She remembered her police training and tried to bring it to the forefront of her mind. She was on her way to meet her ex-husband, but told herself she was going to interview a suspect. Above all, she needed to keep herself safe. She started to think about all the things that could go wrong, and by the time she got into town she was shaking.

She checked her phone and found she was ten minutes early. She must have been walking faster than usual. Not wanting to appear too keen, she went for a walk around the block. She didn't want to give Zak the wrong idea. She got to the coffee shop seven minutes late.

Zak was at the counter ordering himself a double espresso. Nikki hung back, her nervousness returning. She took a deep breath, told herself she was practicing for her sergeant's exam, then pushed open the door.

'Hi, Nikki,' Zak greeted her with a smile, as if things were perfectly normal between them. 'Usual?'

Nikki nodded. They were behaving like an old married couple instead of two almost strangers. She didn't say anything but went to find a suitable place to sit. There was an empty table in the window with two comfortable looking armchairs. When she had cleared all the debris onto another table, she sat down.

A few minutes later, a cappuccino was placed in front of her, and Zak sat down opposite. Nikki tried to smile at him.

'So,' she began, 'how have you been?' It was all she could think of to say.

'Oh, you know.' He did smile. 'You're not bothered about that. You just want to know why we're here.'

Maybe he knew her better than she thought.

'That had crossed my mind, yes.'

'Several things.' He took a sip of his coffee. 'The main one is for me to say sorry.'

Nikki stared at him.

'I married you for all the wrong reasons,' he spoke quietly. 'But I thought it would all work out okay. I didn't bargain on you being so strong-minded.'

'I didn't bargain on having to live with your parents. That was the first thing that went wrong.'

'I know. I should have explained things properly right at the beginning.' He hung his head. 'I wanted to, but I thought I'd lose you. I was right, wasn't I?'

'It wasn't only that, Zak.' Nikki told herself to be careful. She was starting to feel sorry for him. 'I know now I'm too young to be married. I'm not ready for it yet.'

'No, nor me. I wanted to protect my mom. I thought having another woman in the house would help. And a few kids.' He grinned.

'Kids are a long way down the line for me.'

'Yeah, I can see that now. I also thought that having a police officer in the house might make Dad think a bit. Didn't work though.'

'You mean – you married me because I'm a cop?' Nikki's mouth fell open when he nodded. 'You bastard.'

'Yeah. Like I said, I'm sorry.'

'So you should be.' She got to her feet and reached for her handbag.

'Nikki, hang on. There's more.'

She turned and stared at him. 'What more could there be?'

'Sit down, please. I've got something else to tell you about. Something your lot have been looking into.'

Nikki hesitated. Could she believe him? Should she? She sat back in her seat and finished her coffee, hoping he wasn't trying to lure her into a trap.

'I told you I worked in IT,' he stated. She nodded. 'I'd got really good at it and people were starting to head hunt me. When I got approached by one particular person, I just couldn't say no. Now I wish I had. He's evil.'

'What has this got to do with me?'

'Hang on, I'm coming to that. This bloke is into cars. High end ones.'

'Ah.'

'Yes, I thought that might interest you.' Zak reached into his pocket. 'I've got this for you. It's part of my apology.'

He handed her a piece of folded paper. As she went to open it up, he shook his head slightly.

'Look at it later. On there are the names of several people who have been involved with stealing cars.' He lowered his voice. 'I was one of them. I sort of got sucked in, and it was kinda exciting.'

'Oh, Zak, you idiot.'

'I know, but you can't say no to people like – no, I can't tell you his name. Anyone that crosses him ends up hurt. Or worse.' Nikki stared at him. 'Those names should lead you to him, but Nikki – for God's sake be careful.'

She looked at Zak closely, trying to work out if he was telling the truth or not. She eventually decided that he was.

'Whatever you do with that.' He gestured towards the note. 'Please, leave it for a few days.'

'Oh yes?'

'Give me and Mom a chance to get away.'

'Zak?'

'I got in with these people to make money. Lots of it. I've bought a house abroad. Me and Mom are flying out on Wednesday. He looked down now. 'I've got to get her away. Plan A didn't work, so now I'm on to Plan B.'

'Mom was right,' Nikki muttered.

'Eh?'

'Nothing.' She stood up again. 'Good luck, Zak.'

He held out his hand, and she took it. Suddenly he seemed to have grown up and become responsible.

'And you,' he said. 'I'm sorry, Nikki.'

'Two lines under it and walk away.'

'Yes. There isn't really much else we can do, is there?'

'Goodbye, Zak.'

'Yeah.'

Nikki walked out of the coffee shop and didn't look back. All she wanted to do now was get home to her mother. She really wanted to be with Stuart, but he was miles away with his own family. Mom would have to do for now.

She felt guilty at her selfish thoughts as she walked into the small terraced house. Her mother had always done the best she could for her and her two siblings. They rarely visited, so Nikki felt it was down to her to look after her mom.

She walked in to find her tucking into a cheese and pickle sandwich. Mom looked up and immediately asked her if she wanted one.

'I'll do it,' Nikki said with a smile.

'Put the kettle on, love.'

When she came back with her sandwich and two mugs of tea, Nikki could tell that her mom was bursting with curiosity.

'How did your meeting go?' she couldn't wait to ask.

'Good.' Nikki had already decided she wasn't going to give away too many details. If they were going to escape, she didn't want to do anything to jeopardise that.

'What did he have to say?'

'He wanted to apologise. He knows now that we should never have got married. Did it for all the wrong reasons, he said.'

'Did he say anything about Armajit?'

'Not much. Just that he's trying to protect her.'

'He's a good lad really, looking out for his mom. I thought he'd be good to you too.'

'It's alright, Mom. None of this is your fault. You only wanted what was best for me. But if I ever do get married again, I'll choose my own husband. Alright?'

Mom looked at her with tears in her eyes. Then she nodded.

'I know I'm not a very good Sikh,' Nikki added. 'Really, I don't want to be one at all.'

'I know,' Mom said quietly.

CHAPTER FORTY-FIVE

When Nikki got to work on Monday, she handed Stuart the piece of paper Zak had given to her. Stuart drew up his eyebrows in puzzlement. Nikki explained what had been said in the coffee shop on Saturday.

'I promised I'd keep him out of it,' she ended by saying.

'That makes things awkward. Where am I going to tell the Guv this came from?'

'Anonymous tip off?' she suggested.

'Mm. Dunno.' Stuart frowned for a moment. 'Tell you what. Bung it in an envelope and find an excuse to go to Tamworth to post it. A couple of these names have got that town next to them.'

'What's the point of that?'

'Keep Shorty off the scent. If he finds out Zak gave you this, he might go after him as well.'

'That's true.' Nikki looked worried. 'And he did ask me to leave it for a few days.'

The list arrived back in Brodewell two days later, and Stuart took it in to show to Vic.

'Interesting,' Vic murmured. 'Looks like someone in this organisation is getting jumpy.'

'Or wants out,' Stuart said, thinking of Nikki's husband.

'This seems to have Tony King written all over it.' Vic was looking thoughtful. 'Get anything from your old man?'

Stuart shook his head. 'Loads of containers going out, but none containing cars. Another dead end.'

'Not necessarily.' Vic smiled. Stuart could tell he had an idea brewing. 'If this is Tony King, we'll have to find a way to entice him onto our patch. Leave it with me, I'll think of something.'

'If he's such a villain, how come West Mids haven't picked him up?'

'Oh, they have, lots of times, but he's a slippery bugger. Probably got a bent lawyer as well as –' He stopped for a moment. 'Whatever we do, it'll have to be by the book, no cutting corners.'

Stuart looked sideways at him. He wasn't the one who did that, but he didn't say anything apart from, 'Yes, Guv.'

'You get on with looking this lot up.' Vic waved the list. 'Oh, and I think Nikki has found one of the geezers who collected the Bentley. See if you can tie him in with this lot.'

Stuart nodded, and went back to his desk. Nikki didn't look at him. He knew he was going to have to talk to her soon. Find out if she still wanted to go on seeing him, as it was looking as though she was having second thoughts. She must have felt his eyes on her, as she looked up and tried to smile.

'The Guv says you've found the other car collector,' he said, as a way of starting a conversation.

'Oh.' She looked a bit taken aback. 'Er, yes, I think so.'

'Okay. Let's see if we can connect him to any of these.'

An hour or so later they had checked all the names on the list, and found associations between some of them. Now all they had to do was round them all up.

'Not so fast, sonny,' Vic said when he suggested it. 'We've got nothing on any of them, apart from this one. Get him in and we'll lean on him a bit. We'll play good cop, bad cop.'

'Which one are you going to be?' Stuart couldn't resist saying. Nikki couldn't quite supress a giggle.

'Ha, ha.' Vic glared at him. 'What d'you reckon?'

Stuart laughed. He couldn't hold it back either.

'What's this geezer's name?' Vic pointed at Nikki's screen.

'Jonathan Pritchard.'

'I'll go and find him.'

Let's hope he doesn't drop Zak in it, else Nikki's going to have one hell of a lot of explaining to do.

He glanced at her as he left the office, but she didn't respond. Stuart couldn't blame her. It was probably safer that way.

Jonathan Pritchard wasn't difficult to find. He lived with his parents in Brodewell and was slumped in front of the television when Stuart arrived. He didn't make a fuss in front of his mother, and came quietly. Once he got into the interview room he sat staring sullenly at a spot on the wall just above Stuart's head. Stuart said nothing. He was waiting for Vic to arrive.

'Right then, Mr Pritchard,' he said as he came into the room. 'You've got a bit of explaining to do.'

'Oh, yeah?'

'Yeah.' Vic leaned across the table to stare into his face. The lad sat back a bit, a flash of fear crossing his eyes. Stuart smiled to himself. Vic was getting to him already. 'Young lad like you getting mixed up in shit like this. What were you thinking?'

'What shit?' He seemed to have recovered his composure.

'Nicking a Bentley from Riversholme.'

'Where?'

'Don't get clever with me, son. We've got you on CCTV. Show him the pictures, Sergeant.'

Stuart put them on the table in front of him, crossing his fingers behind his back. Afterwards, the youth seemed as sullen as ever.

'Wot you got to say about that, then?'

'Nuffin. That don't prove anything.'

'It proves you collected the Bentley,' Vic persisted.

'It don't prove we nicked it though, do it?'

That was all too true. Vic mentally cursed. This lad wasn't as stupid as he looked.

'You've got a record as long as my arm for theft of this, that and the other.' The youth didn't respond. 'Okay, so who's this Asian bloke?'

Stuart held his breath.

'Just some bloke, I dunno his name. He was new. Right flash prat he was. Didn't like him.'

'So who's running this website for collecting cars?'

'What website? I just got a phone call telling us to collect it.'

'Where did you take it?' Vic was losing patience.

Jonathan shrugged his shoulders. 'To the multi-storey car park in the middle of Brodewell. We were told to leave the keys on top of one of the front wheels and bugger off.'

'And who told you this?'

'Someone on the phone. A man.'

'Brummie accent?'

Jonathan nodded, then said. 'Would have, wouldn't he? There's more Brummie's than enough round here.'

'That's true, Guv,' Stuart murmured.

'I know,' Vic hissed back.

'Can I have a word, Guv?'

'Yeah,' Vic sighed. 'Why not?'

They left the room, and Stuart asked a police constable to keep an eye on him while they talked outside.

'I've got an idea,' Stuart said. 'We could offer to let him go if he gives us the names of all the others, especially the leader.'

'We're gonna need more than that, son. We need proof, evidence. Otherwise that slippery blighter'll get away again. I've got a better idea, but I need to speak to Fatso about it. Go back in and be nice to him. See if he'll give you anything we can use.'

Stuart watched as Vic hurried away. He had that look on his face that could well mean trouble. He had got the bit between his teeth over something. Stuart supposed he would find out what it was eventually.

Jonathan Pritchard gave him no useful information. He had obviously been well briefed in keeping quiet. From what he did say, Stuart deduced that he didn't know much anyway. All his instructions have been given over the phone. He appeared never to have met Tony King. No wonder he was still walking the streets.

Vic came back several minutes later, all fired up.

'Back to the office. We got work to do.'

Stuart looked towards the interview room.

'Leave him to stew for a bit?' he asked. Vic nodded.

Back in the office, Vic went straight to Nikki.

'That car theft website still working?' She looked at him blankly. 'Have a butcher's for me, will you?'

'Okay, Guv.' She fiddled on the keyboard, then waited a moment. 'Yes, it is. Thought they would have shut it down by now.'

Stuart caught her eye. Zak must have forgotten about it.

'Right. Put this car on there.'

Vic handed her a piece of paper. She stared at it with wide eyes.

'Isn't this the Super's car?' she asked.

'It is indeed, Jigsaw.'

'Nikki, Guv,' Stuart murmured.

'Yeah, yeah. We're setting up a sting operation, but what I haven't figured out yet is how to get Tony King to turn up. He's the one we really want. He's been getting away with stuff for years.'

'All I got out of Pritchard was that he's scared of

the boss. Nothing he said as such, but every time I mentioned him, he clammed up. I don't think we'll get Pritchard to dob him in.'

'No. This King geezer seems to be well connected. Probably got half of West Midlands on his payroll. They seem to turn a blind eye to a lot of stuff.'

And they're the enemy. Stuart knew there was a lot of rivalry between the two police forces. Vic was walking a dangerous line. If ever this operation went wrong…

CHAPTER FORTY-SIX

'So – how's life with Mr Boring?'

'Fine,' Michelle answered her lover. 'Things couldn't be better.'

'Ha.' Tony laughed. 'They can't be that good, else you wouldn't be here with me.'

'Bastard,' she muttered.

'Yeah, but that's why you love me, isn't it?'

'Piss off. I don't love anyone.'

'Oh yeah?' He laughed again. 'You told me it was the real thing with lover boy, but I knew you were lying. Don't understand it really. With all the practice you've had, you should be a superb liar by now.'

'Leave me alone. What do you know about anything?'

'I know all about you. Once a whore, always a whore.'

'Fuck off.'

'Speaking of which, put that bloody phone down and come to bed. That's one thing you're good at. About the only thing, really.'

'Fine. Michelle stood up and reached for her bag. 'I'll just piss off now, shall I?'

'You're going nowhere, darlin'.' He glared at her. 'Don't cross me, Michelle. You know what happens to people who do that.'

'A few more years in prison might calm you down a bit.'

'Oh, don't be such a stupid cow, I won't do it myself. I've got plenty of thugs working for me who'd be only too pleased to oblige. Might have a bit of fun with you first, though.'

'You really are a bastard.'

'Yeah, and don't you ever forget it.'

They stared at each other for a few seconds, hatred in both pairs of eyes. Michelle was the first to look away. Not for the first time she wondered what she was doing being back with him. She had moved to a remote village that nobody in Birmingham had ever heard of to get away from him, yet here she was back in his clutches. She couldn't believe she could ever be that stupid. What had she been thinking? She was a complete idiot.

'Anyway.' Tony looked at his perfectly manicured fingernails. 'You didn't answer my question. Where does lover boy think you are at this precise moment?'

'On a shopping trip,' Michelle replied, unable to keep the sullenness out of her voice. 'Not that it's got anything to do with you.'

'That's where you're wrong, darlin', it's got everything to do with me. How would it look if someone were to ring him and tell him where you really are?'

'You wouldn't.' Fear struck at Michelle's heart. It was exactly the sort of thing he would do.

Tony laughed, but there was no humour in it whatsoever.

'You'll never know, will you? Now get upstairs and do what you're good at. Then I'll tell you what sort of cars I'm on the lookout for. Can't have you living in some posh village without me getting something out of it.'

She thought about threatening to go to the police, but didn't say anything. She wasn't so pissed off with her life that she wanted it to end just yet. Yes, Phil was boring but at least with him she would be safe. She wished she was with him right now.

'I've got a headache.'

'Not surprised. Too much gawping into that bloody phone of yours. I'll take your mind off it. Get upstairs.'

Michelle knew she had no choice; she wasn't going to talk him out of it. She went into the hall and started up the stairs. Tony followed close behind. She could feel his hot breath on the back of her neck...

Two hours later, he seemed to have had enough. He had a shower and went downstairs. Shortly afterwards she could hear him talking. Who was he ringing? Phil?

'Oh, God,' she muttered as she hurried out of bed.

Ten minutes later, she was going downstairs herself. Tony was still on the phone, and he didn't sound very happy. She winced, and slid into the kitchen to keep out of his way.

'You up yet, you dozy tart?' She heard him shout from the bottom of the stairs a few minutes later.

'In here.' She quickly filled the kettle. 'Fancy a brew?'

'I could do with something stronger. It looks like one of my men has gone walk about.'

Don't blame him. They aren't all stupid, then.

'Oh?' She pretended to be interested.

'I'll get some of the others out to look for him. I knew I should never have trusted him. Too flash by half.'

The kettle was starting to boil, so Michelle busied herself with mugs and spoons. Tony went back to his phone.

'Daz, it's Tony. You seen Zak?' There was a pause. 'No one? Where the hell is he?'

There was another silence. Tony must have moved, or pushed the door shut, as she didn't hear any more of the conversation. She stayed where she was, wondering how much longer it would be before he let her go.

'That tea ready?' he called from the lounge.

'Yes,' Michelle answered with a sigh as she went to join him.

When she walked into the room, she was surprised to see he was on his laptop. He didn't look up at her but waved towards the office table. She dutifully put his tea down on a scruffy beer mat. He concentrated on the screen for quite some time, then slammed the lid of the laptop down and let out a growl. Michelle stayed where she was on the settee. She could tell he was furious, and that was never a good sign.

'Something wrong?' It was an unnecessary question, but she asked it anyway. She knew she shouldn't wind him up but sometimes she just couldn't help herself.

'You could say that. One of my lot has definitely gone missing.'

'That's not such a big deal, is it?'

'It is when a load of my money has gone missing as well.'

'Oh, dear,' she said, trying not to laugh. If someone had managed to rip off the most powerful villain in the area, then she had nothing but admiration for him.

Well done, I like your style. Wish I knew who you are.

'Any idea who it is?'

'Of course I have.' He glared at her. 'What d'you think I am, stupid?'

Michelle couldn't hold it back any longer. A fit of the giggles came out, and she couldn't stop them.

'You'd better pack that up. It isn't funny.'

The laughing continued. She was crying with it now.

'Get out,' he shouted, his eyes bulging. 'I mean it. Get out now.'

Michelle struggled to her feet and collected up her things. As she left the house, she heard him thump the wall and yell.

'I'll kill the little bastard!'

CHAPTER FORTY-SEVEN

A day or so after Nikki had put the Super's car on Zak's website, she had a phone call. It was being recorded, so she kept the male caller talking for as long as she could. She gave him her superior's address in a fashionable area of Leek, and flirted with him a bit.

Now all they could do was wait.

Joanne Lowe wasn't exactly over the moon at the prospect of her pride and joy being taken away by bandits, but had agreed to go along with it. She had as good as threatened Vic with decapitation if anything went wrong. CCTV cameras had been set up to record the pick-up and a tracking device was already in the car. After it had been collected, the same young PC who had taken Vic to New Street Station drove the Super down to Brodewell like Jeremy Clarkson on steroids. Her face was quite pale when she met up with Vic at the multi-storey car park.

'Who is that young man?'

'Richard Comer. He hasn't been with us long. I've decided to call him Meatloaf.' She gave him a puzzled questioning look. 'Coz he drives like a bat out of hell.'

'He certainly does.' She laughed.

'I've told him to get a bit more training. We need all the bats we can get. That lad could go far.'

'I agree. He's one to keep an eye on.'

Vic smiled to himself. He wouldn't mind young Richard on his CID team, and now he had been brought to the attention of the Super, he might be able to get that to happen.

'All we've got to do now, ma'am, is keep our heads down and wait for your car to arrive. Glad to see you're in plain clothes today.'

'I could hardly see my car off in uniform. They'd have run a mile if they knew I was a police officer.'

'Oh, I dunno.' Vic smirked. 'Tony King would probably love to get one over on us.'

'We don't know for definite he's involved.' She sounded as though she was telling off a naughty eight-year-old.

'We don't know he isn't either,' Vic answered, praying that he was.

They were parked on the opposite side of the car park, in a dark corner. Nikki was outside across the street, and Stuart was half a mile away at the next road junction. West Midlands police were on alert in case anyone strayed into their territory, including armed response.

Vic's radio crackled, then he heard Nikki's voice.

'Target approaching.'

'Received. Stay in position.'

'Check.'

Both Vic and the Super were half holding their breath as her large white car came into view. They were on the ground floor of the car park, amongst the many other vehicles. Vic had no idea on which of the other levels they might take the Audi, but he was ready for them. He had never felt so excited and determined in all his life. He wished he hadn't got to babysit his gaffer. He wouldn't be able to let rip with the language with her sitting beside him.

The Audi entered the car park and drove upwards. Vic had his window down, and could hear the engine for quite a while.

'Reckon they've taken it up the top, ma'am probably quiet up there,' he said quietly. 'Now all we've got to do is wait for it to come down again, then follow it up the yellow brick road.'

'So, we're all revved up with no place to go,' the Super murmured. Vic glanced sideways at her, wondering what the hell she was talking about. She smiled shyly. 'Another Meatloaf title, Victor.'

'You? Meatloaf?' He could hardly believe his ears. 'I'd never have –'

'You'd be surprised.' She was still smiling.

'You're not kidding.' He laughed. 'Ay up, who's this?'

A car entered the multi-storey and drove up the ramp. The Super was looking worried now, and didn't say a word. A few minutes later, the car returned. Followed by the Audi. She gasped, and Vic smiled.

'Target returning,' he said quietly into his radio.

'Received,' Nikki answered. 'Following.'

Stuart had picked up the message as well, and acknowledged. The mystery tour had begun.

'Right,' Vic said as he started the engine. 'Let's see what we shall see.'

'Indeed, Victor.'

There was hardly any conversation as the four cars sped out of Brodewell towards Birmingham. The Super didn't appear to have anything to say, and Vic spent the time trying to remember all the Meatloaf songs he could, in case he could use them to cheer her up some other time. The lack of talk was unnerving. Usually she was the one in control and he was on the back foot, but being in the car together like this made them equals. Vic would never have described himself as the most perceptive or sympathetic of people, but even he could feel the despair coming from the seat next to him. An overwhelming sense of unhappiness and loneliness. It seemed they had more in common than he had ever imagined.

'Mustang to team leader.' Stuart's voice came over the radio. He hadn't lost his sense of humour. 'Overtaking you. Suggest you drop back for a while.'

'Received, Mustang.'

This strategy had already been agreed, just in case the driver of the Audi realised he was being followed. Nikki would take her turn later, if necessary.

'You okay, Jigsaw?'

'Yes, team leader. Still in position.'

Stuart's Ford Fiesta slid past Vic's battered Volvo, and the Super watched with detached interest. Then she broke the uncomfortable silence between them.

'I understand your reasoning for nicknames,' she said quietly, 'but sometimes they seem rather offensive.'

'That's me,' he replied. 'But I don't think that's one of my nicknames.'

'No, yours are worse than that.'

'Anyway.' He didn't like where this was going. 'Today they're useful as code names. In case anyone's listening.'

'This isn't MI5, Vic.'

'No, ma'am, but there's no harm in pretending.'

'Why do men never grow up?' she murmured.

He had an answer, but bit it back. This wasn't the time to be upsetting her. So far today he had got her onside, which was easier to handle than the alternative.

'Target slowing down,' came from Stuart's car, some distance in front of them.

'We're nearly in Birmingham.' Vic noticed. 'For Gawd's sake don't go into West Mids. I want this collar.'

'We are working together, you know.'

'Yeah, but – well, okay, - yes.'

'Turning onto an industrial estate,' Stuart told them. I'm dropping back.'

'Received. Don't lose them.'

The only reply he got was a low growl. The Super let out a small laugh, then turned her face to the window. Vic concentrated on his driving. He kept the Audi in sight, but held back as far as he could.

'It's slowing down again, think we're nearly there,' he said to Stuart a few minutes later. 'Get all units into position, then maintain radio silence, unless emergency.'

'Check,' Stuart said. Then the radio went dead.

'Right.' Vic could see the Audi had stopped. A white van with a picture of a blazing fire and big red letters passed him, going in the opposite direction. This was obviously a working estate, so his car shouldn't draw too much attention. Even so, he parked two units distance away. 'We're here.'

'I can see that, Victor.'

He tutted. He was going to have to speak to her about that, but this wasn't the time. He had butterflies in his stomach. He had villains to catch. He never took his eyes off the gleaming white Audi, telling himself he wasn't the slightest bit jealous. At that moment, he decided he was having himself one of those.

'Ma'am,' he drew in his breath as his excitement bubbled over. 'Look, I was right. Tony King is here.'

CHAPTER FORTY-EIGHT

Vic watched the scene carefully. A huge roller door on the front of the unit was moving upwards. He wished he could see inside. Nikki would be able to as she was parked opposite. He sucked in his breath as the Super's car slid out of view. She had her hand to her forehead, and he hoped she wasn't crying. He could hardly bear to watch either.

Tony King was walking up and down the parking area, as if he was waiting for something – or someone. Vic was intrigued. What else had they got planned? He could see Stuart's car fifty metres away outside a unit selling bathroom equipment. At least there were a few other vehicles outside that one. Vic felt a bit obvious where he was. The only car in front of a warehouse with no writing on it.

King was looking at his phone, and didn't look like a happy bunny. He turned into a hopping mad one as another car arrived, a big black BMW four by four, and a young Asian man climbed out. King moved towards him, his face screwed up in anger. Vic wondered what was going on, so wound his window down halfway so he could hear.

'You've got a flaming nerve.' He heard King say. 'I knew I should never have trusted you. Pritchard was right, you are a flash git.'

'Calm down, boss, we can sort this out.'

★ ★ ★

Stuart was staring through his windscreen. He recognised the man as he got out of the four by four from his photo. It was Nikki's husband, Zak, who was supposed to have done a runner abroad. What the hell was he doing here?

★ ★ ★

Nikki had also seen him, and the blood drained from her face. Had he lied to her? Was he still working for Tony King?

★ ★ ★

'Let's get on with it,' King snarled at Zak. 'I got work to do.'

'Yeah, yeah, I know.' Zak didn't seem concerned about the two heavies, one each side of Tony King. 'But you do realise whose car you've just taken in there?'

'What does it matter whose it is? It'll soon be on its way to Europe. End of.' King looked closely at Zak. 'What's it to you, anyway?'

'I checked the website yesterday. I was gonna close it down, then I spotted the Audi on there. It belongs to a Ms Joanne Lowe.' King was looking bored. 'She's the Superintendent at Brodewell Police Station.'

'So what? It'll be long gone before she finds out it's missing. How do you know this, anyway?'

'The police aren't the only people with access to ANPR.' Zak grinned. 'I was curious, so I hacked into their database.'

'You're a clever little shit, Zak, that's why I hired you in the first place, but you're getting too smart for your own good now. Cut the bullshit, and give me back my money. That's why we're here.'

'What if the police know about this? I'm sure they know about you. You don't exactly keep a low profile, driving around in that thing.' Zak pointed to the Ferrari, which did indeed stand out. Especially in the middle of a quiet industrial estate on the edge of Birmingham.

'You been shooting your mouth off, you cocky bastard?'

'Me? Nah.' Zak laughed. 'But I could. Then again, I could keep quiet if someone paid me enough. How about it?'

All through this exchange, King had been looking angrier by the second. Zak was winding him up, and everyone who was watching independently agreed that he was playing a very dangerous game. They were all wondering what to do.

'You're pushing your luck, Zak.' Tony King's fist was clenched. The heavies took a step forward, one of them reaching into his pocket. Zak laughed again. King turned to the other one. 'You. Search his motor.'

'Waste of time,' said Zak. 'The money isn't in there.'

'You're making me very angry, Zak, and you don't want to do that,' King hissed. 'Now stop pissing about and give me my money.' He took a breath and then yelled. 'Hand it over. Now!'

'I haven't got it with me.'

'That's what we agreed. Cash.' King took a step forward and stared directly into Zak's face. 'I knew I should never have listened to you. You trying to double-cross me? You'll regret it if you do.'

Zak stared back, a big daft grin on his face. 'If I hand it over, it'll be done the same way as I took it. Bank transfer. You don't really think I'm gonna lug dirty great suitcases full of money all over the place, do you? What do you think I am? Stupid?'

'I know one thing.' King growled. 'You'll be a dead stupid if you don't come up with the goods. You won't be the first.' He turned to one of his henchmen. 'Daz, sort him out.'

Daz was standing close to his motorbike, which was parked behind the Ferrari. A moment later, he had a baseball bat in his huge hands and was swinging it round his head. Now he was the one with a beaming smile, and Zak's grin had disappeared.

★ ★ ★

Across the road, Nikki gasped. Stuart reached for his car door handle. Vic's eyes widened.

'Stay here, ma'am,' he said as he flung open the door.

Vic marched across the road towards Nikki's car and indicated to her to open the window. She was looking nervous, so Vic took a chance.

'You know that bloke?' She nodded. 'Gawd. Of all the Asians on the planet, one had to turn up that you know. Who is he?'

'Zak Singh.' Her voice shook. 'My husband.'

'Your -? Oh, bloody hell.'

'Oh no, Guv, look!'

Vic glanced back towards the unit. The Super had a face like thunder as she left his car. Vic gasped.

She was striding towards Tony King.

CHAPTER FORTY-NINE

Joanne had watched Vic go with a look of resignation on her face. Why did the men get all the interesting bits? All her young life she had been ordered about, by either parents or teachers. She had never been given credit for having any brains. Just because she was overweight – and always had been – everyone assumed she was lazy and stupid. She had joined the police to prove them wrong, and thought she had done pretty good so far.

Vic had disappeared across the road. She thought he was going to tackle Daz, but it looked as if he had bottled out. Typical. All talk and no action. Tony King and Zak were still slinging insults at one another like a couple of hormonal teenagers. No one was going to get anywhere at this rate.

'Oh, I've had enough of this. Why are men so bloody childish?'

She opened the car door. Vic let out a yelp when he saw her, and came running over, shouting, 'Ma'am, get back in the car.'

King had seen them both, and stopped in mid-sentence. He looked puzzled, then his brow relaxed as he realised what was going on.

'Cops.' He almost sounded pleased. 'I should have known. Who's the fat bird, then?' He was speaking to Vic, who had reached her, breathless already after his short burst of unfamiliar activity.

'I am Detective Superintendent Lowe,' she said, looking down her nose at him, 'and you are under arrest for stealing not only my car, but an awful lot of others.'

Vic was furious. He had wanted credit for this arrest. This infuriating woman had stolen his thunder, and he felt like punching her. If she had been a man, he wouldn't have hesitated.

Daz lowered the baseball bat, King burst out laughing, and Vic felt a chuckle coming on too. The Super looked ridiculous standing there with her hands on her hips, looking like an old-fashioned school marm. Vic suddenly had another mental image of her, in a leather basque, long boots and holding a whip, and very nearly laughed out loud.

'Hell, mate,' Tony King said to Vic. 'If that's your boss, I don't envy you one bit.'

Now Vic did laugh, he couldn't help himself.

While King was looking at Vic, the Super used the opportunity. She swung a punch at King, not noticing that he was drawing something out of his jacket pocket. Vic saw the gun, but he had no chance to do anything.

The Super's clenched fist caught King on the side of his face. He tottered, swung round like a demented ice skater, lost his balance completely and fell to the ground. Halfway down, the gun went off, and Zak screamed. The bullet had gone through the sleeve of his jacket and grazed his arm. It carried on and clanged into the back of the Audi, parked inside the half open unit.

'My car!' Joanne shrieked.

King was lying dazed on the floor. The two heavies looked confused, not knowing whether to help him up or run like hell. Daz made a bolt for his motorbike but he didn't get far. Two police cars had come out of nowhere and blocked the road, the only exit.

* * *

Stuart had watched all this, feeling like a spare part. When he had seen Vic run across the road, he had gone over to Nikki's car to find out what was going on. He hadn't liked the state she was in. She looked worried and frightened half to death. All the while he had been talking to her, her eyes had never left Zak, and when the gun had gone off, she had gasped and tried to get out of the car.

Stuart reached across her to get to the radio, but she didn't even notice he was there.

'This is Mustang. All units, go, go, go,' Stuart shouted, more out of frustration than anything else.

Within seconds a black van screeched into the road between the two sets of units, and two police cars had blocked it off. The back door of the van opened and the armed response officers from West Midlands Police poured out, dressed in full combat gear and holding machine rifles. They quickly surrounded the group of four men. Screaming at them to get on the ground with their arms spread. Daz stared at them as if they had just landed from Mars.

More police cars had turned up now and officers were running towards them with handcuffs at the ready. These were soon slapped onto the wrists of the three villains, then they were hauled to their feet.

Stuart moved out of the way as Nikki forced her way out of the car and began to walk briskly across to where the action was taking place. Stuart still felt useless, but he followed her. He was just in time to hear Vic speak.

'Tony King, I am arresting you for attempted murder and car theft. Anything you say –'

Stuart wasn't listening. He was watching Nikki, who had ignored everything that was going on as she headed towards Zak. The Super had led him away a few metres and was on her mobile phone. Stuart hardly noticed this. His eyes were fixed on Nikki, and his heart was in his mouth. Zak smiled happily as he saw her, and the Super looked puzzled.

'I know him, ma'am,' Nikki said quietly, 'he's my husband, but I had no idea he was involved in any of this.'

'I'm sure you didn't, Nikki.' Joanne smiled at her fondly. 'I've called an ambulance, but I think it's only a flesh wound. Can you keep an eye on him until it gets here?'

'Of course, ma'am.'

'God, Nikki, this hurts like hell,' Zak said as Joanne moved away.

'Serves you right for getting involved with all this.' Her annoyed tone of voice cheered Stuart up. He carried on listening. 'I told you you were an idiot. What the hell are you doing here? I thought you'd gone abroad?'

'I'm going to, but I had this one thing to do first.' He tried to clutch his arm, but it hurt too much and he cried out in pain. Blood was dripping from the end of his sleeve and he looked as though he was about to pass out.

Joanne reappeared with a plastic chair. Nobody asked where it had come from as she handed it to Nikki with a smile. Zak sank down onto it, and Nikki pushed his head downward between his knees.

'What Zak? Why are you here?'

He didn't answer for a while, but took several deep breaths. Nikki had her hand on his shoulder, and Stuart didn't like the concern she was showing. It was supposed to be all over between them, but it didn't look that way to him. Eventually Zak raised his head and Nikki bent down to be nearer his face.

'I wanted that bastard locked up.' Stuart could hardly hear him. 'I knew you lot would be investigating the car thefts. Jon Pritchard told me he'd been hauled in and I knew it was only a matter of time before you found out about King. He's an evil swine. He's had people killed, you know.'

No, I don't think anyone knew that, Stuart thought.

Nikki was looking shocked. 'So why didn't you get away from him when you found that out?'

'I was in too deep. You don't know what he's like. Nikki.' He looked up at her, and the look on his face tore Stuart apart. 'I was scared he'd come after you. I know it's all over between us, but I wanted to keep you safe. I still care that much.'

'Oh, Zak, you fool,' Nikki whispered. A tear ran down her right cheek. Stuart thought he felt his heart break in two. He looked away, feeling tears coming to his eyes as well.

Nikki stood with her arm round Zak's shoulder and Stuart walked away, his thoughts all over the place. As he did, he heard her last comment.

'I'm so proud of you.'

That's it, it's over. I've lost her. She's still in love with him. What the hell am I going to do now?

CHAPTER FIFTY

Clive was getting himself some lunch and had the television on in the background. The national news had just finished, but he hadn't paid much attention to it. There was never any good news.

The local newsreader introduced herself before reading out the headlines. Clive stirred his saucepan of soup and hummed to himself. He glanced up as he heard some big local criminal had been arrested, and did a double take at the picture that half-filled the screen. He recognised that face.

'–Tony King,' the newsreader was saying, 'was arrested yesterday by Detective Chief Inspector Vic Hardcastle of Brodewell CID on suspicion of attempted murder of a police officer, and car theft.'

Clive didn't listen to the rest of the report. His wide eyes were glued to the face of the man who had been at Phil and Michelle's wedding. He still felt he hadn't sorted that out with Phil. Perhaps now it was time to put it right.

★ ★ ★

As many people as could get in were crammed into the front office at Brodewell Police Station. They too were watching the TV news, and a cheer had gone up when Vic's name was mentioned. As a general rule, Brodewell didn't get much attention, being a small rural police station, but now it seemed that they had been put on the map by their often surly DI. Most of them suspected they might have to think up some more complimentary nicknames for him after this. None of them had noticed him slip into the room, wondering what all the noise was about. The report continued.

'A spokesperson for West Midlands Police has told us that Tony King will be held on remand until his trial, and they would like to thank Detective Chief Inspector Vic Hardcastle and his team for assisting them with their operation to bring this man to justice –'

'Bloody cheek.' Vic nearly exploded. 'Their operation? It was me wot dreamt it up.'

'Hey.' Pete was the first to react. 'Congratulations, sir. Well done.'

'Yeah!' The whole room agreed with him. Hands were clapping and feet were stamping. This went on for some time, and Vic appeared to be lapping it up.

'That's typical of a bigger force,' Pete said, when the noise had died down. The television was being taken back to wherever it had come from. 'Trample all over the little guys.'

'Yeah.' Vic sounded sullen. No change there as far as Pete was concerned. 'Should've known they'd take all the credit.'

'Not quite all, sir,' a young voice piped up. It was PC Comer. 'They've given you the credit for the arrest. That's got to be worth something.'

'Yer right, lad.' Vic smiled at him and Pete raised his eyebrows. 'That's worth a hell of a lot to me. Anyone who messes around in my villages had better watch out.'

With that, he walked away back towards the CID office. Richard looked disappointed.

'Oh hell,' he muttered. 'I wanted to ask him something.'

'Well, you've missed your chance alright.' Pete laughed. 'It ain't just the villains who are slippery around here. What was it?'

'I need someone senior to sign a form for me. I'm applying to do the advanced driving course.'

'Bloody hell, lad, you've only been here five minutes.' The youth was keen, Pete had to give him that. 'Give it here, I'll sign it for you. What made you think of that?'

'I didn't,' he said quietly.

'You'd better get back to work.' Pete looked round the room and noted all the chatter. 'We all had. Come on, you lot, break it up.'

A few minutes later, Pete had his territory back the way he liked it. Well organised and quiet. He was hoping it would stay that way. He had some paperwork to catch up on.

Halfway through the afternoon, he went to the kitchen. He was gasping for a cup of tea. Stuart was there, and gave him a wave, so Pete went to sit with him. There was a ten-year age gap between them, but they had always got on well.

'See the news report?' Stuart asked as Pete sat down.

'Yeah.' Pete nodded. 'At least we got a mention, that's something, I suppose.'

'Did well to get even that.' Stuart laughed. 'The Chief Constable wanted the Super to do a press conference, but West Mids got in first. Don't think she was too bothered. The Guv says she hates doing stuff like that.'

'Think she's pretty shy really.'

'You wouldn't have said that if you'd seen her at the arrest. She packed that King a hefty punch. Put him on the floor.' Pete's eyes were like saucers. 'Good thing she did, else someone could've got killed.'

'Wish I'd seen that.' Pete was totally in awe.

'The Guv tried to stop her but she was too quick for him.'

'Didn't think anyone could get the better of him. He's a bit of a legend round here. Miserable sod, but he gets things done.'

'I don't know him that well yet,' Stuart admitted. 'How long's he been here?'

'Ooh, ten, twelve years, not long after he made inspector.'

'What I can't understand is his accent. I thought he was from Stoke.'

'He may have lived there.' Pete smiled. 'He moved around after he left Tipton, which is where he's from

312

originally. Family trouble, I heard. Now he's on his own, and I can see why. He's got a daughter he never sees, must be awful that.'

'He never saw his son grow up either.'

Pete was all ears. This was a new bit of gossip he hadn't heard. He looked at Stuart, dying to know more. Stuart looked uncomfortable, as though he had spoken out of turn.

'What I meant was,' Stuart said, a little too quickly, 'he doesn't see him either.'

'I wouldn't be without my family.' Pete was very sure about that.

'No comment.' Stuart laughed. 'Anyway, I'd better be getting back. Don't want our legend yelling at me.'

'Just make sure you get that King character put away for a long time. The legend might make out he hates villages, but he'll defend them to the last if anyone starts on his patch.'

'I'll remember that.' Stuart looked thoughtful as he walked away.

Pete glanced up at the clock and realised he should be moving too. He sighed and went back to the delights of the front desk. The first person he ran into was Richard, who was running his fingers through his hair and straightening his jacket.

'What you been up to?' Pete asked.

'Just brought ma'am back from a meeting with the Chief Constable.'

'What's he like?'

'Dunno, I didn't meet him. She was gone ages this time. I'll be glad when she gets her car back. Hey.' He looked as if he'd just remembered something. 'She said when it's all over, she'll show me the bullet. Says she's gonna keep it.'

'Just be glad it wasn't aimed at you, lad, now get about your business. All this driving the Super around is going to your head.'

'Aw, sir, leave off.'

'Is that young PC Comer?' Vic's familiar voice came from the doorway. Pete looked surprised, and Richard looked worried. 'Heard you wanted to talk to me.'

'Oh, yes, sir.' He looked flustered, and was blushing. 'It was a form for a driving course, but the sergeant's signed it.'

'Thought it might be that.' Vic smiled. 'Good lad. Once you've got your driving under control, you'll be dynamite.'

Pete watched in amazement at the exchange. Vic was still smiling. It seemed he liked this young man.

'Thanks, sir.'

'Ar, make sure you do it well, and live up to your name. I got one for you already. Meatloaf, you heard of him?'

'Yes, sir, but –?'

'Bat out of hell. Describes your driving, son. I shall be looking to see how you're getting on.'

Before anyone could reply, he had gone. Pete was the first to speak.

'Ruddy hell, looks like you've got a fan in old Super Dick. You won't go far wrong if you can keep in his good books.'

'Why's he called that?' Richard asked, noticing that several people were smirking.

Pete thought for a second. 'Coz he's a good detective, of course.'

The smirks turned to laughter, but Richard didn't react. He just said, 'oh' and walked away, nearly bumping into a well-built man in his fifties who was entering the building.

'Yes, sir, can I help you?' Pete said politely.

'Yes. I'd like to speak to Detective Sergeant Young. My name is Clive Morrison.'

CHAPTER FIFTY-ONE

Stuart was more than a little surprised when he heard that Clive was at the front desk. He didn't say anything to Nikki as he left to meet him in Interview Room Two. Things between them were still cold, and he wondered when she was going to come to her senses and make a decision. It was him or Zak. She had to choose.

Interview Room Two was larger than the other two they had, and less formal. There were pictures on the walls, a pale green carpet and four comfortable armchairs. Clive was already there when Stuart arrived.

'Mr Morrison. I wasn't expecting to see you again.'

'There's something that's been bothering me. It might be nothing, but I thought I ought to tell someone,' Clive began as Stuart waved him to sit down. 'I saw the news at lunch time. About Tony King's arrest.'

'And?'

'My mate Phil got married not long back.' Stuart nodded. 'Tony King turned up at the reception. He was with Michelle's sister.'

Stuart paid more attention now, this was interesting.

'Michelle froze when she saw him and looked worried. I could tell straight away that she knew him, so I kept an eye on them.'

'Go on.'

'Well, after a while, I went outside. There was an atmosphere and I didn't like it. I heard Michelle talking to him, well, it was more like an argument really. He was saying that they would still see each other, and she was dead against it. He even said keep the dress, we'll use that. He was as good as threatening her.' He stopped and looked at Stuart, who didn't react. 'I thought she was hiding something all along. She was always going off to Birmingham and staying the night. I think even Phil suspected something, although he always wants to see the best in people.'

Stuart thought he had better be careful what he said. He remembered what Nikki had suggested, that there might be something else going on. He might as well find out what he could without giving anything away. He hoped she wasn't right. Their relationship was shaky enough as it was.

'So, you think this has been going on for some time?'

'I don't know. She's only been going to Birmingham a lot for the past month or so, but I think she's known him for longer than that. She seemed to know all about him.'

'This sister of hers, do you have a name for her?'

'Kirsty. She seemed a nice girl, nothing like Michelle.'

'Age?'

'Younger. In her thirties I'd say. She didn't seem the sort to be with him. He was charming enough, but I heard him tell Michelle that he'd only got with her to find out where Michelle was living. It's as if she moved away to get away, and he came after her.'

'It sounds that way, yes.'

'He threatened to hurt Kirsty as well, if Michelle didn't keep seeing him. I'm glad he's locked up. He sounds like a real piece of work.'

'Did you hear anything mentioned about cars? That's why he's been arrested.'

'No, but they moved around the gardens and I'd heard enough. I tried to talk to Phil about it, but he said it was in the past, and nothing to do with him and her.' Clive stopped to think 'Although,' he said slowly. 'There have been cars stolen in Hawksmere and Aldermarsh lately. Posh ones. Was she helping him find them?'

'We have suspicions, but we can't prove anything.' Stuart looked at his worried face. 'If she was, she probably had no choice. You seem very concerned about this, sir. There isn't anything going on between you and her, is there?'

'Of course not.' Clive was suddenly indignant. 'She's not my type at all. All she's interested in is money and I'm sure that's why she married Phil. Tony King said as much. It's Phil I'm worried about. He's my best mate.'

'Is there anything else you can remember?'

'No, that's about it. I just thought you should know, that's all.'

'Thank you, Mr Morrison, you've been very helpful.' Stuart stood up. 'If you think of anything else, please get in touch.'

He showed Clive out, then went back to the office. He could see Vic moving towards the frosted glass panel in his office door, and wondered if he should mention what he had heard. It was all circumstantial, but interesting none the less.

'Had a visitor, I hear. Wot he have to say?'

Bloody hell, he doesn't miss much. How did he find out about that?

Vic smirked at the look on his face, and added, 'there's more than one grapevine around here, son. Come on then, out with it.'

Stuart told him everything. Vic sat for a while digesting the information. Eventually he spoke.

'Do you think he knew they were married at one point?'

'No, Guv. I'm sure he would have mentioned it if he did.'

'Yeah, reckon so.'

'They got divorced years ago, she ditched him. Looks like that didn't go down too well.'

'Some blokes can't let go.' Vic looked thoughtful, then smiled. 'I weren't too sorry to see the back of mine, but that's another story.'

'Shall we pull her in?'

'It's tempting, but what have we really got? Having an affair ain't a crime. We got nothing on her. She's a gold digger obviously, and Phil Bateman's got plenty.'

'So has Clive Morrison.'

'Yeah, she could be playing them off against each other, but we still got nothing on her.'

He's as bad as Nikki. Looks like I'm outvoted here.

'I was thinking, Guv. Hazel didn't mention any of this, did she?'

Vic snapped to attention, his lips pursed.

'No, she didn't. Lot of use she was undercover.' He scowled. 'Go and have a word with her, save me ripping 'er head off.'

'You putting me in training?' Stuart couldn't resist saying.

'Don't tempt me.'

Stuart left to see Hazel, smiling to himself. It appeared Vic had been cured of his crush on what he had previously referred to as a tasty bit from Lichfield. Sure, she had the looks, but brains were a bit thin on the ground. Stuart wondered what her excuse would be this time.

She didn't even try to make one. She admitted to getting off with one of the waiters instead of concentrating on her job, and begged Stuart not to tell Vic. Stuart made no such promise and she was close to tears when he left her. He hadn't shouted at her. There didn't seem to be any need.

On his way back he noticed Vic in front of him, heading for the stairs. That meant he would be alone with Nikki in the office.

'He's gone to see the Super,' she said as he walked back in. 'Muttering something about getting rid of Hazel.'

'Not before time, either. She was larking about with one of the waiters at the wedding. Not what she was being paid to do.' Stuart hesitated. 'Nikki – we need to talk.'

'Looks like it.' The look she gave him was only one step away from a glare. 'You've been acting really weird lately. What's wrong?'

'You and Zak. You getting back together?'

Now she looked amazed. 'What on earth gave you that idea?'

'The way you were with him at the units. You were all over him.'

'He'd been shot, someone had to help him.'

'It wasn't only that. You're still in love with him, aren't you?'

'Stuart, I've never been in love with him, I told you that, and no, we're not getting back together. He'll go off abroad and I'll never see him again.' She did glare at him now. 'And I'm glad. It was over a long time ago.'

Stuart wanted to believe her, but was finding it difficult. He couldn't get the images of her and Zak out of his head. The look in her eyes on that day was haunting him. She could deny it all she wanted, but he knew the truth. He didn't believe she would ever forget Zak, and he would always be second best. He couldn't live like that. His heart sank as she turned away from him. Even when Vic came back grinning all over his face, he couldn't feel any happier.

He was beginning to wonder if he should put in for a transfer.

CHAPTER FIFTY-TWO

Joanne was sitting next to Vic in the court, listening to the proceedings. They didn't both really need to be there, but she had dragged him along out of curiosity. She watched as the offences against Tony King were read out, and he was eventually remanded in custody. All attempts to get him bail were refused and she was glad. At least everyone would know where he was now.

'Come on.' She nudged Vic's arm. 'Let's get out of here.'

They left quietly as Tony King was led away. Never to be seen again, she hoped.

'Happy now?' Vic asked as they walked back to his car.

'I'll be happier when I get my car back. That bullet has done a lot of damage.'

'See, if you'd got an old banger like this, you wouldn't

be so worried about it.' Vic laughed. 'If it had been mine, I'd have thought he'd have done me a favour.'

'I suppose so.' She smiled. 'At least I've got young Richard to drive me about locally. The courtesy car I've been given is alright for getting to and from work, but I'd look a right idiot going to see people like the Chief Constable in it. I mean, why shocking pink?'

Vic had seen the car in question, and could only agree. It was a miracle to him that she could even get into it. It wasn't called compact for nothing.

'You got to see him soon?'

'Yes, this afternoon. He wants an update on this case. He's chuffed to bits that we got the arrest, but he isn't too happy about West Mids involvement. He says these rivalries should stop, but I can't see that ever happening.'

'Nah, it's an inbuilt part of the system. And anyway, we couldn't have done it without them. We haven't got the manpower.'

'I know. That's one of the things I want to discuss with him later.'

'Best of luck, ma'am.'

She nodded. She knew she would need it.

When she rang down later to summon Richard she nearly asked for Meatloaf, but thought better of it. Vic's habit of giving everyone nicknames was starting to rub off on her. She had been spending more time with him lately, and had to secretly admit she had enjoyed it. His approach was unconventional but really rather refreshing. This afternoon would be much more difficult, and would involve a lot of pussy footing around. Sometimes she hated the politics that came with rank.

She was quiet on the short journey to see Chief Constable Edison Poole, whom she had only met a few times before. He was everything Vic wasn't. Tall, good looking, athletic and teetotal. She couldn't imagine what he would make of her Detective Inspector.

'Good afternoon, sir.' She greeted him as she was shown into his office by a young black woman in civilian clothes.

'Ah, Detective Superintendent Lowe, come in, sit down, coffee?'

'Thank you, sir.'

The woman nodded and smiled, and left them for a few minutes.

'My PA,' the Chief Constable said as she closed the door behind her. 'She's from an agency, but she's very good. How did court go this morning?'

He got straight to the point, and she liked that. Maybe the tiptoeing around wouldn't be so bad today.

'We got the result we wanted. Remanded in custody. That'll keep him out of trouble while we build the case against him.'

'Mm.' He looked thoughtful. 'Pity we couldn't have been in control of the press conference, but at least we got a mention, it's a start. I intend to put this county on the map. I want it to become the most talked about in the country.'

The Super didn't like the sound of that, but when she thought about it, perhaps introducing him to Vic might be a good idea. He always managed to get himself noticed, one way or another.

'Yes,' she began slowly. 'My small CID team at

Brodewell are very proud of their connections to Staffordshire.'

'So they should be.' He smiled. 'Oh, one bit of good news. West Midlands have taken over building the case against Tony King. They have a lot of information and evidence that they can probably now tie to him. All those loose ends and bits and pieces that slowly build up a true picture.'

'Plus.' Joanne thought she had better get in quickly. 'They have the manpower. We are more than a little short staffed.'

'Yes. To that end, I am running a new recruitment campaign.' He hesitated. 'In line with national policy, we need to promote diversity. Some aspects of our society are under-represented, as I'm sure you realise.'

'We're lucky that we have Detective Constable Singh.' The hairs on the back of Joanne's neck were beginning to bristle. There was something about his manner that she didn't like, and she felt an overwhelming urge to defend herself. 'She is a very good police officer, and we all regard her as an extremely valuable member of our team.'

He didn't answer right away, and she could see the wheels of diplomacy going around in his head.

'Of course,' he began slowly, 'I'm sure you know that the annual assessment procedure is coming up soon, which means you could easily be promoted to Chief Superintendent. A woman of your abilities should be rewarded.'

'All the work was done by my team, sir. They deserve the recognition.'

'Of course.' He smiled, and she thought there was something rather reptilian about it. 'But remember the higher up one becomes, the more power one gets. Promotions in your team would be a lot easier.'

Bribery, that's what he's doing.

And there was more to come.

'How is PC Johnson coming along?' He didn't wait for an answer. 'A very bright young woman. I'm sure she would make a much more valuable contribution to your team than the DC you've got at the moment. I suggest you encourage her to study for her sergeants exam, I'm more than sure she's ready for it.'

The Super took a deep breath as her temper flared. She could feel the colour coming up in her face, and her hands were shaking. She tried to control her emotions, while thinking how to answer him.

'Actually.' She used the word deliberately. She knew it often annoyed. 'PC Johnson hasn't fitted in at all well. She seems to have ideas way above her capabilities, and neglects her duties because of them. Yes, ambition is to be nurtured, but I don't consider she is ready to go into CID yet. She needs a little more experience and maturity before that happens.'

'I value your opinion, of course, Joanne, but I am a great believer in the fast-track programme. Officers such as Johnson need to be encouraged before they become disillusioned and leave us. Recruitment is difficult enough as it is.'

'Sir.' She didn't trust herself to say anything else. This had been the first time he had called her by her given name, and she didn't like the implication. For a fleeting second, she felt as if she was back at school being told off by the Headmistress, and she wasn't enjoying the experience.

'Well, we are both busy people.' He was getting to his feet. 'Let's leave it at that for the moment. When we've both had time to think things over, we'll meet again. I shall look forward to it.'

The Super made her escape as quickly and politely as she could. There was only one thing on her mind now.

She needed to talk to Vic.

As soon as possible.

CHAPTER FIFTY-THREE

'He's horrible!'

Vic stared at the Super's outburst as he came back to the table in the window, carrying a pint of bitter and a large wine. He had been a bit surprised when she invited him for a drink, and had wondered if there was more to it than a social occasion. He hadn't seen her since her last visit to the Chief Constable, and only now realised how on edge she was.

'Get that down ya.' He put the wine glass in front of her. 'Then you can tell me all about it.'

'Oh, Vic.' She reached for her drink with a shaking hand. 'I don't know what to do.'

'Yer can calm down fer a start off. Sure you don't want a brandy?'

'Are you trying to get me drunk, Victor?'

'Ma'am. Please, for Gawd's sake, don't call me that. I bloody hate that name.'

'He called me by mine. He called me Joanne.' Her voice was bordering on hysterical.

'Nice name. Better than mine.'

'I was brought up to use proper names, but there is no way I'm ever going to call him Edison.' She stared into Vic's face. 'I'm sorry, Vic. I won't call you – you know – again.'

'Thank you, ma'am.'

'I need a codename.' She was suddenly calm. 'For occasions such as this, when we're off duty. And before you say anything.' She pointed an accusing finger into his face. 'I know what the one is you've already dreamed up.' He winced.

'I've got another one for you now.' He'd been thinking about it for a while. 'Lighthouse. Coz you show us the way.'

'It's certainly better than the other one.' She almost smiled. 'And you are to be Eagle. Always swooping in on the criminals.'

'Oh, ma'am, thank you.'

'Getting back to the Chief Constable. I'm worried, Vic.'

'I can see that,' he murmured.

'That – that – man.' She nearly spat the word. 'Is trying to get rid of our Nikki. He wants Hazel in CID instead.'

'Over my dead body.' Vic was horrified. Then he stopped to think. 'Hang on a minute. How would he even know Hazel? She's a PC and he's the Chief Constable.'

'You've got a point there.' She frowned as she slurped her wine. She would need another one soon the way she was going. 'In any case, we need to keep Nikki's involvement with the King arrest very quiet. If he finds out about that, she'll be out of the door without her feet touching the ground.'

'I ain't having Miss Marple on my team, no way. And I ain't going back to Stoke neither. If that happens we'll all resign, see how he gets on then.'

'That might be what he's after, Vic.' She gave him a sideways glance. 'And none of us wants to give him what he wants, do we?'

'I know wot he wants.' Vic growled. 'Stuffing with –'

'That's enough of that.' She gave him one of her death stares. 'Do something useful, and get me another drink.'

'Yes, ma – Lighthouse.' He grinned.

He heard her sigh heavily as he went back to the bar. He had to wait a couple of minutes to get served, and used the time to think. What was this new bloke up to, exactly?

He looked back towards the window, and could see the Super had her hand to her forehead. He would have to watch himself. He was feeling sorry for her, and worse: lately, he had even begun to like her. He reminded himself that they were on the same side and for once, they had a common enemy.

'Seems to me,' he said when he came back, 'we've got someone here wot's trying to prove himself. Trying to make a big splash. Impress somebody.'

The Super stared at him as he sat back down. She was frowning, but eventually she smiled as his words sank in.

'Of course,' she murmured. 'I think we need to find out a little more about Edison Poole. Oh yes, I'll enjoy that.'

'In the meantime.' Vic reached for his pint with hungry eyes. 'We need to shift Miss Marple back to Lichfield pronto, before he gets any more daft ideas.'

'Has she finished what she was brought here to do?'

'Probably not, but I wouldn't trust her to do it right anyway. She's a slacker. More interested in skiving off for a fag and chatting up the lads than doing any work. We'll be well rid.'

'That will put us under pressure.' She looked worried.

'Better that than wot he's on about.' Vic was sure about that. 'If we do have someone new, I know who I'd rather have.'

'Meatloaf? 'The Super was smirking now.

'Any day. He's a good lad.'

'He is. I'm becoming rather fond of him in a funny kind of way.'

'You, ma'am? Never.'

'Lighthouse, if you don't mind.'

'Yeah, sure. It's gonna take me a while to get used to that.'

'Changes everywhere, Vic. We'll all have to get used to it.'

'Ar.' His thoughts were dark as he got stuck into his pint.

He went to work the next day with mixed thoughts. He had enjoyed the company last evening, but had been a bit alarmed at her suggestion of going for a meal next time. He had realised some time ago that she was lonely and was reaching out. So was he, but he would rather be seen in public with something a bit younger and tastier. That reminded him. He had something to do in the front office.

He felt Stuart's eyes on him as he went to send Hazel packing, with a smirk on his face. The business didn't take long, and she had seemed pleased about it. That suited Vic. He wasn't any good with tearful women. When he got back to the office door, he could hear a conversation going on between Stuart and Nikki. He hovered outside to listen in. There was something wrong between these two, and he wouldn't find out what it was if he went barging in there and disturbed them.

'It won't get out, you're talking stupid,' Stuart was saying.

'That's all you've done lately, is call me stupid.' Nikki sounded upset. 'First the business with Michelle Bateman, and now this.'

'Nikki, you're not stupid, I didn't mean it like that. All I meant was, no one's going to drop you in it. The Guv won't say anything.'

'What about the Super? She was there too, and you know what a stickler for detail she is. I don't know why Zak turned up like that, he's really messed things up. It's bound to come out during the investigation, and how do I explain what my husband was doing there?'

'How many Singh's are there in the country? Thousands. Stop worrying.'

'I can't help it.'

Vic sighed as he heard her crying, and stayed where he was.

'I never thought I'd ever see him again, I didn't want to.'

'You sure about that?' Stuart said quietly.

'Positive.' She snivelled. 'I was proud of him at the time, putting himself at risk like that, but I meant it when I told him he was an idiot. He's ruined everything, that's all he's any good at.'

'So, you're not going back to him?'

'Of course not, now you're being an idiot.'

Oh, come here. Let's be idiots together.'

Vic raised his eyebrows as the room went quiet. All he could hear were subdued murmurs. At least now he knew the truth. There was more going on between these two than he had ever imagined.

CHAPTER FIFTY-FOUR

A week had gone by since Tony King's arrest, and Michelle was starting to relax. At last she was free of him and was looking forward to the future. The only thing in her way now was Phil. She was watching him, spark out in front of their large flat screen television, and sighed. Before she had married him, she'd had no idea how boring life was going to be.

Now it was time to do something else.

All along, Phil hadn't been the target of her affections: she had seen him as a means to an end. Now that Tony was out of the picture she could put her plan into action, and get what she really wanted. His best friend. Clive.

She collected up her handbag and car keys, and slipped out of the back door. With a bit of luck, she wouldn't be coming back. She checked in the car boot before getting into the drivers' seat.

Still got my escape bag handy. Wow, the times that's come in useful.

These thoughts reassured her as she started the engine and drove slowly away. Clive was in for a very pleasant surprise. She had waited a long time for this. She had no doubt that he would fall into her arms; no man had ever said no to her.

It didn't take long to drive to Clive's house on the other side of Hawksmere. He had no immediate neighbours, so they wouldn't be disturbed. And Phil would never know. She parked round the side of the house, out of sight. Then she took a deep breath, and rang the doorbell, her heart hammering against her chest. She had lived in the shadows for long enough. It was time to shine.

'Michelle,' Clive sounded surprised as he opened the door. He looked past her, then back at her. 'On your own?'

'Yes, Clive.' Her knees were beginning to shake. 'I've got something to tell you. Something important.'

'Oh.' He looked puzzled. 'You'd better come in, then.' He stood aside to let her enter. She breathed in his after shave as she walked past him. 'Phil alright?'

'Eh? Oh yes, he's fine. This has got nothing to do with him.'

'Oh,' he said again. He looked worried now. There was no need, her thoughts ran, she was about to make him a very happy man. 'Come through to the lounge.'

Michelle followed him quietly, her heart still clanging against her ribs. She was wondering how to begin. She had rehearsed this speech so many times in her head, but now it came to it she was all of a dither.

He offered her a drink, so she asked for a gin and tonic. She watched from the settee as he poured two, then handed one to her.

'So …'

'Yes,' she breathed. 'Do you remember the first time we met?'

He shook his head. 'Can't say I do.'

'It was in the Red Lion. I hadn't been with Phil long, then you appeared. I didn't know what had hit me. I never believed in love at first sight, until it happened to me.'

Now he was looking more than worried: it was more like horrified. Michelle thought she had better explain.

'I've been round here before, you know. Debs invited me.'

'I didn't know you knew Debs.'

Michelle smirked. 'No one did, that was the clever part about it. I met her in the Co-op a few times, and we got chatting. Then I took her to The White Hart to get to know her better. Boy, could she pack the vodka away.'

'I know.'

From the expression on Clive's face, she could tell he was wondering where all this was leading but she was enjoying keeping him dangling and watching his reactions.

'Anyway,' she continued. 'She seemed glad of my company. Said she didn't have any friends round here. She was bored. And lonely.'

'Yeah. I suppose so.'

Now he looked slightly guilty. There was no need. In a few minutes, he would understand everything.

'We used to meet up every now and then, either in Burton or Lichfield. Retail therapy and lunch. You know the sort of thing.'

No, he didn't. His face was blank.

'Why are you telling me all this, Michelle?'

'I'm coming to that.' She smiled. 'On your birthday, she rang and invited me round. Sort of bring a bottle thing.'

Clive stared at her, his mouth beginning to fall open.

'It was a nice day, so we went into the garden. She was pretty well out of it when I arrived, so the rest was easy.' She let her eyes roam around the room. 'I must say, this is a very nice house you've got here.'

Clive seemed thrown by this comment. He tried to say something but no sound came from him.

'I brought a bottle with me, two in fact. Polish vodka. You know, the strong stuff.'

'And?'

'I got her to drink a load of it.' Michelle laughed. 'She'd had enough really, but I wanted to make sure. I was tipping mine away when she wasn't looking, which was most of the time really. She started to fall asleep, so it was easy to ram the bottle down her throat. I just poured the rest in. She struggled but I was too strong for her. She was making some weird noises, but not for long. I left the bottle where it was to make sure, and waited.'

'Waited?' Clive looked confused, amongst other things. She wanted to put her arms around him and comfort him. 'Waited for what?'

'To make sure she was dead, of course. In the meantime, I had a look round your house and then a tidy up. Wiped all the surfaces I had touched, that sort of thing.' She reached for his hand. He snatched it away. 'This really is a lovely house. I know we'll be happy here.'

Clive stared at her in real horror now. That wasn't the reaction she had been expecting. Maybe she wasn't explaining this properly.

'Don't you see, Clive? I love you. I've loved you since the first time I ever laid eyes on you. The only thing in the way was Debs, and you said yourself you were sick of her. All I did was get rid of her for you. I helped you. I set you free.'

'Oh my – fucking hell,' he muttered.

'So now there's nothing to stop us being together.' She smiled at him, her heart swelling with what she supposed was this thing called love.

Clive stood up and ran one hand through his hair. He looked as though he didn't know what to do with himself. He turned to face her, but she couldn't read his eyes.

'You crazy evil cow,' he said quietly. 'I knew you were a wrong 'un from the start.' He took a step closer to her, and she held her breath. 'How could you do such an awful thing? You – you – murderer.'

'I saw it more as an act of kindness.' She smiled up at him. 'She was unhappy and so were you. I couldn't let that go on. I did you a favour.'

'Michelle, for God's sake!'

He walked away from her, heading for the kitchen. She got up and followed him. He didn't seem to understand; she needed to reassure him.

'It's just a bit of a shock at the moment, that's all. You'll see,' she said, as softly as she could.

'I could never be with anyone like you.' He turned to her. 'All you're interested in is yourself and money. You're a devious scheming cow, and I want you out of my house.'

'We were meant to be together. I'll divorce Phil and we can get married.'

'You don't get it, do you? You're crazy. Raving mad. I was going to marry Connie. She's the only woman I wanted.'

Michelle's eyes flew wide open. She stared at him as he glared at her, his eyes full of hatred and disgust.

'Connie? Connie!'

'Ten times the woman you are.' He went to the back door and flung it open. 'Now leave. Get out.'

Michelle couldn't believe her ears. No man had ever turned her down before. And this one wasn't going to do that now. She stayed where she was, close to the sink. He came towards her, looking as if he was about to physically throw her out. She reached behind herself for one of the kitchen knives she had spotted on the way in, and carefully took hold of one of them. When he got close enough, she plunged it into his chest. She felt nothing. No anger. No love.

'There's something you need to know about me,' she hissed as she began to pull the knife out. 'I don't take no for an answer. If I can't have you, then no one will.'

She stabbed him again. Over and over, grunting and screaming as she did so. For the first time in her life, she had lost control.

The last stab was in his stomach, and Michelle stopped. She was exhausted. She was covered in blood, and it was even in her eyes. She couldn't think. All she could see was red, and it wasn't all because of his blood. She let go of the knife and staggered backwards.

A horrible gurgling noise was coming from him. He clutched at the long handle of the knife, as though he was trying to pull it out to save his life. He got both hands round it, then his eyes glazed over. He fell to the floor and landed on his front.

There were no more noises.

Clive Morrison was dead.

CHAPTER FIFTY-FIVE

Hush had fallen over Brodewell Police Station when the news came in, and Vic was furious. Another murder in one of his villages. Looked like it was howling at the moon season, and he had never realised how dangerous villages could be. PC Comer had been one of the officers attending the call, and had been a bit shaken: he had never seen a dead body before.

'Michelle Bateman is in Interview Room One,' Stuart told him. 'She called it in. She was at his house.'

'With her old man?'

'No. Just the two of them.'

'Oh, ar. Looks like she *was* playing both of them.'

'You going to talk to her, Guv?' Stuart asked. 'I've got my report ready, from the house search.'

'Anything interesting?'

'Yes. Looks like she was a regular visitor to the house.

I found women's clothes in one of the wardrobes, and toiletries in the bedroom and bathroom. The log burner was going, which seems a bit unusual, coz it hasn't been that cold lately.'

'Maybe they were planning a bit of afternoon delight on the settee,' Vic suggested. A subdued noise came from Nikki across the room, and Stuart raised an eyebrow. 'Don't look so surprised. I've had my moments.'

'It's just that I – never mind.'

'Right.' Vic decided it was time to change the subject. 'Let's go and see wot she's got to say for herself.' He glanced at Stuart. 'Coming?'

'Yeah. We leaving her husband in Interview Room Three?'

'We'll get to him later. Looks like one of them killed Morrison. All we've got to do is work out which one.'

'Piece of cake.' Stuart grimaced as he said it.

'Good luck,' Nikki said quietly as he followed Vic out of the room.

It was Vic's turn to raise his eyebrows when he saw Michelle Bateman. She was dressed in a tee shirt which was several sizes too big, baggy shorts and a pair of flip flops. Added to this, her hair was damp. He made no comment as he and Stuart sat down opposite her.

'Right then, Mrs Bateman.' Vic said once the introductions were out of the way. 'Would you like to tell us what happened?'

She looked up slowly and Vic almost shuddered. There was no life in her eyes at all. It was as if someone had switched her off and taken the batteries out.

'I don't remember,' she said quietly. 'Where am I?'

'You're at Brodewell Police Station, ma'am,' Stuart said in a similar tone. 'You rang the police to say a man had been killed.'

She looked puzzled.

'Clive Morrison,' Vic said.

Michelle's eyes widened, and some sort of recognition flashed into them. She put one hand to her forehead and took a deep breath.

'Clive,' she said slowly, then shrieked. 'Oh God, Clive.'

She began to shake. Vic had seen this before and realised it was delayed shock. He shot Stuart a warning glance which said – don't say anything.

'Clive. Phil killed him. I'm next, he'll come after me next.'

'Just tell us wot happened. Take your time, and talk us through it.' Vic was genuinely being patient. He had a feeling this story was worth waiting for.

'Clive and I were in love.' Vic could hardly hear her. 'We were planning to go away together.' She took another deep breath. 'I went round to see him, I often went there. Sometimes I even stayed the night. I went upstairs to have a shower to get ready for – you know.' Both Vic and Stuart nodded. 'I got dressed in these clothes, they're Clive's clothes. It's a game we liked to play. Master and servant, that sort of thing. We take it in turns.'

Vic was trying to get rid of the image of Clive Morrison that had just come into his mind. He really must get out more.

'I suppose I was gone a while.' Michelle hesitated. 'When I came down, there was no sign of him. I thought he was playing about. He likes to tease me.' She smiled. 'Quite a lot really.'

'And then?'

'I went into the kitchen and – and –'

The tears started. She had broken through the shock barrier. Vic was believing every word. If there were any lies in there, then she didn't realise that's what they were. To her this was the truth, and always would be.

Vic let her be for a while. Stuart sat beside him and didn't utter a word. They didn't even look at each other.

'So, you were both alone. How long for?'

'I don't know. I didn't rush. We never rush things.'

She was slipping away from him again.

'You found him dead on the kitchen floor, stabbed several times.'

'Phil. It was Phil.' She looked up at Vic with wild eyes which were difficult to read. 'He must have found out. We tried to be careful.' She looked away and stared at the wall. 'Always so careful,' she whispered.

She sat like this for several minutes, tears rolling down both cheeks. Vic knew they were real. He had seen enough crying in interview rooms to last him a lifetime. Most of them had been for show, but these weren't. From the look of things, they weren't about to stop any time soon either.

'Phil said if he ever found out I was cheating on him, he'd kill the pair of us. He told me that more than once. I'd been married before, years ago, but I could never tell him that. I was his princess, his little girl. He was like a big daft kid with me. Like we were teenagers, starting out on our first love affair. All innocent and virginal.'

Vic was having trouble seeing her as either of those things, especially with everything Stuart had told him about her past.

'Phil loves me so very much,' she continued. 'Too much. I knew being with Clive was going to be hard. We were trying to think up a way to get away from him, but now it's too late. Too late!'

She put both hands over her face as the sobbing noises started. Vic reached for a shelf behind him and grabbed at a box of tissues. He looked at Stuart, and grimaced. It didn't look as though they were going to get anything else out of her. She was still shaking, and Vic suspected that now it was out of fear. He nudged Stuart and stood up.

'I think that's enough for now, Mrs Bateman,' he said quietly. He spoke to a constable on the way out. 'Get someone to fetch her a strong cup of tea with plenty of sugar. And make sure someone is with her at all times.'

'Sir.' The officer nodded.

'Please,' Michelle said as he was leaving. 'Put me in a cell. Lock me up so Phil can't get at me.'

Her voice was high and she looked panicky. Vic agreed, and when they were in the corridor, he saw her being led away.

'Think all that's true, Guv?'

'Yes, I do. But we'll talk to her husband next.'

'She's a tough cookie. She might just be a good actress.'

'Looked pretty real to me.'

'And me,' Stuart agreed. 'She's scared stiff. Don't think she was as frightened as that when Tony King was around, and he's a nasty bastard.'

'Mm.' Vic was deep in thought. 'All we've got to do now is find out how nasty a bastard Phil Bateman is. It's right wot they say. The quiet ones are usually the worst.'

CHAPTER FIFTY-SIX

Phil Bateman was a different matter altogether. He was sitting at the table in Interview Room Three, with an empty cardboard cup in front of him. As Vic and Stuart entered, they saw him cross his arms over his chest and sigh. He looked bored and angry.

'Mr Bateman,' Vic said breezily, 'sorry to keep you waiting.'

'What's this all about? Why have I been dragged in here?'

'All in good time, sir.' Vic sat down. 'First, can you tell me where you were this afternoon? Say between noon and four o'clock?'

'What? What's going on?'

'Just answer the question, sir.'

'I was at home. In front of the telly, if you must know.'

'Was anyone with you?'

'Yeah, my wife.' He hesitated. 'Well, most of the time.'

'Yes?'

'I must have dozed off. When I woke up, she'd gone. I saw the car wasn't there, thought she'd gone to the Coop.'

'And what time was this?'

'God, I dunno, never looked. What is all this?'

'I'm afraid we have some bad news for you,' Stuart said quietly.

'Michelle, is she alright?' Phil looked worried now. The anger had disappeared completely.

'She's fine, sir. It's your friend, Clive Morrison.' Phil was staring at him, his eyes wide. 'He's dead.'

'Dead? But –'

Stuart exchanged glances with Vic. Now the acting might start.

'Was it his heart?' Phil said quietly.

'No, sir,' Stuart answered. 'He's been murdered.'

'And you think that I -? He's my best friend.'

'Yes, sir, we know. How friendly would you say he was with your wife?'

Phil's body language changed immediately. His body stiffened and his face hardened. This didn't go unnoticed, by Stuart in particular. He had done an online course on the very subject.

'He didn't like her,' Phil said, after what seemed like a long time. 'He tried to hide it, but I could tell. We had a bit of an argument about her at the wedding. I told you about that.'

He was addressing Stuart. Vic kept quiet.

'So, it's interesting, don't you think, that it was your wife who reported his death? She was at his house.'

'No, no, she's gone to the shop.' Phil tried to laugh, then gave up and looked Stuart in the face. 'Why the hell would she be at his house?'

'That's wot we're trying to find out,' Vic said quietly.

Nah, that can't be right. I know she's been no angel in the past, but Clive? No. She wouldn't.'

'Did you know she used to be married to Tony King?'

Stuart sighed. He hadn't been going to mention that, it hardly seemed relevant.

Phil shook his head, his face starting to crumble. His whole world was being ripped apart bit by bit. There wouldn't be much left of it by the time Vic had finished.

'I knew she knew him,' Phil eventually said, 'but not that well.'

'It seems there's a lot about your wife that you don't know.'

Stuart wished Vic would shut up and let him do the talking. The look he gave him tried to send that message.

'She says they were having an affair. Even that she was going to leave you for him. She rang the police from his house.'

'I want to talk to her.'

Stuart shook his head. 'I'm afraid that won't be possible.'

'God, he was right,' Phil whispered. 'I have been a fool.'

Neither Stuart nor Vic knew what he was talking about, so they both kept quiet. Phil looked as if he was

349

sinking into himself. Slowly disappearing under the weight of the truth. No one spoke for a while, but it was Phil who broke the silence.

'So, who killed him?'

'Who indeed,' Stuart answered.

'She says it was me?'

Stuart didn't say anything. Vic sighed.

'She does, doesn't she? Oh, God.' He put his head in his hands. 'If I'd known about this, the one I would have killed would have been her. How could she do this? All I wanted to do was look after her.'

Phil began to cry. Vic looked embarrassed. Stuart stood up.

'Yeah.' Vic looked at him. 'Think we'll leave this for a while now. We'll be back to speak to you again later.'

They left the room quietly, and went into the monitoring room. They got there just in time to see Phil thump the table. The empty coffee cup leapt into the air and then fell on the floor. A watching police constable was moving towards the door. He threw it open and yelled as Phil picked up the chair he had been sitting on and flung it at the wall. He screamed as he did so.

'Temper, temper,' Vic murmured.

'He's upset,' Stuart pointed out.

'I get upset, but I don't throw chairs around. Gawd, look at him go.'

Phil was now tussling with three burly police officers, who were trying to restrain him but weren't having much success.

'Aw, those were the days.' Vic was watching the scene with a dreamy expression on his face.

'You've been watching too much old telly.' Stuart tutted. 'Looks like he's off to the cells.'

'No.' Vic's attention had been brought back into focus. 'We've only got two, and she's in the other one. We don't want 'em talking.' He was halfway out of the door. 'Let's see if Burton can take him.'

Half an hour later, Phil was manhandled into a police van with his wrists handcuffed behind his back, and taken off to Burton nick. He was likely to stay there for the duration. Stuart and Vic were back in the CID office, and Stuart had just finished telling Nikki all about the interviews.

'I thought she was hiding something about Clive Morrison,' she said.

'Looks like you were right. See Guv, there is such a thing as female intuition.' Stuart couldn't resist having a dig at him.

'Never said there wasn't.'

'Yeah, right,' Stuart muttered, and winked at Nikki.

'Anyway, two pains in the arse have gone now. Miss Marple's on her way back to Lichfield, and he's off to Burton. Reckon he did it?'

'Dunno, Guv, it's an odd one.'

'Told you these bloody villages are weird. Two murders in the same one, in the same house. And it's likely we'll never know who did either of them, not for sure.'

'Our only hope is the knife, the murder weapon,' Stuart said thoughtfully. 'We'll have to see what Forensics come back with.'

CHAPTER FIFTY-SEVEN

The forensic report seemed to take forever to come through, and when it did, the results were inconclusive.

'Bloody hell,' Vic complained. 'You seen this?'

'Yes, Guv,' Stuart said. 'Not much help, is it?'

'You're not wrong there, son.' Vic still had the file in his hand. 'The victim's fingerprints on the knife handle. Wot the hell was he doing? Others underneath, but too smudged to be positively identified.' He slammed the folder onto Nikki's desk. 'Gawd.'

Nikki flinched as the file just missed her hand.

'Someone'll have to tell the Super.' Stuart didn't help matters by saying.

'Yeah, guess who.' Vic sounded sullen. 'In a bit. I need a strong coffee.'

The others looked after him as he stormed out of the door.

'It's tough at the top.'

'Stuart!'

Vic returned five minutes later and looked a lot happier. He rubbed his hands together and smiled

'Feel about ready to face her now.'

He was heading for the corridor when the phone rang in his office. Still smiling, he went to answer it.

'Everyone on their best behaviour,' he said a minute later. 'Lighthouse wants to see all of us. In her office, now.'

'Oo-er,' Stuart muttered.

The three of them were heading for the stairs as Ella was on her way back from the kitchen. She said hello, and smiled at Stuart.

'Thanks for –' She nodded towards the front office.

'Everything alright?'

'Will be when I've finished checking through it all. She wasn't very thorough.'

'Best of luck,' Stuart said.

'Come on,' Vic called. 'Onwards and upwards.'

'The Super.' Stuart pulled a face.

Ella nodded and went on her way. Stuart hurried up the stairs after the other two. He was the last one to enter the office, and was surprised to see a tray full of tea, coffee and cakes on her desk.

'Ah, the famous CID team,' she greeted them. 'Please, sit down, all of you. Can I offer you a cup of tea, Nikki?'

'Oh.' Nikki sounded surprised. 'Er, yes, ma'am. Thank you.'

'I'm sure the others can help themselves to coffee.' Joanne smiled as she lifted the teapot.

They could, and they did. The cakes looked far too good to be ignored.

'Wot's all this about, ma'am?' Vic voiced the thought for everyone.

'Are you charging anyone for the murder of Clive Morrison?'

'Ah, bit difficult, that. No conclusive evidence. We're pretty sure Phil Bateman did it, but we can't prove it.'

'What are your thoughts, Stuart?'

'He changed completely when we mentioned his wife, and later became violent. I agree with the Guv. He had more reason to kill him than Mrs Bateman. She came over as genuine at her interview, especially when the conversation got round to her husband. She seemed terrified of what he might do. Burton are holding him for now.'

'Mm. Sounds like they had better continue to do so for the time being. I've read through all the reports and I agree with your conclusions. However, as you say, proving Phil Bateman killed his friend is likely to be difficult. I shall recommend he be held in custody while further enquiries are made. The wife, I think, can be released. We know where she'll be if we need to speak to her again.'

'Your decision, ma'am.' Vic shrugged his shoulders.

'That's settled, then. Well, I have to say, you've all done very well. Even the Chief Constable said so, I had him on the phone earlier.'

Stuart noticed the glance that went between her and Vic, and wondered what it meant. He looked at the Guv, but he was giving nothing away.

'I'm sure I speak for him as well when I say you have an excellent team here, Detective Chief Inspector Hardcastle. They each have their own talents, and compliment one another perfectly. You should all be very proud of your achievements.'

'Thank you, ma'am,' Stuart and Nikki murmured in unison, while looking at each other. Did she just say -?

Stuart glanced at Vic waiting for his reaction, but he was too busy getting stuck into a large slice of fruit cake. With a big daft grin on his face.

'Also it appears that Andrew Ferguson will be going to trial soon.' Joanne had a beaming smile. 'The CID team from Glasgow send their thanks to you all. He was well known to them.'

She was looking at Vic as she spoke, and he swallowed hard.

'I'm sure he is.' He chuckled, when his mouth was empty. 'Here, 'ang on a minute – did you just say Chief Inspector?'

'Yes, I did. You did well at the annual assessments, so it's no more than you deserve, Vi –' She stopped herself just in time. 'Effective immediately.'

Oh.' Vic was glowing. Stuart had never seen him look happier. 'Thank you, ma'am.'

'So. Congratulations all round. Please everyone.' She waved to the drinks. 'Help yourself to refills.'

Vic was first in the queue.

'To the Guv and his team.' Joanne held up her bone China cup, and Stuart noticed her wink at Vic. 'The best little set-up I've ever had the pleasure to work with. Here's to many more successes.'

Vic smiled and raised his cup of coffee.

'I'll drink to that!'

Want to know how the story really ends?
HARDCASTLE & YOUNG –
CONFLICTING CASES
Coming soon…

This book is printed on paper from sustainable sources managed under the Forest Stewardship Council (FSC) scheme.

It has been printed in the UK to reduce transportation miles and their impact upon the environment.

For every new title that Troubador publishes, we plant a tree to offset CO_2, partnering with the More Trees scheme.

For more about how Troubador offsets its environmental impact, see www.troubador.co.uk/sustainability-and-community